MALCOLM ARCHIBALD

LAST TRAIN TO WAVERLEY

Fledgling Press Ltd,
7 Lennox St., Edinburgh, EH4 1QB

Published by Fledgling Press, 2014
www.fledglingpress.co.uk

Cover Design: Graeme Clarke
graeme@graemeclarke.co.uk

Printed and bound by:
Bell & Bain Limited, Glasgow

ISBN: 9781905916856

For Cathy

PRELUDE

BOTANIC GARDENS, EDINBURGH,

June 1919

Despite the early morning sunshine that threw long shadows from the Lebanese cedar, dew still lingered on the stalks of the grass. A gardener worked diligently with his hoe, barely looking up as the man and his woman eased past. Her arm was hooked into his, but whether out of affection or to support him, the gardener could not tell. The man wore the uniform of an army officer with the three pips of a captain, but as they passed beyond the shadows, the sun gleamed briefly from the three gold wound stripes on his sleeve.

The gardener paused to lean on the haft of his hoe as his interest was briefly roused. The officer was tall and he limped heavily and stopped frequently as if in constant pain. His face was drawn and his eyes haunted, as if the war had not yet left him; although he was physically among the peace of the Botanical Garden, mentally he was still trapped in Flanders mud.

The gardener sighed and returned to his work; Edinburgh was full of injured men recently returned from the War; it was not his concern. This week's crop of weeds was more important to him. He ducked his head and sliced the hoe through the dark soil.

The couple walked past. They did not notice the gardener at all. Gillian pulled the silk scarf tighter over her throat and took hold of Ramsay's arm.

"It's cold this morning." She shivered and huddled closer, her eyes lifting to his.

Ramsay squeezed her hand in the crook of his elbow. "You may have been better advised to wear a longer skirt," he said.

"You like it?" Gillian looked down at her sky blue dress. She straightened her left leg so the serrated hem rose even higher up her shin. "Shorter skirts are the height of fashion this season, Douglas."

"Of course they are," Ramsay agreed. He tried to lengthen his stride slightly but that damned wound caught him again and he winced and returned to his now-familiar but still frustrating hobble.

Gillian had automatically hesitated when he faltered and now she looked enquiringly at him. "Are you all right?"

Ramsay nodded but said nothing. God! He hated this weakness of his body. He looked up suddenly and ducked his head as something exploded from the shrubbery on his left. It was a magpie: only a magpie. He grinned to hide the embarrassment he felt at having betrayed his ragged nerves.

Gillian patted the stripes on his cuff. "It will get better, Douglas. You will get better in time."

He watched the bird flutter toward the domed glass of the Palm House, black and white against the green leaves. He saw its reflection in the polished panes and then it was gone, disappeared behind the glittering roof as if it had never been. Here one minute, gone the next; it no longer mattered. The only things that mattered were those that were before you at that second: the here and now. All the rest was unimportant. The past had happened and could not be altered and the future may never happen. Only the present mattered, and that was Gillian. He inhaled deeply, very aware of her perfume mingling with the soft scent of earth and new-cut grass.

"Douglas?" Gillian pulled lightly on his sleeve. "Are you with me?"

I think so Gillian but hold onto me or I may drift away back to the trenches.

The sun had risen in the short time they had been walking. It emerged from the fringe of the shrubbery and eased its light on to the Palm House, caressing each pane of glass as the Earth continued its inexorable orbit around that mysterious yellow globe. Ramsay thought of how the sun had looked on other mornings, in another country, in another world far removed from this place of false tranquillity. Maybe he had left a part of himself there; maybe the memories and the guilt would follow him forever.

"Douglas?" Gillian was leaning into him, trying to catch his eyes. She asked again: "Are you with me?"

"Of course I am with you." Ramsay forced a smile. He watched as the sun caught the penultimate pane on its gradual spread over the Palm House. There was no sign of the magpie now; nor was there a lark singing. But there should be a lark; there was always a lark. He looked down at Gillian; her eyes were bright, but the concern was also there.

"I think you are getting tired now." When Gillian spoke in that kind tone, her voice washed over him like warm soapy water, loosening the visible hurt but unable to penetrate to the depths beneath.

She tightened her grip on his arm. "Come along, Douglas; time we were getting back home I think." She held out her left hand and allowed the sunlight to glint on the central and largest diamond of her engagement ring. "We have a wedding to arrange."

Ramsay nodded. "We have indeed, Gillian." He lengthened his stride to match hers, rode the pain and tried once more to concentrate on this strange life of peace, where a sudden noise was more likely to be somebody dropping a cup rather than a dreaded coalscuttle bomb exploding, and men wore dark suits or flat caps rather than mud-coated uniforms stinking of lyddite and sweat.

He heard the whistling before he saw the source, but automatically his mouth formed the words of the song and he joined in, softly.

> *"Après la guerre finie*
> *Soldat Ecosse parti*
> *Mademoiselle in the family way*
> *Après la guerre finie"*

Gillian saw the movement and smiled. "You looked happy there for a moment, Douglas. Please sing louder for me."

Ramsay shook his head as he realised what he was doing. "It's a trench song, Gillian. It's hardly suitable for your ears."

"I'm not made of glass you know!" Despite Gillian's smile, the words retained enough of a sting for Ramsay to recognise her hurt.

He saw the residual anger in her eyes and shook his head. "I know that," he said softly. "I know you have seen plenty and heard plenty, but I still think of you as that young girl I fell in love with a lifetime and four years ago."

"I am still me, silly." The hurt faded from Gillian's eyes. "And you are still you, under that uniform, Douglas. The war was only an episode."

Ramsay nodded. "Yes," he said. "It was only an episode."

The whistling continued to the tune *Sous les Ponts de Paris*, jaunty and sharp but with an undertone of bitterness. Ramsay stopped and waited for the whistlers. They came around the corner of the Palm House, three men in blue hospital suits and scarlet neckerchiefs. One pushed a wheelchair in which the second sat; the third hobbled behind on a pair of crutches; his single remaining leg heavily bandaged. The badges on their caps advertised membership of three different regiments.

They stopped when they saw Ramsay and two of them saluted. The man in crutches tried to balance long enough to lift his arm but staggered so the wheelchair pusher had to hold him upright.

Ramsay returned the salute. "Stand easy, men." The words came automatically, as did the instinctive relaxation of the three men. They had stopped whistling and stood as if waiting for orders that Ramsay was not inclined to give. He nodded to the man in the wheelchair. "Where did you get that?"

The man glanced down, where his legs should have been. "Ypres, sir; gas gangrene."

"And you?" Ramsay nodded to the man on crutches.

"Hindenburg Line, sir." The accent was East End Glasgow, the cap badge HLI.

"And you?" Ramsay nodded to the wheelchair pusher.

"Amiens, sir." The man bore himself with some authority and Ramsay guessed he had been a corporal, perhaps even a sergeant. Blue eyes met Ramsay's in a gaze that was neither obsequious nor challenging.

"Well done, men," Ramsay said. "Carry on." He watched them pass, noting they still had their shoulders squared and their heads up; they were soldiers, but more than that, they were men. They started to sing, the words soft but distinguishable as they continued with their defiant, tragic song.

"Après la guerre finie
Soldat Ecosse parti
Mademoiselle can go to hell
Après la guerre finie"

"Well," Gillian watched them disappear behind the bushes. The song returned to whistling, which gradually faded away. "The guerre is après now, but there is not much partying from these Scottish soldiers." Her voice lowered. "Not without legs." She sighed and rubbed her hand up and down his sleeve. "I am very glad you came back intact." She touched the ribbons sewn on his breast, "and decorated. You are a hero, you know."

"I am no hero," Ramsay denied. "And I am not sure if I am intact. The true heroes were the men who did not come back."

Men such as Edwards, Niven, Aitken, Mackay . . . the list is endless.

"What nonsense!" Gillian said. She touched his ribbons again. "These prove your heroism and that's all there is to be said . . . no!" She held up her hand, palm toward him. "I won't hear another word, Douglas; not another word. You are intact, just a wee bit hurt and I can cure all of that, I promise you."

She slipped her arm into the crook of his elbow and they continued to walk, slower now, toward the western entrance gate. A trick of the breeze brought the sound of whistling back toward them and then there was silence, save for the rustle of leaves and the sad refrain of blackbirds.

Ramsay stopped abruptly, and Gillian staggered slightly.

The woman stood just inside the gate with a child at her side and hope shorn from her face. The high polish could not disguise the battered state of her shoes and her clothes that had gone out of fashion at least four years before. The child stared at Ramsay, pointed and whispered something briefly to his mother. The woman shook her head.

"Do you know that woman?" Gillian asked.

Ramsay spared her a cursory glance and looked away quickly. "No." He hesitated for a moment, swore softly and tapped his right hand on his leg. "Excuse me, please, Gillian." He disengaged his arm and walked over to the woman. She watched him approach, her face disinterested.

"That is a fine boy you have there," Ramsay tried to smile.

"He's not bad." The woman pulled her son back and held him close.

"His father must be very proud of him."

"His father is dead," the woman said bluntly. She looked at the medal ribbons on Ramsay's breast and pursed her lips.

"In the War?" Ramsay asked. He put out a hand but the woman pulled the boy out of his reach.

"Where else?" The woman sounded too tired to be bitter. There were dark rings around her eyes and deep lines between the edges of her mouth and her poverty-sharp nose.

Ramsay nodded. "That must be hard for you."

"It's hard for everybody." The woman barely shrugged. "Why should it be any different for me?"

"Of course." Ramsay looked closely into the eyes of the boy. They were brown and wide. "How old is he?"

The woman pulled him closer. "He's four come August."

"Oh." Ramsay pulled out his wallet. As the woman watched, he extracted a pound note and held it out. "To help," he said. "Take it, please."

"I don't take charity." There was a surge of pride in the woman's voice, despite the desperation in her eyes.

Ramsay shook his head. "It's not charity," he said, "your husband might have served with me. Please," he repeated, and lowered his voice, "please. For the boy's sake if not for your own."

The woman glanced down at her son and then slowly took the money. She held it as if it was red hot. "Thank you," she said. She stuffed it away inside some recess of her coat, turned and walked, round shouldered, out of the gate. "Come on, William." She looked back once, as if to reassure herself that Ramsay was serious, and hurried away.

"That's the third woman to whom you have given money in the past two days." Gillian's eyes were soft. "You can't support every war widow you know, Douglas. The government does provide for them."

Ramsay said nothing. He watched the woman scurry across the road to the tall stone pillars that marked the entrance to Inverleith Park.

"Why do you do that, Douglas? The war was not your fault."

"No," Ramsay agreed softly. "The war was not my fault; but some of the killing was." He began to sing again, the words soft as the tear that brightened his eye.

> *"Après la guerre finie*
> *Soldat Ecosse parti."*

But there were no larks.

CHAPTER 1

FRANCE

19 March 1918

Even in Albert there was always the sound of guns. Wherever he was near the line the guns formed an unremitting backdrop, so regular that it became part of life, unheeded unless the unseen gunner targeted him personally. Mostly the rumble came from the north, where the salient around Ypres was constantly under siege, but today they came from the French sector to the south. Lieutenant Ramsay disembarked from the train, lit a cheroot and allowed the sergeants to organise the unloading of the draft reinforcements.

A stocky NCO with the face of a boy and the eyes of an octogenarian stepped past him. "Right lads. I want the Royals to form up on the right, the Durhams to form in the centre behind me and the Fusiliers to the left!" The stentorian roar echoed around the railway station, competing with the sound of the train as it voided steam over the shifting mass of men.

"Should we not be taking charge?" Second Lieutenant Kerr adjusted his Sam Browne belt slightly and checked the holster of his revolver.

"I always find it best to allow the sergeants to do this sort of thing," Ramsay said. "They do it so much better than us. It's what they're made for."

Kerr forced a smile. "Yes, sir." He straightened his cap so the peak was exactly square on his forehead.

Did I look as young as him when I first came out here?

Encouraged by the sergeant's bellowing, the khaki-clad men filed into their respective units. The veterans stood at ease, their faces expressionless, while the recruits looked around in nervous excitement. The stocky sergeant was joined by two others; a taller, slender man who Ramsay guessed was in his late teens and an average-sized man with a greying walrus moustache.

"You're with me, Durhams." The tall sergeant barely raised his voice above a conversational tone yet when he gave the order to march the Durhams immediately moved out of the station towards the town outside.

The stocky sergeant blasted the Fusiliers in his wake, leaving the Royals standing, watching the officers with a mixture of frank curiosity and total disinterest. Ramsay noted the difference between the wide-eyed recruits who scarcely halted chattering even when the moustached sergeant barked at them, and the wary eyes of the silent veterans.

The Durhams and the Fusiliers filed into lorries, hauling themselves over the tailgate and taking their seats with non-stop noise and the clatter of equipment. One by one the lorries jerked away, leaving a blue cloud of exhaust fumes and rising dust. Kerr watched them go. "Is there transport for us, sir?"

"No," Ramsay told him. "From here on, we march."

Kerr indicated the disappearing files of lorries and the slowly dropping dust. "I thought they were all coming with us," he sounded disappointed.

"They are replacements," Ramsay explained, "to fill the gaps caused by casualties and sickness. They are fortunate that they are going to their own regiments. If there was a big push on, they would be spread out wherever they are needed along the whole line." He glanced at the train. Already empty, it was heading back for more men. The front always demanded more men, like some starving dragon that devoured human bodies and drank human blood. Ramsay shook away the horrific images and glanced up as a new body of men marched past, arms swinging and rifles slung over their shoulder. They were singing, the words familiar, jaunty with sardonic humour.

"Après la guerre finie
Soldat Ecosse parti."

Ramsay noticed that many looked terribly young, younger even than Kerr, and his face had never experienced the sliding hiss of a razor. Others were little older in years, but their mouths were hardened from experience and eyes embittered by the sights they had seen. Some had socks fastened over the muzzles of their rifles in preparation for the mud ahead. Many had one or more gold wound stripes on their sleeve; few of these were singing and then only softly; more as in prayer than with vigour. Their steel helmets seemed pitifully inadequate protection against the howitzers and mortars that would soon be targeting them. Yet still they marched and still they sang, with the veterans joining in one by one as they slid into the routine of the march.

Ramsay turned his attention to the single body of men who remained. They stood in the fading evening light, some with the patience of cattle, others lighting the ubiquitous Woodbine cigarette and talking quietly among themselves,

3

a few staring at their surroundings in something like awe.

"That's the men ready, sir." The moustached sergeant saluted. "The guide is waiting for us." He nodded to the station exit, where a tousle-headed corporal lounged against the pillar, smoking a cigarette.

The corporal lifted a single hand in acknowledgement and slouched forward. He eyed Kerr's Sam Brown, raised a weary eyebrow and threw a casual salute to Ramsay.

"I am ready whenever you are, sir." He was all of eighteen years old.

With the men formed in a short column of four abreast, the replacements for the 20th Battalion, the Royal Scots followed Ramsay toward the front. He felt the familiar mixture of emotions; the slide of despair that he was returning to carnage, the fear that was so constant a companion he had almost learned to control it and the strange exhilaration that he was returning to what now felt like home. This was his regiment; this was the First of Foot, the oldest regiment in the British Army outside the Guards; the right of the line, Pontius Pilate's Bodyguard: he was returning to his family.

There was the clatter of hooves on the central pave.

"Clear the road, lads!" The sergeant ushered the men to the mud in the verges. They moved reluctantly and the younger faces watched as the field ambulance hurried past, the red cross bright against the spattered background of mud.

"Blighty!" one of the veterans yelled. "Blighty!" He turned to the man next to him. "There's another lucky bastard got a Blighty."

His companion grunted. "Lucky bastard," he echoed, and shifted his grip on his rifle. Neither mentioned the slow drip of blood that fell from the tail of the ambulance.

"Right, lads," the sergeant stepped back on the pave. The corporal guide was watching, his eyes unreadable as he lit one cigarette from the glowing tip of the last. He led the way, shoulders hunched and feet sliding rather than marching.

The column trudged on, slower now as more vehicles approached. An ammunition limber growled past, then a water carrier. They marched through a village where every second house bore signs of shell damage. Many were uninhabited, but others contained civilians who watched the marching soldiers with no interest at all. A mother cradled her infant son as the men passed; a young girl skipped alongside for a few yards and laughed when one of the privates tossed a biscuit to her; she stuffed it in her mouth and ran away. The village slid away as they marched on, the drum beat of their feet monotonous on the cracked pave.

"How far is the front?" Kerr asked.

"Not far now; it's just a few miles." Ramsay recognised Kerr's excitement. "You will know when you get there."

The sudden roar made the recruits jump and Ramsay was not the only veteran who flinched as the battery of six inch guns fired.

"Give them hell, boys!" somebody shouted, the words lost in the concussion of the blast.

"That's bon," a smooth-faced veteran said, and looked to the horizon where the shells were travelling.

"I didn't even see them there!" Kerr shouted. He held a hand to his ear. "What an infernal noise!"

The gunners threw aside the empty brass shell case and slammed in another. Stripped to the waist and perspiring, they did not look around as the infantry marched past. Ramsay watched them fire again and then looked away; the first shot had taken him by surprise, the second was a familiar entity in this world. He knew that each successive round would be less important until the shellfire became just part of the psychological landscape, accepted and ignored.

Ramsay glanced up as a shell ripped overhead. The sky above stretched to infinity, a void of nothingness marred only by the vapour trail of a single patrolling aircraft, thousands of feet up. The aircraft looked so innocent up there, harmless, almost angelic, that Ramsay had to force himself to remember what horrors such a flying machine could unleash. The devil had sent his winged emissaries to soil the purity of heaven.

At noon they stopped for a break. The men lit pipes or slender Woodbines, chatted in undertones or looked around in dismay at the increasing devastation. Ramsay bit the end off a cheroot, lit carefully and inhaled slowly. He looked forward, hoping the fear did not show in his face. With every step his excitement lessened.

Oh God, here we go again. Please, God, let this nightmare end soon.

They moved off again, trudging now as weariness settled on them. There were more gun batteries, more ambulances, and the occasional dispatch rider on a snarling motor bike. There were perspiring store men and a red-tabbed staff officer in a motor car, heading away from the front. They passed a cemetery where new planted crosses seemed to blossom like some obscene crop. One young soldier tried to count them but gave up after a few moments.

"Don't look, son. Leave the dead in peace." The sergeant sounded almost gentle. "You concentrate on staying alive." He was only a year or two older than the recruit, but his eyes were timeless with fatigue and responsibility. The corporal guide watched and said nothing. He murmured something to the sergeant, glanced at Ramsay and altered their direction; they headed east, away from the dying sun.

The column moved on, relentless, the sound of their boots on the pave like the rhythmic clatter of some subterranean caterpillar, hollow and sharp, mocking the men who were so blithely marching to meet death. Ramsay counted his steps, each one was a millisecond of this life easing away, each one brought him closer to that other existence. Each one took him further from Gillian.

There was another battery of guns, eighteen pounders this time, firing slowly at the unseen enemy, the gunners moving like machines and the pile of empty brass shell cases head high at their side. Only the recruits turned their heads to watch; the veterans had returned to their front line selves, they had seen artillery before. There was a sound like an express train overhead and a sudden eruption in the flat fields, a hundred yards away to their right. The recruits ducked, some held on to their steel helmets, others stared open-mouthed at this ugly growth that subsided in a roar of falling mud and stones.

"What was that?" Kerr's nose wrinkled at the reek of lyddite. He peered through the brown haze of dirt.

"That was the bloody receipt, sir," one of the veterans explained, to be quickly hushed into silence by the sergeant.

"That's Fritz replying," Ramsay explained. He raised his voice. "Split the men up, Sergeant. Spread out the column."

The sergeant nodded, wordless, and gave quick orders. The column spread out, men looking uneasy as they were deprived of the comfort of close companions who had been strangers only a few hours previously. The sky was darkening overhead, with the flare of shellfire bright on the southern horizon.

"Why did you split the men up?" Kerr asked. "They don't like it at all."

"Minimise casualties," Ramsay said shortly. "If a shell lands in mud it will plunge underground before it explodes. The mud dissipates most of the force. If it lands on this pave," he tapped his boot on the road, "it will explode on contact and spread shrapnel and shell casings and bits of stone for scores of yards. One Jack Johnson could wipe out the entire column."

Kerr nodded. He looked around at the Royal Scots who now marched in a long, extended line.

"You take the rearguard, Kerr," Ramsay ordered. "Try and bring them in safe."

There were more ruins now, the shattered shells of houses, some sheltering small groups of soldiers on mysterious errands of their own. Behind one wall lay the bloated corpse of a horse, its flesh furred with flies. Behind another wall lay three soldiers sleeping in a heap, their uniforms so muddy and torn it was impossible to identify to which unit they belonged. An occasional gust of wind carried a smell of human waste, putrefying flesh and lyddite; the stink of the Front.

Ramsay halted the column in a muddy field. "The boys are marching by their chin straps now, Sergeant." He raised his voice. "Bed down for the night, men," he said, and watched the veterans show the recruits how to use straw and grass as a makeshift mattress. He lit another cheroot and looked up at the uncaring gaze of a million stars, already accepting the constant grumble of the guns as part of life. He leaned against a tumbledown wall at the edge of the field and drew on his cheroot until the tip glowed red.

Kerr joined him, shivering at the bite of the March night. "How far is the front?" Kerr asked again.

"Not far," Ramsay said. "This is the support area. We will be in the front line tomorrow." The words had the ring of doom about them. "But before you think of what tomorrow will bring, do your rounds – check your men. As an officer, the men are your first priority."

"Yes, sir," Kerr threw a smart salute.

"And please don't salute when we are near the front." Ramsay knew his nerves were showing. "It lets the Hun snipers know who the officers are."

With the eastern horizon intermittently scarred by the brilliant flashes of gunfire, and an occasional distant star shell illuminating the sky, Ramsay found no sleep that night. He lay hard against the rough stone wall and fought the fear that mounted within him. *I cannot go back again*, he thought. *I cannot go back again.* But he knew he must. There was no choice. The alternative was disgrace, ruin and the loss of Gillian. He reached into his inside pocket, pulled out the silver hip flask and unscrewed the cap. The aroma of whisky was sharp in his nose. He tipped the flask into his mouth and swallowed. *If I drink enough it will all go away for a while.* Each time though, it got worse.

He listened to the sweet call of the larks and envied them their freedom.

Ramsay felt the flask tremble as he held it. The mouthpiece rattled against his teeth as he tipped it further back. *Please God, if I am to be killed make it quick.*

They marched on next morning, with Ramsay's head throbbing in time with the pounding of iron-studded boots on the cracked pave. Sleep had refreshed the men and they marched faster now, the veterans keeping their heads down and the recruits looking around them, exclaiming at the shambles and flinching at even the most distant shell burst.

"Is this the front?" Kerr asked.

Ramsay grunted. "Not yet." He kept silent for a few more minutes before he relented. "This is the area the Germans vacated when they retreated to the Hindenburg Line." He waved his hand around. "Behold the civilisation of the Hun." He stepped aside and looked around.

There was mile after mile of devastation. All the houses

had been pulled down, all the wells filled in or polluted; even the trees were stripped – the branches were bare, naked fingers entreating pity from an uncaring sky.

"They make a desert and call it peace," Ramsay flicked ash onto the ground, "to misquote Tacitus."

"It's frightful," Kerr said. He ducked as a 5.9 inch exploded a hundred yards away. "We *must* win this war."

Two of the passing veterans threw him looks that combined disgust with pity. Ramsay noticed but did not comment. He could appreciate their point of view.

"Oh, yes. You keep that thought in your head, Kerr, when the whizz bangs are falling."

He looked upwards, to where two aircraft were pirouetting together, their vapour trails creating white patterns on the grey sky. It could have been pretty except for the distant chatter of machine guns. Somewhere the lark was still calling, the sound melancholic against the unheeded grumble of the guns. *There are always bloody larks. I hate those birds.*

Ramsay pulled hard on his cheroot. It was the smell that he objected to most. It seemed to seep into every pore of him; it stuck to his clothes and refused to leave. It was not a single smell, but a compilation of a hundred; from the sickening stench of decaying meat created by the dead and buried bodies that lay in No Man's Land, to the stink from the latrines, socks: weeks unwashed and men's lice-infested bodies, and the vicious stink of lyddite and phosgene gas. The stench remained with him long after the sights and sounds had vanished.

They reached the first trenches at seven in the morning, passing a battery of artillery whose gunners glistened with sweat as they fired a continuous stream of shells toward the German lines.

"The morning hate," Ramsay explained as Kerr flinched.

"You'll get used to it."

There was another small cemetery here; the crosses plain, with the name, number and regiment of each soldier the only sign that the grave beneath held a man who had lived, breathed and loved, who had planned for his future, who had a mother and perhaps a sweetheart or a wife. Now they were empty carcasses mouldering in France with the vitality and personality that had made them unique gone and already fading from memory.

Not all the dead were buried yet. There was one body lying outside the wall, covered in a single blanket. As they passed a twist of the wind flicked open the cover and the corpse glared out. He had not died easy; shrapnel had sliced him open, his intestines had escaped and he had tried to replace them with clawed hands. Fear and agony furrowed his face.

Ramsay watched as Kerr gagged, recovered and moved bravely on, muttering, "Frightful."

"You'll get used to that as well," Ramsay said quietly.

"Here's the Communication Trench, sir," the guide said, and slipped into an entrance of muddy sandbags. "We call it Leith Walk." He thrust a Woodbine between his lips and slouched on, his feet straddling the sludge of mud in the centre of the trench.

"Just keep behind me, sir," the guide sounded bored, "and duck when I do." He led them along the trench and through a maze of shoulder-high ditches, some with deeper trenches that led to the front. On either side the slimy mud was riveted by planking, with a wall of sandbags on top. Occasionally there were pools of water to negotiate, some crossed by duckboards, others without. There were dugouts from time to time, some containing groups of weary men, others piled with equipment or stores, with a bored sentry to prevent pilfering. The gunfire seemed muted down here.

"Watch yourself here, sir." The guide ducked his head. "A shell knocked the sandbags to glory." He jerked a thumb in the direction of the German lines. "It's not bon because Fritz occasionally sprays the gap with a machine gun."

Ramsay nodded and passed the information back. He remained at the gap in the sandbags, waving his men through one by one until the sergeant at the rear nodded to him. "That's them all, sir."

"Make sure there are no stragglers," Ramsay ordered, and pushed through to the head of his men.

A shell burst overhead, scattering shrapnel over a wide area. The veterans ducked into what cover there was, pulling the recruits behind them. "Come on, you!"

Nobody was injured, but the recruits grasped their shrapnel helmets closer and looked around, fear and anger replacing excitement. Somebody whimpered. Someone else shook a fist in the direction of the German lines and shouted a challenge. Something metallic thudded into the sandbag, a foot from Ramsay's head. He looked at it without interest. He did not care about near misses, they did not matter.

Kerr had crouched down in the bottom of the trench. "Will our guns fire back?"

"That was one of ours, sir," the guide said. His voice was flat.

"Keep going, boys," Ramsay ordered. "But keep your wits about you."

Twice the guide stopped them to warn of areas where snipers were active. The replacements ran past at irregular intervals, ducking low beneath the sandbag parapet. The gash in the back wall of the trench with the dribble of sand onto the ground beneath told its own story.

"No casualties?" The guide glanced over the replacements. "Bon. Now keep your heids down, eh?"

As they neared the front line the guide moved more slowly, checking every traverse of the trench until he arrived at the entrance to a dugout. The gas curtain was pulled back, revealing a long flight of steps descending into the dark.

"Here we go, sir. Major Campbell will look after you now. You too, Mr Kerr."

Without bothering to salute, the guide ducked away leaving Ramsay and Kerr to negotiate the steps. Ramsay sniffed the familiar aroma of candle smoke, sweat and whisky, tinged with the cheerful scent of fried bacon. He pushed through a second gas curtain and stepped into the interior of the dugout. There was a single deal table, much stained, with three hard-backed chairs arranged around it and a larger, occupied armchair in the corner. A single candle burned low from its perch in the neck of an empty wine bottle.

"Ah! Douglas Ramsay I presume!" The major was short, stout and red-faced. He lifted himself from his lopsided armchair and advanced with his hand outstretched. "Welcome to the 20th Royals!"

"Thank you, sir," Ramsay saluted, and accepted the proffered hand.

Campbell looked at his two pips, then at the wound stripes on his sleeve. His eyes narrowed slightly, but he said nothing. He glanced at Kerr; "And you must be Simon Kerr?"

"Yes, sir." Kerr stiffened to as near attention as the low ceiling of the dugout permitted. He threw a salute that would have made any guardsman proud.

"There is no need for you to stay, Kerr," Campbell said. "The sooner you get used to things the better, so just jog along after the guide, eh? There's a good chap."

Kerr flushed a little, but recognised the dismissal and withdrew toward the door.

"Oh, and Kerr," Campbell called him back. "Lose the

Sam Browne would you? There's no sense in advertising to the Huns that you're an officer."

Kerr blinked, glanced at Campbell's shoulder, bereft of any Sam Browne. "Yes, sir."

Campbell waited until he was gone. "There is no need to scare the lad yet, but your timing is excellent, Ramsay. We're expecting Fritz to try a push soon and we need all the experienced men we can get."

Campbell's eyes were weary, half-hidden beneath a spider's web of wrinkles.

"Yes, sir," Ramsay said. "I heard the rumours before I came."

Campbell's smile dropped. "This war is full of rumours, Ramsay, but this one may be true." He shrugged. "I wish the defence line was completed, but if wishes were horses we'd all win the Derby, eh?"

"Yes, sir," Ramsay took the chair that Campbell offered.

"Since we took over this section from the French we have done a lot of work to it, but it is far from completed yet." Campbell shrugged again. "We will just have to manage as best we can."

Ramsay realised he was supposed to comment. "Yes, sir. I am sure we will."

"Have you brought your servant with you?" Campbell looked at the dugout entrance as though expecting a private to emerge from the dark. "Obviously not. We can get that arranged tomorrow."

"Yes, sir." *Only if Fritz allows us the time.*

Campbell grunted, leaned across to the table and opened a drawer. He produced a half-empty bottle of Glenlivet and two glasses. "This is just to take the trench taste away." He sloshed whisky into both and slid a glass over to Ramsay.

"Your health," he said quietly. "Try and avoid bullets this time, Ramsay, and may God be with us both."

The whisky burned its way down Ramsay's throat and exploded in his stomach. He gasped and took a second swallow.

Campbell finished his glass in a single gulp, poured himself another and drank that too, before replacing the bottle in the drawer. "Now that you've been christened, Ramsay, have you any questions?"

Ramsay glanced at the map of the front line spread over one entire wall of the dugout. "Where are we, exactly, sir?"

Campbell unsheathed a bayonet that hung in its scabbard from the back of his chair, looked at the glittering blade for a second and jabbed it in the map.

"We are here, between the Durhams and the Northumberland Fusiliers. As you know, most of the Front is no longer a continuous line of trenches, but a system of strongholds – we call them keeps – which should be mutually supporting with interlocking fields of fire." Campbell raised his eyebrows and waited for Ramsay's confirmation.

"Yes, sir," Ramsay said.

"Except the keeps are not complete yet," Campbell said, "and we are lacking machine guns and artillery." He opened the drawer again, looked at the whisky bottle and closed it with a bang. "How up to date with the situation are you, Ramsay?"

"I have been recovering from wounds for the past few months, but I have kept in touch with events in France."

Campbell nodded. "You are quite experienced for a lieutenant. Remind me where you were wounded, Ramsay?"

Ramsay ignored the implied criticism of his rank. "Passchendaele." He heard the flat intonation of his own voice.

Campbell heard it too. "That was a bad one," he said. He glanced at Ramsay's two pips and pushed harder. "Was that your first action?"

"No, sir." Ramsay shook his head. "I was at the Somme as well."

Campbell glanced again at the two wound stripes. "You were injured there as well?'

"Yes, sir." Ramsay did not explain further.

Campbell nodded. "I will be blunt, Ramsay. I would expect an officer of your experience to hold a higher rank than lieutenant." The weary eyes held Ramsay's gaze.

"Yes, sir," Ramsay sighed. "I was wounded on the first day of the Somme. I hardly cleared our own trenches before I was hit, so there was little time to gain promotion."

Campbell nodded, but his eyes remained hard. "Was that your first action?"

"Yes, sir," Ramsay said.

"And your second?"

"Passchendaele," Ramsay told him. "In between I was recovering and then based in southern England."

"Hence no chance of promotion," Campbell agreed. "Even so, it's good to have an officer of your experience here, Ramsay. We are fighting a different war to the one you knew at the Somme, and with different men." He returned his attention to the map. "As I was saying, the front line should consist of a series of strong points with interlocking fields of fire, so in theory every inch is covered by machine gun and artillery fire." He tapped the point of his bayonet on the combination of lines and dots that marked the British front line.

"We are here, in the centre left of General Gough's 5th Army. I want you to take over this section of the firing line, from here, to here." He moved the bayonet slowly across the map. "We are still creating our strong points, but we have a partially completed small keep which you will command." Campbell sat back down, put a hand toward the table as if reaching for something, changed his mind and began tapping his fingers on the arm of his chair. "As soon as you are settled in, Ramsay, I want you to send out an observation patrol. Tonight will do. See if old Fritz has anything planned, listen for anything unusual. Try and see when Fritz is coming."

Ramsay nodded. "How many men do I have, sir?"

"Thirty three," Campbell said quietly, "and you have three traverses with one Lewis gun. There is support behind you, of course. We have two Vickers machine guns, as well as artillery, so your front is well-covered if Fritz decides to call.'

Ramsay nodded. "Thank you, sir, that is good to know."

"We call your section of the line Gorgie Road," Campbell gave a wry smile. "I hope you are not a keen follower of the other Edinburgh football team."

Ramsay did not smile at the Edinburgh connection. "I prefer rugger sir. How are the men?" he asked.

Campbell shrugged. "Mostly very young, with a stiffening of veterans," he said. "You have a few originals and you will need Sergeant Flockhart and Corporal McKim." Campbell shook his head. "McKim is a bit of a rogue, but there is no better man when things get rough, except perhaps Flockhart."

"Sergeant Flockhart?" Ramsay started. He felt the blood rise to his face but took a deep breath. *Calm down; it's a common enough name. There's no need for worry.*

"That's the man," Campbell confirmed.

"Sergeant James Flockhart?"

Oh God, no! Of all the people to bump into out here!

"You know him?" Campbell looked up, smiling.

"Not personally, sir, but I have heard the name," Ramsay lied easily. He tried to still the increased hammering of his heart as the memories crowded back into his mind.

Fresh spring grass; puffy clouds painted white against

17

a blue washed sky, with trees waving only the tips of their boughs in the lightest of breezes. She looked up into his face, wide eyes of light blue laughing with him as they made soft love.

"Happy?" he asked, and she nodded her head, and then opened her mouth in a cry of ecstasy.

He smiled and allowed the sensation to linger as he gazed down at her, with those wondrous breasts now exposed to the kiss of the sun that highlighted the faint down on her arms.

In a few years, Ramsay knew, the breasts that gave him so much pleasure would be ponderous and her eyes hardened with toil and poverty, but for the time being she was all that he desired in a woman: young, willing and free.

He climaxed and lay there, panting slightly as she moaned in his ear. The world was good.

He listened to the sound of her breathing and reached out for her again.

"Do you love me?" she asked.

"That's not surprising," Campbell's words brought Ramsay back. The major studied a section of the map for a second. "Flockhart is a good man – one of the originals – a veteran of Mons, Ypres and the Somme. He's seen it all and done it all, he can be trusted. McKim is an old soldier from way back. He's been promoted and busted back to the ranks so many times the regiment has lost count. He was in the Boer War from Bird's River to Paardeplatz, the siege of Wepener and with Dawkins in the Transvaal. He knows all there is to know about soldiering." Campbell touched the two gold wound stripes on Ramsay's sleeve. "Junior officers have to earn the trust of McKim and Flockhart, but these will help."

The sergeant's name had startled Ramsay but he glanced down. "Yes, sir."

Campbell returned his attention to the map. "So you're back for another helping of Fritz, then?" He sat down again before Ramsay could reply and waved his bayonet at the map. The twelve and a quarter inch long blade seemed to waver in the flickering glow of the candle. "Let me elaborate on the set up we have here. It's not like it used to be, Ramsay. Now we have three distinct defence lines. The rear line that we can defend in depth. You have just come through that. There is the battlezone of strongpoints and redoubts, this is where we will hold any push by Fritz. Lastly, and most exposed, is the forward zone of small outposts and larger strongpoints." He waved the bayonet vaguely at the map. "As our sector is not complete yet, we still have sandbagged trenches as well, while the strongpoints are not as strong as I would like them to be."

Campbell held Ramsay's eyes; his face was expressionless. "I am sending you to the forward zone."

Ramsay nodded. *Back again. Back with the mud and slaughter, back to the scene of my earlier failures.* "Yes, sir."

"Just leave my office here," Campbell smiled at his attempt at humour, "walk down Gorgie Road for half a mile and you will reach your new home." He held out his hand. "Well, good luck, Ramsay. You had better get out to the forward zone and look after things." He smiled, briefly, but his eyes were still weary. "I repeat, I am glad to have an experienced man with us. These young lads like Kerr are good stuff, keen as mustard and brave as they come, but the men prefer an officer who's been through it." His smile was bleak as an Edinburgh November. "There are not many of us left."

With that reminder of their own vulnerability, Campbell sat back down, glanced at Ramsay and recovered the bottle of Glenlivet. Raising it in Ramsay's direction, he asked, "More?" and shrugged when Ramsay shook his head.

"You won't mind if I do." He poured whisky into his glass and did not stop until the liquid slopped over the rim and overflowed onto the table that bore a hundred similar stains. Ramsay left him to the sanctuary of alcohol and stepped into the sinister dark.

How long this time? How long before I catch a bullet and the men despise me?

A flare drifted across the night sky, casting a red light over the surreal landscape, momentarily highlighting a barrier of sandbags with crimson shadow. *Like blood. Like the blood of a million dead men.* Ramsay shivered, pushed the thought away and concentrated on finding his way through the shambles of barbed wire that linked the strongpoints together. What had seemed so clear cut on the map was only confusion on the ground.

"Are you looking for somewhere, sir?" The voice came out of the dark.

"I'm looking for Gorgie Road," Ramsay said.

"You've found it, sir," the voice said. "You'll be Lieutenant Ramsay then?" A compact figure emerged from the shadow of the sandbags. When a signal flare soared up above No Man's Land, he withdrew to the trench wall, but not before Ramsay had seen he was a stocky man with steady eyes and the three stripes of a sergeant on his sleeve.

That's him. Oh, God, that's Flockhart.

"Careful now, sir. There's a sniper about. He's a persistent bugger and he loves it when somebody lights us up with a flare."

Ramsay stood still until the flare died away. He knew that movement meant death if a German sniper was on the prowl. Of the British, only the Lovat Scouts could outmatch the German snipers and there were none in this sector of the line.

"Can't we deal with him?" Ramsay moved on, with the sergeant slightly behind, his feet quiet on the sparse duck boards. "I might send out a patrol of picked men and watch for him."

"Not bon, sir. Your predecessor tried," the sergeant's voice was flat. He gestured over the wall of sandbags with a jerk of his head. "He's still out there," his face twisted in the sudden light of a flare, "hanging on the old barbed wire."

Ramsay nodded. "I see. You will be Sergeant Flockhart, then?" He tried to keep his voice neutral as he narrowed his eyes against the glare of the flare. His hand edged to the flap of his revolver holster. *Did Flockhart know who he was?*

"The very same," Flockhart agreed. "If you don't mind me saying, sir, would you like me to show you to your dugout? You look dead on your feet."

The flare faded and fell to earth, leaving them in blackness that seemed more intense in contrast to what had gone before. Ramsay started at the sudden clamour of a machine gun. The noise echoed in the dark. "Sorry," he said, "my nerves are not what they were." He flicked open the catch of the holster. *Do it now. Nobody will know. It will be one shot among a thousand.*

"Nobody's nerves are what they once were." Flockhart had not moved. "That was up north, not in our parish." He stepped onto the duckboards in the centre of the trench. "Come this way, sir. Mind and keep your head down."

The trench was shallower than those Ramsay remembered, with sandbags making up more than half the wall. Rather than forming a permanent barrier across the whole line of the front, it served as a link between a number of more heavily fortified strong points, where Lewis gunners crouched behind castellated parapets and Vickers machine guns swivelled to cover all possible access points. As always, there were men on duty, standing on the firing step, peering through periscopes into the dark or crouching in the shelter of the sandbags as they gripped their rifles. Some looked up as he passed, others ignored him. Only one man jumped to attention and tried to salute. Flockhart pushed him back. "Don't be stupid, Nesbit! If Fritz is watching you'll have Mr Ramsay marked off for the sniper!"

"Oh God, I'm sorry, sir!" Nesbit appeared to be about fifteen years old.

"Just something else to remember, Nesbit," Ramsay said. "You get back to duty, son." He felt suddenly ancient. He was barely twenty-three, but it was hard to remember a time when his life had not been regulated by gunfire and punctuated by the wary eyes of private soldiers. Either that or the heavy smell of antiseptic in the white-painted wards of a military hospital, among the regulation blues that hid the wreckage of what had once been fit young men.

Ramsay borrowed a trench periscope and eased it over the parapet to survey No Man's Land. At first his eyes could not penetrate the dark, but a providential flare drifted across the sky, casting a greenish hue over the landscape and reflecting from ten thousand barbs in a hundred coils of wire. Ramsay winced at dark memories.

Kerr joined them, his face tinted green by the flare. He said nothing as he filed behind them, but his breathing was heavy, indicating nerves.

"Good man, Kerr," Ramsay encouraged.

Flockhart nodded to him, "If you just bear with us, sir," and led them round a corner of the trench to where a wall of sandbags soared into the hostile sky. "Here we are sir. We call it Craigmillar Castle. This is our own private keep."

The sandbags were six deep around this section of the trench, with firing positions every yard and a raised platform for the Lewis gun. One glance through the periscope revealed an eighteen foot deep barrier of barbed wire. "It's not perfect, sir," Flockhart said. "We could do with a heavy machine gun in our section and at least two more Lewis guns." He gave a wry smile. "And a couple of Fritz's pill boxes."

Ramsay nodded. He looked around, assessing how his section of trench could be improved. "How has Fritz been behaving recently?"

"Tres bon, quiet as a baby on laudanum, sir." Flockhart jerked his head back to indicate the German lines, a scant two hundred yards away. "No patrols, no morning hate, nothing. It's like they are on holiday over there."

"They are definitely planning something then," Ramsay said. "We can expect a raiding party tonight or at dawn tomorrow. Is there a listening post in No Man's Land, Sergeant?"

"There is, sir. It's manned day and night in case the Huns try anything. We have Second Lieutenant Mercer there now, but it's time for his relief." Flockhart rolled his eyes toward Kerr.

Now! Now I can get rid of him. Ramsay nodded and turned to Kerr, who had been a silent spectator to the conversation. "Kerr, I want you to take Sergeant Flockhart and four men to the listening post. If you hear anything unusual, report back. Follow the advice of Sergeant Flockhart. I don't want any heroics now."

Kerr grinned quickly, "Thank you, sir."

Thanking me for sending him into danger. That boy should still be at school.

"Remember what I said and don't be a hero, Kerr. Do as the sergeant advises. He was cutting barbed wire when you were still cutting your milk teeth. "

Flockhart did not look as pleased. He raised his eyebrows

briefly, nodded and said, "Very good, sir." He seemed to be studying Ramsay's face, as though trying to recognise him

Yes, it's me you bastard, your nemesis. Die!

Ramsay watched as Kerr divested himself of all his surplus equipment and followed Flockhart into a deep, sandbagged bay. There was a crooked tunnel that led into a sap which zig-zagged forward. Flockhart slid into the sap, with Kerr following eagerly and four anonymous privates who followed more slowly and with less enthusiasm.

Set ye Uriah in the forefront of the hottest battle and retire ye from him, that he may be smitten and die. Ramsay shook the betrayal from his head. "Good luck," he said. Kerr looked back and smiled and then the privates shuffled forward and they disappeared behind a dogleg in the sap. There were faint sounds of feet scuffing on duckboards and then silence. Suddenly it seemed lonely in the keep.

What have I done? Self-loathing uncoiled in Ramsay's stomach and he turned away in disgust. He turned again, opened his mouth to call them back and a corporal hunched past, pipe between his teeth and his eyes as calm as midsummer. "Evening, sir," he said. "Don't you worry, you'll soon settle in." He stopped and removed his pipe but made no attempt to salute. Ramsay saw that he wore the King's and Queen's Boer war medal ribbon as well as the purple and green of the North West Frontier.

"Thank you, Corporal. . .?"

"McKim, sir." The corporal appraised him frankly. "Kenny McKim. You'll be the new lieutenant, then." He grinned. "Welcome to Craigmillar Castle, sir."

"Thank you," Ramsay repeated. "Hardly a castle, is it?" He looked up as another flare soared into the night. The light illuminated this section of trench, showing the heavily sandbagged emplacement for the Lewis gun with its six man team trying to grab some sleep around its base. The barrel pointed skyward but the drum of ammunition was fitted in place and one man had his hand on the stock, as if holding the hand of a favourite child.

"Let's hope Fritz stays at home for a few days," McKim placed his hands in his pockets and sauntered down the trench. Although he did not look down, his feet found the driest places on the duckboards. "Here's your own personal snug, sir." He jerked an elbow toward a dugout. The top step was supported by sandbags and the side wall riveted by broken duck boards.

"Wake me in two hours," Ramsay paused at the entrance, "and I will do my rounds."

"Yes, sir," McKim said. "Although the guns will wake you first." He raised a hand in farewell and stepped around the traverse of the trench. His rifle was slung casually over his shoulder, but a canvas cover protected the muzzle and what Ramsay could see of the mechanism was bright and clean.

Ramsay negotiated the five steps that led to his dugout. It was not as luxurious as that enjoyed by Campbell, being little more than a depression scooped out of the ground, roofed with corrugated iron and protected by layered sandbags. Despite the chicken wire that lined the interior walls, mud and soil had seeped into the room and lay in small piles, while the smell of stale sweat from the last occupant was noticeable, even above the normal stench of the front. There was a garish picture on the wall, a scantily clad woman with ample breasts and a big smile – the accompanying script was in French and Ramsay did not bother with a translation. The table was small, unsteady and unwashed; the bed consisted of a duckboard plank balanced between two sandbags and a straw mattress on top. There was a telephone with a wire snaking up the steps, presumably connecting the dugout to Major Campbell. Ramsay lifted the receiver and heard the faint buzz that confirmed his connection; there was nothing else in the room, save mud.

I sent a man to the most dangerous post possible today, and I am safe and well.

Lying fully clothed on the damp mattress, Ramsay tried to close his eyes. The images returned to haunt him, reactivated by the sights and smells of the trenches. Images of men drowning in mud; images of fragments of men pleading for death; images of men mown down by the dozen, the score, the hundred; images of that deep shell hole filled with poisonous green water in which he had survived until the stretcher bearers came for him. He shook his head, feeling the sweat start from his pores and the familiar maddening itch that the memories always brought. He was back in the environment he loathed yet could never escape from, among men who were as doomed as he was. This was his reality and anything that had occurred before did not matter. Even that day did not matter, although it had nagged at his conscience with tearing claws and those accusing eyes were in his mind every morning he awoke.

All the horrors of the war formed a veil, behind which that reality cowered, but night always eased back a corner of the curtain and the guilt peered through. He screwed his fists into tight balls and writhed on the rustling straw.

CHAPTER TWO

FRANCE

21 March 1918

The roar of the guns woke him. He rolled from the mattress onto the muddy duckboards as the enamel mug on the plank table jumped and rolled beside him. He looked up as McKim poked his head through the gas screen of the doorway.

"Two hours, sir," McKim said cheerfully. "That's our counter preparation wishing Jerry a good morning."

Ramsay picked himself up from the floor. "Sorry, I fell off the bed."

"So I see, sir." McKim grabbed his helmet as a shell burst short and red hot shrapnel clattered down the steps. One piece ripped through the gas curtain and fell onto the ground. It glowed a dull red for a few moments then gradually faded to black. McKim scuffed it aside. "I think the brass hats want to break up any possible German attack before it starts."

Ramsay nodded. "Thank you, McKim."

"We'll sort out a servant for you today, sir." McKim glanced around the dugout. "We'll soon have this place looking like home. In the meantime, here's a mug of char and a chunk of bungy."

"Thank you, McKim." He stuffed the cheese in his mouth and sipped the tea. "Blighty tea," he said, and glanced up. "Let's get topsides."

Ramsay ducked through the gas curtain and up into the firing line. A quick glance behind him revealed flashes in the misty darkness; the muzzle flares of the British guns that were firing at the German positions. The shells arced overhead, ripping through the air with a relentless noise that made it hard to hear and harder to speak. Ramsay looked north and east and saw the results, the orange bursts over and on the German positions, only a few hundred yards away across No Man's Land.

"Poor buggers," McKim mouthed the words and shrugged. "Better them than us."

Ramsay nodded but said nothing. He remembered all too well what it was like to be on the wrong side of such a bombardment. He also knew that however impressive the fire and fury looked, the Germans had taken far worse at the Somme and had emerged unshaken to wreak havoc with the British attack. He leaned closer to McKim and spoke in his ear. "Fritz is a tough bugger, he will be dug deep underground, laughing at us."

McKim screwed up his face. "That's not bloody bon, sir."

"No," Ramsay said. He tightened the chinstrap of his helmet. "That's not bloody bon at all, McKim."

"The fog's increasing, sir," McKim said. "I would not like to be out there in that." He nodded toward No Man's Land where the mist clung to the closest coils of barbed wire. A patter of soil landed around them; debris from an under-shot British shell.

"No," Ramsay agreed. For a moment he thought of Kerr and Flockhart and then dismissed the thought. They would have to take their chances, just like everybody else. This was war. He commandeered a trench periscope and surveyed the lines before him. The fog made visibility nearly impossible and if it had not been for the orange flash of explosions he would not have been able to make out where the German front lines were. He moved the instrument from side to side, noting the shell bursts through the fog.

"Once the barrage lifts, McKim, I want you to take out a patrol. Liaise with Sergeant Flockhart in the listening post, see if he has heard anything significant and then probe toward the German lines. Don't get into a fight, just see if there is anything happening out there."

McKim grunted. "Kitchener wants me, does he?" He nodded. "Yes, sir."

Despite the shelling the fog intensified and by three in the morning Ramsay could hardly see as far as the nearest edge of the barbed wire. At four o'clock the barrage lifted. One second there was the hellish drumbeat of shells and next there was a mind-numbing silence that pressed down upon him, punctuated only by the sound of a lark hidden somewhere in the fog.

"McKim?'

The corporal had already detailed two men to accompany him into No Man's Land.   "Ready, sir."

They stood with blackened faces, carrying rifles, bayonets and short, vicious knobkerries for close combat, but bereft of packs or belts. McKim wore an empty sandbag over his helmet so the steel would not reflect the light of flare or shell flash. Ramsay watched as McKim led the two privates over the top and crawled forward. Within seconds they vanished into the mist and perils of No Man's Land.

It was nearly dawn, the dangerous time. If the Germans were coming, this was the best time for them, when the men who had been on guard all night were tired and the others not properly awake yet.

"Stand to," Ramsay ordered, quietly. "Come on, lads." The men stumbled wearily from their dugouts and shallow shelters. They took their positions in the firing bays and removed the Lee-Enfields from their covered positions set into the side walls of sandbags. A few of the men handled the rifles with the expertise of veterans, but most had the clumsy movements of the half-trained recruits they still were. "Fix bayonets, lads."

There was a sinister click as the Royal Scots prepared themselves for any possible German attack. The veterans probed makeshift periscopes of penny mirrors tied onto lengths of wood above the sandbagged parapet and a few bold men inched cautious heads into the castellated gaps above the fire steps. The steel shield of a loophole reflected the light of a weary flare for a second. There was the single sharp crack of a sniper's rifle to the south, followed by the chattering reply of a machine gun. Then silence.

"I hate this waiting," one man complained.

"Keep your mouth shut, Cruickshank!" an NCO snapped.

The Royal Scots waited for whatever No Man's Land would bring. Some looked eager, others resigned, a few hid their fear behind nervous grins, but all held their rifles. Ramsay glanced along the line. One recruit was trembling while his neighbour, a man of nearly nineteen, touched his arm.

"Steady, Tam. If they come, then they come and we can kill them. If not, then we just wait."

It was just half light; obscured by the swirling mist, Ramsay patrolled his section of the trench. There was a strange beauty here, a Hieronymus Bosch surrealism of dim figures partly seen; magnified or decreased by shadow and form, with the twinkling of matches and the soft glow of cigarettes or pipes hazy through the mist and the slow awakening of another dangerous day. The dark eased westward, chased by relentless dawn.

"Cannae see a bloody thing in this mist," a tall private broke the spell in the uncompromising accent of Leith.

"Something's moving," his neighbour said. He pushed his rifle forward on the sandbag, the barrel made a small hissing sound, the bayonet snaking forward, pointing towards the enemy lines.

"Who's that on the Lewis gun?" Ramsay whispered.

"Black, sir." The voice was tense.

"Keep a good watch, Black," Ramsay ordered. "As best you can in this muck."

"Aye, sir," the voice was patient and the simple phrase revealed that Black was fully aware of the necessity of keeping a good watch. The Lewis gun team clustered around him. They said nothing but Ramsay could hear their tense breathing. A breath of wind shifted the mist, obscuring the Lewis gun team.

On either side of him the Royal Scots levelled their rifles. A man began to pray. Another sang softly between his teeth,

> *"Après la guerre finie*
> *Soldat Ecosse parti*
> *Mademoiselle in the family way*
> *Après la guerre finie"*

"God save us, God save us," another man mumbled.

"Come on, you bastards," a dark-haired corporal grunted. "Come on so I can kill you."

There was the subdued rattle of bolts being pulled back. Somebody swore, somebody muttered an obscene joke, there was a short burst of laughter. The breeze dropped, the mist thickened.

"Ready, boys." Ramsay unfastened his holster and pulled out his revolver. It shook in his hand. He remembered buying it in John Dickson's gun shop in Edinburgh.

"Do you have a Webley Fosberry?"

Gillian had widened her eyes in surprise. "I did not know you knew anything about guns."

"The Fosberry is renowned for its reliability," Ramsay said. He did not tell Gillian that his knowledge came from the catalogues he had read the previous evening.

The gunsmith nodded. "Off to France, sir?"

"Yes, eventually."

The revolver was heavy and clumsy in his hand.

"Would you care to try it out?" The salesman showed him how to load the revolving chamber.

"No, I'll just take it." Ramsay tried to appear nonchalant, as if he bought a gun every day of his life. He hoped that Gillian was impressed.

That seemed a very long time ago. Now he was in France once more, over three years later, and he held the revolver in a shaking hand. He took a deep breath and tried to control his nerves, or was it fear?

I am not scared; I am an officer of the Royal Scots. I am not scared; I am an officer of the Royal Scots. I must show no fear in front of the men.

A figure loomed up, giant in the mist; the legs elongated, the helmeted head shaded by heavy moisture. It stood for a second at the lip of the trench, the tails of its greatcoat sliced off and it appeared like some form of fancy dress. Shreds of mist wisped from the broad shoulders and the blade of the bayonet was darkened by smoke and caught no light.

"Jesus, it's Fritz!" Private Aitken, tall and lanky and with the hint of a moustache, levelled his rifle.

"Wait!" Ramsay knocked up the barrel as he recognised McKim.

"Stand easy, boys." McKim almost dislodged the top sandbag as he slithered into the trench. The two privates followed him, landing with audible relief on the muddy duckboards. "Nothing happening out there, sir," he reported. "Fritz is behaving himself."

Ramsay nodded. "Thank you, McKim. How was Sergeant Flockhart?" *Is he dead or alive? Have I killed my own sergeant? Am I free of that day? Am I a murderer in all but name?*

McKim looked sideways at him. "All bon, sir. He's still there. Lieutenant Kerr and he have had a quiet night, despite the bumps."

Ramsay nodded. "Good for them." *Why am I relieved at that? I tried to kill him; I failed. I should be disappointed.*

McKim hustled his privates past Ramsay. "Come on lads, time to get some scoff."

Ramsay looked to his right. Second Lieutenant Mercer was heading toward the furthest traverse. A tall, thin youth with pimples on his chin, he gave Ramsay a quick smile. "My post is round there, sir."

"Off you go then, Mercer. Good luck."

Mercer hesitated at the corner of the traverse. He looked over his shoulder, adjusted the chin strap of his helmet and stepped into the mist. He looked like a school prefect inspecting a dormitory, perhaps a bit younger.

The first shell was a whizz-bang. It exploded without warning, a hundred yards to the left, scattering splinters over the neighbouring trench. The next landed in the midst of the barbed wire entanglement, thirty yards in front of them. It lifted the supporting stakes and dropped the whole lot in a tangled mess. Ramsay swore. "Here we go!"

CHAPTER THREE

FRANCE

21 March 1918

After the first few sighting shots, the shells came in force. A score, a hundred, a thousand shells screaming over from the German positions to smother the British positions. At first they landed in groups of six, and then in scores and the volume increased until the air was full of flying shells and the ground was a confusion of orange flames and flying pieces of shrapnel.

"Dear God!" A private stared at his arm, which lay on the ground at his side, neatly severed. There was no blood, a sliver of white hot metal had cauterised the wound. He was still staring as a second shell fragment cut his head in half. Pink and grey matter oozed onto his shoulder as he slowly toppled onto the duck boards at the bottom of the trench.

Another private tried to hold in intestines cascading in an obscene pink stream from his belly. He made small mewing noises as he watched his life slip away. When he looked up, Ramsay saw the hopeless fear in his childlike eyes.

"Stretcher bearer!" Ramsay's roar was lost in the maelstrom of noise and the confusion of ten thousand shell bursts.

The boy began to scream, endlessly, in a high-pitched falsetto that reached above the roar of the bombardment. "Help me, sir," he mouthed, as he pushed his intestines back inside his body. "Please, help me." The words were unheard amidst the hellish din of the bombardment, but the message was clear.

Ramsay knelt beside him and stuffed handfuls of slimy guts back in the ragged hole in the boy's stomach. "You'll be all right, you'll be all right," he muttered, again and again. *Oh God, you poor wee boy. Die quickly, please die quickly.*

The boy stiffened, gave a convulsive shudder, vomited blood and died. Ramsay cowered as a shell exploded just on the far side of the sandbag wall and showered him with dirt. A pebble clattered from the crown of his helmet, making him wince and his head ring. He remained crouched in the bottom of the trench beside the dead boy until his head cleared, and then looked around his command.

There was no need to order anybody to take cover. Ramsay saw that his men were hunched into the deepest corners of the trench or had dived into the dugouts. A shell exploded directly behind the firestep, throwing a score of sandbags in the air as though they were packed with feathers. The dead boy vanished completely, a crater occupying the space where he had died. Other shells exploded overhead, scattering shrapnel down upon the men sheltering below.

"Gas! Gas! Gas!" There was panic in Aitken's voice and Ramsay scrambled for the gas mask that hung around his neck. He fumbled with the fastenings, slid the apparatus around his face with shaking hands and stared out through an eyepiece that was already beginning to mist over. All around him, men were doing the same. They hated the masks only a little less than they feared the invisible killer, the German gas.

"Bastards," Ramsay mumbled, "bloody Hun bastards." He looked at the thick white mist, wondering how much was natural fog and how much gas. *The scientist that invented gas as a weapon of war should be choked to death by mustard gas and condemned to the deepest pit of hell.*

The bombardment increased. Ramsay could no longer distinguish the individual shell bursts. He existed within a constant roar of noise punctured by shrill screams and the whistle and clang of ricochets and whirling shrapnel. He slithered through the gas screen and fell head first into his dugout, lying on his face, his hands holding the steel helmet tight on his head, trying not to scream. There was a man beside him, but he did not look to see who it was. It did not matter. In this situation there was no rank, all were merely men in terrible danger of maiming or death.

"Bastards, bastards, bastards," his fellow sufferer repeated the single word in a continuous monotone. "Bastards, bastards, bastards."

The noise continued as Ramsay lay there with the ground shaking beneath him and sand sliding through the corrugated iron roof from the piled sandbags above. He lost all track of time. Seconds merged into minutes and minutes into hours but none of that mattered. There was only the noise and the slow seeping gas that lay around him. That and the fear. Ramsay felt the shakes return like an old friend, or a newer enemy. Fear was worse than the Germans. He could see the Germans, he could understand them. They were men like him; solid tangible, creatures of flesh and bone and blood, animals that breathed and spoke and ate and slept and bled; they were him but in a different uniform. Fear was different; insidious, intangible, unseen. He could feel it creeping up on him, slow and soft at first but gradually building up with every bursting shell and every tremble of the ground. There were screams somewhere, but Ramsay did not move. To leave the dugout was to ask for death.

The private removed his gas mask. "They're throwing everything at us, sir!" He was an anonymous man, with mingled excitement and panic in his wide blue eyes. Ramsay could only nod. He did not trust himself to speak. A near miss shook the dugout and dirt cascaded from a ruptured sandbag above.

"This isn't just morning hate, sir. This is to destroy us!"

Ramsay grabbed the private's mask and rammed it back on his face.

"There's a gas curtain sir. We're safe."

Ramsay ignored the protest and yanked the strap tight. He pushed his face against that of the private and glared though the eyepiece. "Keep it on!" He yelled, knowing that the words would not be heard.

Even as he pushed the private away, Ramsay knew he had been correct. He could distinguish the different calibres of shells as they pounded the British positions and knew that this was far more intense than the usual morning hate, or a box barrage for the trench raid. He cringed at the horrible, heavy sound, like an express train, made by the large shells as they rushed overhead to pummel the rear. He recognised them all by sound or sight. There were the Jack Johnsons that exploded with a pall of greasy black smoke, the hated 'oilcans', the woolly bears and the fast and deadly whizz-bangs.

Ramsay tried to counter his fear by identifying each explosion as the German artillery lashed the positions of the Royal Scots, from the barbed wire entanglements in front, to the supporting trenches in the rear.

Dear God will this nightmare never end? How long has it been now? Two hours? Two days?

Ramsay checked his watch. Four hours and still the shells hammered down.

The sudden silence was a shock. It entered Ramsay's consciousness like the blow of a hammer and he looked up, confused after hours of continual bombardment. He felt the tears on his face beneath the gas mask, but experience had taught him never to remove the mask if there was even the remotest chance of gas. He had seen too many men choking on their own vomit, gasping for agonised breath and with eyes and noses streaming with scalding fluid, to ever want to chance it.

Small sounds seeped in to the dugout, gradually taking the place of the hellish roar of the guns. Somebody was screaming in a high-pitched keen, the sound unnerving. There was the distant popping of musketry, on and on; that was no mere display but a full scale battle. There was the slither of sand from above. Ramsay looked up and saw the mist-smeared sky. The roof of the dugout had been torn asunder by a shell. He had been cowering beneath an open space without realising it.

His ears ringing from the bombardment and his head dazed and numb, Ramsay glanced around the dugout. The telephone lay shattered in a hundred pieces. There was no way to call in reinforcements when the Germans attacked, as they would. They were alone. Ramsay stumbled for the steps leading upward to the trenches; they were gone. There was only an uneven mess of churned-up mud and ripped sandbags lying askew, partially blocking the entrance.

Ramsay had no desire to stand in the firing step, but the intensity of the bombardment argued for more than a mere trench raid – Fritz had begun his push. He stepped onto the first of the torn sandbags and looked upward into the thick smoke and fog. *There could be anything up there.*

"Sir . . ." Ramsay had forgotten about the private who had shared his dugout for the past ... how long? He checked his watch, it was half past ten. The bombardment had lasted five and a half hours. It could have been five minutes or five days.

"Sir." The private looked up. He had ripped off his gas mask again and the eyes that stared out were red-rimmed and weeping.

"Put your bloody mask on!" Ramsay roared, his own gasmask muffling the words. He pointed vigorously to get his message across.

"Come on." Ramsay was aware his words would be unheard. He grabbed hold of the man's sleeve and hauled him to his feet. "Get up and get to a firing bay. Fritz will be here in a minute. Come on, man!" Ramsay stepped into the gap and swore as the ragged gas sheet tangled around his legs. He threw it aside. "If Fritz gets into the trench he will toss a potato masher down here and that will be us."

The bombardment had obviously disorientated the private, he stared at Ramsay with his mouth open.

"Come on, man!" Ramsay repeated, and stepped toward the door, pulling the private behind him. The trench was above them, the steps had been obliterated by the shellfire. There was only a ragged slope, half-covered in mud and split sandbags. There was a human arm lying at the top. Ramsay pulled himself up, reached down and hauled the private up.

"Get to a firing bay!" Ramsay bellowed, and pushed the man in what he hoped was the right direction. He looked around and tried to focus through the clouded eyepiece and the thick gas fog. He had emerged into an unfamiliar landscape, one that bore little resemblance to the trench line he had taken over only the previous day.

The shelling had been devastatingly accurate. In a dozen

places the sandbag barrier was only a memory, with great gaps blasted in the defences and holes gouged in the barbed wire beyond. Gas and smoke merged with the mist, clinging densely to the corkscrew stakes that held roll after roll of savage barbs.

Recognisable only by his jaunty swagger and the stripes on his arm, McKim nodded to Ramsay. His eyes were calm through the gas mask and his rifle looked as clean as ever.

Ramsay jerked a thumb to the corporal. "Get the men out of the dugouts and on to the fire bays immediately. Fritz won't be long." He knew his words could not be heard but spoke automatically. As McKim nodded, instinctively understanding, Ramsay glanced at the devastation. There were few fire bays left. The shelling had scattered the sandbags and destroyed the parapets and men crawled to whatever cover they could find. Not all of the men were able to do even that. There were three crumpled bodies in this section of what had been the trench, and an ugly smear of blood within a smoking crater that told of another casualty. Others were wounded, quietly or noisily, with the stretcher bearers already busy on their endless job.

Men grabbed at those rifles that had survived. They removed the canvas covers protecting the bolts and peered into the shifting grey fog. McKim lay prone amidst a scatter of sandbags, staring into the mist. He looked alert and yet casual, the very image of the veteran soldier he was. He checked the magazine of his rifle and slowly slid the weapon forward. Every moment was measured. Not slow, but unhurried; he was a man at home with his job.

The pop-popping of musketry was louder now, coming from left and right along the remnants of what had been the British positions. Ramsay squinted forward, there was movement in the mist, figures threading quickly through the shattered tangles of wire. The first man came out in a rush, a huge figure in field-grey with a flame-thrower in his hand and a gas mask over his face.

Ramsay snapped open his holster, but before he could draw his revolver McKim had fired, worked the bolt of his rifle and fired again. The bullets slammed into the petrol canister on the German's back. The man spun with the force of the bullet and McKim fired again. The petrol ignited with a whoof that was audible even through the gasmask and the man screamed, high pitched and terrible, as flames engulfed him. Ramsay stared as the German tried to beat out the flames with flailing arms, but succeeded only in fanning them further. He ran in agonised circles and collapsed on the ground where the orange glow of the flames reflected in the surrounding fog and gas. Ramsay's horror lasted only for an instant and then the rush of grey-clad men that burst from the fog took his whole attention.

"Shoot them down, boys!" Ramsay yelled, knowing his voice would not carry through the gas mask. He looked to where the Lewis gun should be – there was nothing left but a crater and a rubble of burst sandbags. The Vickers guns were also silent, their positions blasted away by the bombardment, and only a scattering of British artillery pieces challenged the German advance.

Ramsay levelled his pistol, swallowed hard and fired. The sensation of the revolver kicking back into his wrist was good. *At last. At last I am firing back!*

The grey mass seemed undaunted by the rapid fire from the Royals. They were faceless, inhuman in their gas masks and their silent, rushing advance; men the size of giants who appeared through gaps in the mist and disappeared just as quickly. Ramsay fired six quick shots into the grey tide that poured over No Man's Land, ducked beneath the remnants of the parapet and fumbled for cartridges to reload.

"There's thousands of them." A young private had torn off his helmet. He hauled himself onto the top of the parapet, levelled his rifle and emptied his magazine into the mist.

Ramsay clicked closed his revolver and lunged at the private, who was ramming another magazine into his rifle. He grabbed the man's sleeve, but the private shook him off and looked around, his eyes wild.

"We've got to beat them, sir!" He clicked home his bayonet and ran forward, screaming, into the mist.

The barrage had blown holes in the barbed wire and the attacking infantry were pouring over. They moved quickly, large groups of men racing forward and not stopping to care for their wounded as the Royal Scots fired into them.

Ramsay counted eight men in this section of the trench, and judging by the rifle fire coming from the traverses on either side, there were about the same there as well. A quick count told him there were sixteen surviving men under his command. Seeking revenge after the five hours of hell the Germans had put them through, the Royals had no mercy for the attackers.

McKim was firing like the old soldier he was; fifteen aimed shots a minute, working his rifle bolt like a machine. The Germans were bunching at the holes torn in the barbed wire and that is where they fell in droves. Ramsay fired his six shots and reloaded; fired and reloaded; fired and reloaded, but still the Germans came on.

Kill them, kill them. At last I have fired back, at last I am a fighting soldier. Come on you Hun bastards, come on and die.

Ramsay saw the German advance hesitate as the Royals fired non-stop. Some men wavered and turned back into the mist. Some stood static, to be mowed down like corn beneath a skilful scythe. Some threw down their weapons and fled;

the Royals shot them as well. One tall, grey-uniformed man charged forward, his rifle levelled and bayonet thrusting forward. McKim barely moved as he shot him through the forehead. The man fell on the lip of the trench line, the furthest forward of that German advance.

A sudden shaft of sunlight glinted on the coiled wire. It reflected on a discarded bayonet and the buckle of the belt of the tall German soldier; the words *Gott Mitt Us* mocked the twisted corpse it adorned. Flames from the burning soldier flickered orange through the haze. A slight breeze shifted the mist and the day began to clear.

The firing died down. Ramsay felt his heart thumping, there was sweat dribbling down his chest. He reloaded with trembling hands, dropped a cartridge and saw the brass glitter in the sandy mud of the trench floor. He lifted it, slid it into the empty chamber of his revolver and looked around.

A volley of shells exploded a quarter of a mile to the south. Nobody noticed.

The mist was shredding now as the breeze increased. Some of the men were loosening and removing their gas masks, cautiously breathing in the relatively fresh air.

"Was that it?" a young soldier asked. He stared at Ramsay through wild, wide eyes. "Have we beaten them?" He grinned and raised his gas mask in the air. "We've beaten them, lads!"

The bullet sliced the top of his head clean off and he died still with the grin on his face. His body crumpled into the bottom of the trench.

"Here they come again!" McKim roared and fired into the mass of grey uniforms that crammed once more into the gaps in the wire. The Germans still wore gas masks and moved quickly, silently, efficiently. They died by the score but kept coming with a courage that Ramsay could only admire.

"Death and hell to you!" McKim yelled as he reloaded. Ramsay knew that each British infantryman carried 220 rounds of ammunition, but judging the volume of fire the Royals were unleashing, even that number would not last them the day.

The breeze increased, aiding visibility so that Ramsay could distinguish each man who advanced. In the dark and the mist they had been inhuman monsters, but now they were men with two arms and two legs, much as he was. The enemy, the dehumanised Hun, was exposed as vulnerable flesh and blood. They advanced bravely in long lines that bunched as they came to the gaps, and fell in writhing heaps as the Royal Scots emptied their magazines into the mass.

"Up the Royals!" McKim yelled. "Royal Sco-o-o-o-ots!"

As the mist cleared more men yanked off their gas masks, becoming equally recognisable and more vocal as they joined McKim in yelling at the advancing German soldiers. Ramsay unclipped his mask again, and took a deep breath of air thick with lyddite and the stench of raw blood.

"It's like shooting targets," a freckle-faced private said as he worked the bolt of his rifle with frantic speed. "We can't miss!"

"But there's thousands of them," a swarthy youth shouted. "They're coming on forever."

"Pay them back for the Somme, boys," McKim shouted. "Mow the bastards down." He looked over to Ramsay, "How's the ammunition, sir? I'm running short."

Ramsay checked his own supply. "You there, that man!" He pointed to the swarthy soldier. "Search for ammunition."

"Check the dead, Hepburn," McKim ordered. "Check their bandoleers and magazines, and then go to the stores bay. If we're lucky, Fritz won't have hit it."

"This is pure hell," somebody was sobbing, "this is pure hell."

"Quiet!" Ramsay cracked out. "If you can't say anything useful, then keep your mouth shut!"

"Die!" another man said softly. "Die you German bastards!"

"That's the way, Cruickshank," McKim encouraged.

The next wave of Germans formed up behind the barbed wire, their uniforms merging with the returning mist to form an amorphous grey mass beneath featureless white faces.

"These Fritzes are brave men," McKim said. "They keep coming even when we shoot them to bits." He raised his voice. "Any news of that ammunition yet?" He checked the magazine of his rifle. "I'm about empty here!"

The Germans came forward in a rush, throwing themselves at the gaps in the wire as the Royals fired, worked the bolts of their rifles and fired again. There was no need to aim, the Germans were so densely packed that it was impossible to miss.

"Ammo!" McKim shouted, "where's the bloody ammunition!" There was no chanting or cheering now, only gasps of effort and the occasional curse as the Royals fired, worked their bolts and fired again. Flames still flickered from the burning man and the stench of his charred flesh was sickening. The field-grey bodies piled up in heaps and drifts; a writhing carpet of suffering. Eventually the advance faltered, fewer men pushed over their own dead to face the aimed musketry of the Royals.

"Cease fire!" Ramsay yelled. "They're turning, save your bullets!"

The grey mass was wavering again and then it broke and fled, pushing back through the wire. Only one man emerged from the anonymity of the crowd. He swayed forward in a half crouch, his greatcoat flapping around his legs and a gas mask concealing his face. He dropped his rifle as he came forward, dodging from side to side as he neared the battered British trenches. As he passed the final concertina of wire he ripped off his gas mask, threw it on the ground and began to shout, but the words were lost in the terrible noise of battle.

Ramsay aimed his revolver and began to squeeze the trigger, but McKim knocked his arm up. 'Sorry, sir, but that's Flockhart in a German coat!"

"What?"

I thought he was dead. I thought I was safe!

"Dinnae shoot boys! It's me! I'm coming in!" Sergeant Flockhart slithered over the top layer of sandbags and landed with a soft thud in the bottom of the trench. His face was brown with mud, smeared with blood and his eyes stared through red rims.

"About time you got back, Jim," McKim said. "Leaving us to do all the fighting while you skulk in a bon shell hole."

Flockhart swore at him and shrugged off the German great coat, the bloodstained hole in the chest told its own story.

"Mr Kerr and the others?" Ramsay already guessed the answer.

"Dead, sir. They were blown to atoms," Flockhart said. He glanced at the sleeve of his tunic where a tear showed the raw scar of a new wound. "We were lucky that the German shelling was so accurate. It went right over us, but one dropped short, right on top of the listening post." He took a deep breath and coughed as the lyddite-laden smoke entered his lungs. "The lads had no chance sir. There was nothing left of them but a smear."

Ramsay nodded. He felt sympathy for the dead men but there was no time to mourn. *There is never time to mourn.*

Flockhart looked along the shattered line of the trench. "How do we stand?"

"Badly, Sarge," McKim said. "We have enough

ammunition for one more attack and then . . ," he shrugged. "That's us." He glanced around. "I already sent Hepburn to scrounge what he could, but he has not come back."

"He could have been killed," Ramsay said. "Send a runner to Major Campbell. Choose a good man and tell him to take care of himself."

"Aye, sir," McKim said. "That will be you, Niven. Off you go, lad. Tell the major we need men and ammunition but we are holding out well. Keep your head down, son."

Niven was a steady-eyed man of around twenty-five. He nodded, ducked as a shell exploded some thirty yards away and headed for the communications trench.

No sooner had Niven vanished than the swarthy private appeared with his helmet held in both hands and a mixture of magazines and loose cartridges rattling inside. "It's all I could get, sir," he reported to Ramsay. "The store bay is blown to pieces."

"Well done, Hepburn. Let's hope Niven brings us more." Ramsay handed the cartridges round, just as a renewed roar came from their left and a group of gape-mouthed privates swarmed into their section of trench.

"They've broken through!" the first man gasped in the accents of North East England. "Fritz is everywhere! In the trenches behind us. They're everywhere!"

McKim grunted and looked to the rear. "I can't see any Germans," he said.

"They're everywhere!" The private repeated. He had lost his rifle and his eyes were wild.

Ramsay grabbed hold of the man's shoulders. "Calm down! There are no Germans in this trench and we have no intention of allowing any in!" He held the man for a moment, "Take a deep breath, man! Who are you? What's your name, rank and number?"

The familiar order snapped the panic away from the private. He snapped to attention. "Smith, sir. Private, 3827."

"That's better, Smith." Ramsay let go and Smith stepped back slightly. He was breathing deeply as he tried to keep control. Ramsay raised his voice, "The rest of you, keep watch in front! Sergeant Flockhart, check the next traverse, but be careful. McKim, have a decko in the rear, see if you can see Fritz."

With the situation temporarily calmed, Ramsay concentrated on Smith. "Tell me what happened, Smith, where is the rest of your unit?"

Smith shook his head. He looked back over his shoulder as if he expected an immediate onrush of Germans. "They're gone, sir. There's nobody left. We got shelled to hell and then they sent over storm troopers. They came out of the mist and used flame-throwers and bombs. They came between what was left of the strong points. We tried to hold them, but there was hardly any of us left, sir. They had hit the machine gun posts and the keep. We only had our rifles."

Ramsay nodded. "You were overrun?"

Smith shook his head. He ducked as a machine gun opened up from the German lines. Bullets spattered along the sandbag ridge, raising a thin film of sand that pattered back into the trench,

"Were you overrun?" Ramsay repeated the question.

Smith shook his head. He breathed in short, shallow gulps and his hands constantly closed and opened. "Not then, sir. They ignored us and ran right past. They jumped over the top of the trench and pushed onward without even looking down. There were not enough of us left to stop them, sir. Then more came, line after line of them. They just kept coming out of the mist. We killed and killed them. . .

"I understand," Ramsay said. "Well, Smith, we have held

them here so far, so find yourself a rifle and join the line."

Smith nodded, just as the German machine gun rattled from the front again. The bullets lashed the battered sandbag barrier or skipped through the gaps to thud horribly against the reverse wall. A spray of sand rose along the length of the trench, shimmered for a second and fell in a soft sheen. The air smelled of lyddite and brimstone, with the ugly stench of phosgene and death.

The thud of feet landing on the duckboards made Ramsay turn around.

"Sir!" Niven threw a quick salute. "I could not get to Major Campbell, sir. The Germans are behind us. They're everywhere, sir!" He glanced at Smith. "The Durhams are gone to glory, sir."

Jesus! My bad luck again. Wounded on the first day of the Somme, wounded on the second day at Passchendaele and now, on my first full day back in the line, the Huns get behind our position.

Ramsay swore loudly and looked skyward as a flight of aircraft passed overhead. The black crosses on the underside of their wings were clearly visible. They banked abruptly and swooped down on the lines to the rear. Ramsay saw the bright muzzle flashes from their machine guns as they concentrated on some position to the rear.

"Sergeant Flockhart," Ramsay shouted, "put up an SOS rocket. The Germans are behind us."

"I don't think I can, sir," Flockhart said calmly. "I don't think we have a Very pistol left." He indicated a blasted section of the trench with a languid wave of his hand. "It was kept in the stores bay, sir, but that's gone west."

Ramsay nodded. "No SOS rockets, then." He glanced around. His men were edging closer, trying to listen to the conversation. "Keep watch, boys, Fritz will be back. Watch the rear of the trench too. Is McKim back yet?"

49

"Not yet, sir," Flockhart said.

There was the unmistakable guttural cry of a German fire command, followed by the whizz-bang of an explosion and the bark of taunts from the German side of the lines. "Die, Tommy bastard!"

There were more explosions behind them, the size of the bursts and thick green smoke indicating that the shells were 5.9 inch.

"Fritz is making sure of us, is he not?" Niven ducked and held onto his helmet as dirt showered down. "This is his big push." He looked upward at the tortured sky and added, "Bastards," to nobody in particular.

"Well, Niven." Ramsay flinched as a shell exploded overhead. "We'll make it as hard as we can for him."

"Yes, sir," Niven agreed. "Just like the Somme, sir."

Is that insubordination? Is this private hinting that I did not do my best at the Somme? What has Niven heard?

Ramsay looked hard at Niven, but the private was looking levelly ahead, his expression unreadable.

"How long have you been at the Front, Niven?"

Catch him by surprise; if Niven is trying to be insubordinate, then undermine his confidence.

"Three months, sir." His face remained impassive but his eyes slithered sideways, just slightly, enough for Ramsay to sense his unease at being questioned by an officer.

"What were you before you were called up?" *Remind him that he is only a part-time soldier.*

"I drove a tram sir, in Edinburgh." The eyes flickered again.

"Good man. Let's all get through this and you'll be driving one again." Ramsay forced a smile that he hoped looked natural. "Maybe you'll be driving me along Princes Street one day soon, eh?"

"I hope so, sir." Niven's mouth clamped shut again and he faced his front, as regulations demanded.

"Well done. Carry on." Ramsay started at the sound behind him and his fingers stretched to the flap of his holster.

"Bloody Fritz is bloody everywhere!" McKim slithered over the rear wall of the trench and landed with a thump on the greasy duckboards, slipped but recovered by putting a hand on Ramsay's shoulder. "Oh, sorry, sir!"

Ramsay opened his mouth, ready to snarl at the corporal for this affront to his rank, but closed it again. "Was there any sign of Major Campbell, McKim?"

McKim shook his head. "I couldn't get that far, sir. There are Jerries all over the shop. There was no way through."

We are trapped, surrounded by the Hun. I have failed again. I must not let the men down a third time.

"We will just fortify this position then and wait for our lads to counter attack," Ramsay said.

McKim raised his eyebrows. "I dinnae think they will be here soon, sir," he said. "Fritz is in force behind us and advancing fast."

Ramsay forced a yawn. It was a reaction that gave him a few seconds in which to think. "We will stay put, McKim, and hold out. Fritz may have broken through the regiments on either side, but he's not breaking us." He glanced along the trench, littered with burst sandbags and dead men. "Get this place cleaned up and gather all the ammunition we can. We are not leaving." He nodded to the furthest end of the trench. "Find a couple of knife rests if you can, McKim, and draw them across the edges of our sector. Jerry will have to fight to get us out of here…"

"Watch, sir!" Flockhart pushed Ramsay unceremoniously aside and into the shelter of a sandbagged bay. He pointed upward to the dark shape that swung end over end above them.

The men watched, some cursing, one praying. Niven aimed his rifle and fired upward, as if to try and explode the thing prematurely, but it continued on its evil passage across the sky.

"An oilcan." McKim watched its progress. "Christ, but I hate these things."

"We all do," Ramsay said. He pressed hard against the mud and sandbags of the trench wall. *This is a terrible way to die, trying to burrow into damp earth in the middle of France. The smell of the earth is so familiar, yet so alien. It's earth, but not my earth.*

They watched it turn end over end until it was positioned a dozen, fifteen, twenty yards behind the line, directly over the communications trench. It exploded in a nightmare of red hot nails and shards of sharp metal that showered down in a wide diameter, some landing in the trench where Ramsay pressed hard into the French mud. Men crouched down, grabbing hold of their helmets or trying to burrow into the side of the trench. One man screamed as a long sliver of metal thrust into his back, another fell silent as his head was sheared in two.

"Stretcher bearers!" Flockhart yelled as the wounded man writhed on the ground and a stocky private tried to remove the hot metal from his friend.

"Lie easy, Willie! We'll soon have you in Blighty!" The stocky man looked up, his eyes wide with concern. "Stretcher bearers! For the love of God, stretcher bearers!"

"Here they come again!" The yell came from the firing bay. "There's bloody thousands of them!"

Ramsay glanced up. The Germans were seething across No Man's Land, stepping over their own crumpled dead as they advanced like a field-grey horde.

"Stretcher bearers!" The stocky private shouted again. He

knelt beside his comrade. "It's all right, Willie, I'll stay with you."

"Leave that man!" Ramsay ordered, "We need everybody at the firing step!" He pulled his revolver from its holster, checked the cylinder and waited for the enemy to get closer.

The Germans were as tenacious as ever, sweeping forward towards the line, bunching at the killing zone of the gaps, falling in droves as the Royal Scots fired into the mass, and then pushing through after. The first wave was shot flat, with scores of new bodies joining the previous casualties on the ground, but the press continued and the firing slackened off.

The Germans roared in triumph as they approached the battered trench line of the Royals. They were tall men: Prussians or Bavarians, apparently uncaring of the casualties that they stepped over and obviously determined to cleanse this small group of British soldiers off the map.

"Ammunition!" a private yelled. "For God's sake, has anybody got any bullets left?"

Gradually, one by one, the men stopped firing as the ammunition ran out. The Germans took heart and rushed on, cheering in short angry barks.

Smith screamed, dropped his rifle and turned round, scrambling for the communication trench to the rear. He would never have heard the report of the rifle, and would not have been aware of the passage of the bullet that killed him. It entered the back of his head and burst out between his eyes in an explosion of brains and bone and blood. He died instantly.

"Bayonets and bombs lads!" Flockhart roared above the hellish din of battle. "Don't let Fritz into Craigmillar!"

The first bomb came from the German side, a stick grenade that bounced from the duckboards and lay, ominous until McKim kicked it down Ramsay's empty dugout. The explosion was muted, but a cloud of dust and smoke gushed from the entrance. Flockhart raised himself on to the trench wall and threw a grenade toward the advancing Germans.

"Come on, lads! Send the bastards back!"

Ramsay lifted the rifle of the newly-killed Smith and leaped on to the parapet. The Germans advanced in a solid wave of field-grey until Flockhart's grenade exploded. Three men fell, another screamed and clutched at his stomach and then Flockhart was amongst them with his bayonet and rifle butt and boots. Ramsay joined him, yelling to hide his fear. He saw McKim in front, smashing his helmeted head against the face of a German, he saw a German thrust a bayonet into the belly of a British soldier, he saw a Royal Scot duck under a German's swing and stab him in the groin.

The world was a nightmare of grunting, terrified, angry men, desperately trying to kill each other and hoping to survive the next few moments of life. Ramsay ducked the savage thrust of a Prussian bayonet, levelled his revolver and fired. He was so close to the German that there was no need to aim, the soft lead bullet thumped into the man's chest and threw him a yard into the air. Another German took his place, and another; tall men, shaven-headed and brave, but Ramsay shot them too, remorselessly. He saw McKim leap into the air to smash the rim of his steel helmet across the nose of a yelling German. He saw Aitken duck and thrust his bayonet into the groin of a huge enemy soldier, he saw Niven falling as a German smashed a rifle butt into his stomach.

Another German rush surged through the gap in the wire. Ten, twenty, thirty men advancing with lowered bayonets and yelling voices. Ramsay pointed his revolver and squeezed the trigger, again and again until the hammer clicked on an empty chamber.

"Out of ammunition!" he yelled and reached into his pouch for more. His fingers scrabbled uselessly against the hard leather. "Jesus! Bloody Jesus!"

The Germans came on. A Royal Scot leaped on the closest, his hands closing around the German's throat, but a second German thrust sideways with his bayonet. A tall German Hauptmann finished off the British soldier with two rounds from his pistol and they marched on, pressing the crumpled body of the Royal into the mud with their steel-shod boots. When the officer looked directly at Ramsay, his eyes were chill, blue and calm as a spring morning.

"There are just too many of them," Aitken gasped. He was bleeding from a wound in his neck and his tunic was ripped in three places. "We can't stop the bastards."

Ramsay swore, shoved his empty revolver into its holster and lifted a discarded rifle. He checked the magazine, saw it was empty and held it as a club. "Royal Sco-o-o-ots! Come on, you Fritzy bastards. We're the Royals!" He stared back at the German officer and gestured for him to advance. The German nodded back, obviously recognising a fellow officer and Ramsay squared up, ready to meet him face to face.

The deep-throated snarl took Ramsay by surprise as an aircraft came low overhead, its machine guns rattling. Men fell in ones and twos and dozens, some Royal Scots, but mostly Germans, and the attack wavered again. The field-grey tide halted like waves on a muddy shore, and men at the back pulled back from the killing zone in front of the battered trench.

The plane banked, waggled its wings and soared upwards. Green ribbons streamed from its struts as a stray slant of sunshine struggled through the rapidly thinning mist. For a fraction of a second Ramsay saw the head and shoulders of the pilot, there was a gleam from his goggles as he glanced back over his shoulder at the men struggling in the trenches. Then he was gone, vanished into the sanctuary of the mist, leaving only devastation and death and the stink of fuel as a reminder of his fleeting visit.

British and German stared at each other for a second across the writhing carpet of bloodstained khaki and field-grey. The Germans had reeled back, but the officer stood erect amongst the shambles of his men. Even as Ramsay watched, he holstered his pistol, removed a monocle from the breast pocket of his uniform and slowly placed it into his left eye. A scar across his left cheek moved as he opened his mouth and began to shout orders, but McKim had recovered just as quickly.

"Bomb them back, boys!" McKim shouted. "Bomb the bastards to hell and gone!" He poised and threw a Mills bomb that exploded with an orange flash and an arc of deadly fragments. "Death and hell to you, German bastards!" McKim hefted his rifle to the high port and would have followed up the German retreat if Ramsay had not pulled him back.

"Let them go." He looked into McKim's eyes. They were wild. "Let them go, Corporal!"

Sanity slowly returned to McKim. "Aye, sir." He glowered across the few yards to where the German officer was slowly backing towards the gap in the barbed wire, keeping his eyes fixed on the British position.

"That one is not giving up," McKim said. "I've seen the type before. Prussian of the Guard, him. Definitely not bon."

"Ignore him, McKim," Ramsay said, but he watched until the German officer vanished into the smoke before he spoke again. "Back to the trench, boys," he yelled, "back to the trench! Take back any weapons we can use – rifles, ammunition, anything at all, British or Fritzes!"

There were five Royal Scots prone on the ground as Ramsay ordered the remainder back to the shattered trench.

They slid over the lip and into the comparative security between the ripped and dishevelled sandbags. Ramsay waited until the last of the men were safe and then followed. He felt an amazing sense of relief when his boots thumped onto the wet duckboards. The men looked at him, waiting for orders. Some were gasping for breath, most were wounded in some manner; all were tired. One man coughed as he nursed the bayonet slash that had ripped his tunic across the chest, blood easing between his grimy fingers.

"We're holding out, sir," Niven said.

"We showed the bloody bastards," said somebody else.

"Bon show." Flockhart had been second last to enter the trench and already he had lifted a periscope from the ground and was peering into No Man's Land. "How long do you reckon it will take for reinforcements to reach us, sir?" He looked at Ramsay, his eyes steady.

"We'll hold until they get here," Cruickshank said. He looked around. "Once we get the Lewis gun set up again, Fritz can whistle for his supper, eh?"

Ramsay shook his head. He raised his voice against the unremitting background noise of artillery and rattling machine guns, but a sudden lull caused his words to boom out around the trench. "Fritz has broken through the line, lads," Ramsay said, "he's behind us and in front of us and on at least one side." He watched their reaction. They looked stunned, but accepting.

"So what do we do now, sir?" McKim asked. He had swapped his rifle for a German Mauser and was pressing rounds of ammunition into the magazine.

Flockhart said nothing. He was counting and checking the men. "We've lost twelve men, sir, and three more are badly wounded." He ducked as a salvo of British artillery shells ripped overhead to explode amidst the tangled barbed wire in No Man's Land. "If we don't get them medical aid soon, they won't survive."

Ramsay nodded. *They are my men. I am responsible for them.* "Do your best for them, Sergeant."

"Will our boys get through to us in time, sir?" Flockhart asked bluntly.

Ramsay looked at the three men who lay on the ground. One was unconscious with half his insides blown away. Another was blinded, his face partly gouged away by the burst of a bomb. The third stared at him through huge, pleading eyes. He had no arms.

Ramsay knelt at his side. "You'll be all right, lads. Just hang on there."

He stood again, feeling like a traitor; he could do nothing for these men. The soldiers looked to their officers for everything, but he was as fragile as they were and with as little power over things that matter.

Flockhart was waiting for an answer.

"We hold fast as long as we can and then break out and head for our new front line." Ramsay tried not to think of the three men who suffered on the bottom of the trench. "I am not surrendering to the Huns. Nor are you."

"And these lads?" Flockhart lowered his voice "What about them?"

They are better dead.

"Fritz will look after them. The Germans always care for the wounded as best they can."

"The Huns used the wounded for target practise at Second Ypres," Flockhart reminded quietly. "I don't want my men murdered as they lie helpless in the bottom of a trench."

"We shot their wounded too," Ramsay reminded. "There is no bitterness on this front. Fritz will look after them." He looked at the small body of men that was gathered around him. They looked back through eyes that showed various stages of exhaustion, pain, anger and fear. "We will defend this trench as long as we can." Nobody protested. These were Royal Scots, they were not given to extravagant displays.

"Right lads, you heard the officer." Flockhart's discipline took over. "Let's make this place defensible. Niven, Aitken, make a wall across the traverse so Fritz can't take us in flank. Blackley, Edwards, see if you can find some ammunition. Anderson and Mackay, look for German weapons. McKim, you make sure the parapet is more secure. Donald, see if you can check on the Lewis."

"And you men," Ramsay pointed to a group of men. He did not yet know their names. "Check behind our lines and see what the situation is."

The chatter of a machine gun made them duck and bullets sprayed the parapet, some thumping into the sandbags at the rear wall of the trench.

"Come on, lads! Get moving!" Flockhart lifted a sandbag and threw it on top of the parapet. For a second Ramsay contemplated acting the officer and merely watching, but instead he lifted a sandbag and manoeuvred it to the wall.

"Sir!" Aitken almost had to duck to stand in the trench; he favoured the wound in his neck and the recent thump in his stomach. He had a deep voice and there was a recent scar still healing on his jaw. "What shall we use for the barrier? There are not enough sandbags that haven't been ripped by the artillery."

Ramsay glanced around. Most trenches had a barbed wire barrier ready to thrust into place but the German guns had shattered that to pieces.

"Use the corpses," Flockhart said at once. "They don't mind, they're dead. We did that at second Ypres." He gave Ramsay a meaningful glance. "When the Germans murdered the wounded."

"Jesus." Aitken's mouth dropped and he stared at Ramsay. "We can't do that, sir." Flockhart ignored him, grabbed the nearest body and dragged it to where the trench turned. A khaki-clad arm flopped to the side, a ring scraping on the duck boards.

"That's Jackie, sir. Davie Jackson." Aitken stared at the hand. The ring slipped off the end of Jackson's finger and lay, glinting silver, on the ground. "We trained together."

"Jackson's dead, Aitken, but his body may save your life," Flockhart shouted. "Keep working, lads!"

Obviously reluctant, the men lifted the crumpled bodies from inside the trench, and those closest to the parapet on the outside, and built a barricade across the corner of the trench. Corpse on corpse, the wall grew, a macabre structure of broken bodies that had once been alive, with a bootless leg protruding at right angles and an array of hands and arms and gape-jawed faces.

One red-haired private puffed smoke from the Woodbine that protruded from the corner of his mouth and shook hands with one of the dead. "Good luck to you, Willie, I never liked you alive, but you are a useful man dead."

One or two of the privates gave a small laugh. Nobody objected. The wall grew taller, with field-grey bodies among the khaki and blood seeping and dripping to form a mutual pool that greased the duckboards and seeped into the mud on either side.

"Poor buggers," Aitken said as he looked at the wall. There was a tremor in his voice and for a second Ramsay thought he would break into tears.

"Lucky buggers," Niven corrected and spat on the ground. "At least their troubles are over." He flinched as an aircraft roared overhead, the great black crosses ugly on the underside of the wings, but it continued on its way without

paying any attention to the battered survivors of the Royal
Scots. "They're well out of all this now."

"None of that talk!" Flockhart snapped. "Attend to your
duty, Niven!"

Ramsay left Flockhart to it. He lifted a makeshift trench
periscope and eased it over the parapet. "Fritz has been quiet
for too long. It won't be long before he's back, and he knows
all about us now."

"They should have been hammering us with artillery
between the attacks," Flockhart said, "and leaving much
shorter times between the rushes as well. This is not at all
like Fritz."

*He sounds as if he disapproves that the Germans are not
more efficient.*

Ramsay nodded. "I think we don't matter much, Sergeant.
If he is already behind us, then we are just a nuisance. We are
not holding up his advance."

"So what purpose do we serve here, sir?" Flockhart asked.

*None. We are just waiting for the Germans to notice
us and wipe us out. If you are dead, Flockhart, then I am
free. . .* "Not much, Sergeant. We may delay their advance
by a few hours."

"Not if they are already behind us, sir. Listen to the guns."

Ramsay listened. The rumble of artillery was constant,
but to the rear. "It sounds as if we are stuck well in front of
our own lines."

"I'd agree with that, sir."

Ramsay considered for a moment. "We are serving no
useful purpose here. We would be better back in our own
lines." He could see movement in No Man's Land. "The
Germans are strolling around as if they own the place,
Sergeant."

"I think they do," Flockhart said. "All the patrols we sent

out give the same picture, sir. Fritz is everywhere, back, front and on both sides."

Ramsay nodded and swivelled the periscope in a 360 degree arc. The mist was nearly clear now, with only thin tendrils swirling around ruined dugouts and clinging to the shattered remnants of gun emplacements and corpse-strewn trenches. There were men moving, striding openly in their field-grey uniforms. Somebody shouted in guttural German and there was an outbreak of loud laughter.

Ramsay looked toward No Man's Land again. "There's a whole column marching across towards us, Sergeant. Hundreds of the bastards." He passed over the periscope.

"There's thousands, sir," Flockhart said. "And with our lack of ammunition we would hardly dent them."

Ramsay took back the periscope.

We could take them in flank and kill a score or more before they knew we are here. We can do something to dent the advance. But afterward they will wipe us out.

He looked up the length of his trench where his men were. Some were trying to sleep, Blackley and Edwards were playing crown and anchor; Niven was cleaning his rifle; McKim was whetting his bayonet and muttering dark threats to himself; the stretcher bearers were kneeling beside the badly wounded.

I can't condemn these men to death merely in a show of bravado. Anything we do here will not influence the result of their push in the slightest.

He checked the advancing Germans again. The column was four abreast and coiled across No Man's Land like a never-ending field-grey snake that broke for craters and reformed on the far side, halted at the artillery-torn gaps in the barbed wire and then marched on. They were singing, the words bold and confident: a German military marching song that roared ominously at what had once been the British front line.

McKim lifted his rifle and eased back the bolt. "I could get that big bastard of a Sergeant." He aimed at a burly NCO who marched just to the side of his men.

"No," Ramsay pushed down the barrel of the rifle. "We can't stop them. Get down on the bottom of the trench. Play dead, pass the word along. Everybody play dead. Quick!"

McKim's glower echoed the sentiments of the men.

"Don't argue. We can't stop them and if they see us they will wipe us off the map. If we survive this we can kill more of them later." Ramsay glanced up. The Germans were only a hundred yards away now and marching strongly, still singing, with the sergeant striding alongside his men. There were officers in front: tall, young, and as erect as guardsmen as they led their men toward victory.

"Down, and look dead," Ramsay ordered.

One by one, reluctantly, cursing softly, the men lay on the duckboards or adopted artistic positions across the sandbags. Flockhart was the last of the ranks. He lay on his side with his rifle cradled in his arms and the muzzle pointed toward the German lines. Only when he was sure that all the men were down did Ramsay slide onto the duckboards. He lay on his side with his head resting on his right arm, facing the wall of bodies.

The sound of singing increased; the German voices raucous, arrogant in victory, confident that they finally had the British on the run. Ramsay felt his anger rise as he heard the tramp of boots and then there was a single unmistakable command to halt and the singing and marching ended. The abrupt silence was as unnerving as the previous drumbeat of marching feet.

Ramsay heard a soft thud and guessed that a German

had jumped into the trench. He opened one eye. A German officer stood between him and the wall. His boots shone as he turned around, obviously inspecting the corpse wall and the Royal Scots dead.

He barked an order and another man jumped down. His boots clicked on the duckboards. The two men spoke loudly, one laughed. Ramsay froze as one stepped right over him and walked on, deeper into the length of the trench. He heard more boots thump on the damp duckboards; heard a staccato order from the other side of the wall of corpses and forced himself to remain still, with his eyes open. The urge to blink was overpowering.

The German officers spoke together, their voices casual, and then there was a low moan from one of the badly wounded men. One of the officers raised his voice to bark an order and even from his restricted viewpoint, Ramsay saw a number of German infantrymen clambering into the trenches. The moan sounded again, louder, and there was the sound of a single shot.

"You dirty Hun bastard!" That was Cruickshank's voice.

Oh God; now we're all dead. I have to lead these men now; take the Germans by surprise and kill as many as we can before we are killed.

There was a short, startled silence as Ramsay rose up from the ground. "Royal Scots!"

He had no need to say any more. That single shot had roused the anger of the British infantrymen and they rose from their positions as one man. Cruickshank had been the first to react, thrusting his bayonet into the belly of the German private who had shot the wounded Royal. Ramsay grabbed the nearest German officer by the throat and wrestled him to the ground, gasping with the effort as he tried to strangle the man. The German was tall and strong, but Ramsay had the advantage of surprise and desperation. As the German put his hands up to break Ramsay's grip, Ramsay let go and thrust his thumbs into the man's eyes, bursting the eyeballs. The man screamed in his agony, writhing helplessly until Ramsay hauled the German's pistol from its holster, pressed the muzzle against his chest and squeezed the trigger.

The German officer fell. Ramsay looked around. His Royals had disposed of the Germans within their section of trench, but there were many hundreds more just beyond the corpse wall. He thought quickly. If they remained where they were, the Germans would be on them in seconds, and with their lack of numbers the outcome would not be in doubt for long. They only had one chance for survival.

"Come on, lads!" Ramsay yelled as the madness of battle came upon him, "Charge the bastards. Roar your loudest, throw bombs and blast the Huns back to Berlin! Up the Royals!"

"Royal Sco-o-o-o-ts!" McKim scooped up a stick grenade from a dead German and ran to the wall, priming the grenade as he moved.

Flockhart stepped back. "Follow the officer, boys. Up the Royals!"

Ramsay saw no more, for he was already climbing over the wall of bodies. The Germans on the other side were already advancing, some with their rifles slung over their shoulders, others carrying them at the high port, bayonets pointing wickedly upward. Ramsay aimed his captured pistol and opened fire, aiming at the nearest man as he slid over the unsteady wall of the dead. The Germans hesitated as he jumped into them, firing and shouting.

"Up the Royals!" He heard McKim's raucous roar at his back, but did not flinch as the grenade exploded a few yards away, the vicious splinters scything into the Germans packed into the narrow trench. He ignored the high screams and stepped forward, squeezing the trigger and watching his targets fall down. Their faces were anonymous, their suffering irrelevant in his new found battle madness. "Royals! Up the Royals. Push the Huns back to Germany!"

Ramsay saw the levelled rifles, he saw the muzzle flash and the jerk of the recoil against the field-grey shoulders, but he neither knew nor cared where the bullets went. He fired until the hammer clicked on an empty chamber and then he threw the pistol in the face of a square-jawed NCO. "Come on the Royals! Charge!"

Hoping his men were behind him, but not daring to even glance over his shoulder in case he was alone, Ramsay lifted a bayoneted rifle that lay beside a dead German soldier and walked on into the reeling mass of soldiers. He fired without compassion, uncaring of the danger, knowing only that he had to kill Germans until he was killed in his turn. He heard voices behind him, he knew the roaring was in Scottish accents as well as German, but he walked on, firing, working the bolt of the Mauser and firing again. German bodies piled up, grey and red, still or writhing, dead or wounded; they were human beings, but Ramsay thought no more of them than of the duckboards on which he trod.

"They're running!" Flockhart stood at Ramsay's side, panting; the bayonet on his rifle dripped with blood. "You've done it, sir. Dear God but you've done it."

Ramsay glanced at him. *Why are you not dead? Why have you survived, you stubborn bastard?*

"We've done it, Sergeant, but not for long. Look." He pointed to the lip of the battered trench over which the Germans were scrambling to melt into No Man's Land.

The Germans were running, some even dropping their rifles in their haste to escape from what they may have believed to be a major British counter attack. There were scores of them; an irregular mass of men in field-grey vanishing toward the shambles that had been No Man's Land. But it was not that to which Flockhart was pointing. The retreating men were splintering around another formation entirely, a body of marching soldiers who were advancing steadily toward the line of trenches. Even as Ramsay watched, the officer who led the Germans looked up and for a second their eyes met across the shambles and horror of the front. The manacled face of the German officer he had encountered earlier that day stared back at him. The officer lifted a hand in cold salute as if he also recognised an earlier protagonist, and Ramsay looked at the ranked men who marched at his back.

Each soldier was well over six foot tall, erect as if they were on parade and moving in perfect unison despite the littered mess of the battlefield. Their long grey coats hung precisely from squared shoulders on which their rifles slanted at precisely the same angle and the dying sun glinted from buttons that were burnished until they glittered. On a single bark from the officer, they halted as if they were a multi-legged machine rather than hundreds of men with their own individuality, thoughts and aspirations. They stood at attention, facing the battered British trenches, as immobile and unwavering as statues even as a shell burst overhead and rained shrapnel on their ranks. Three of their number fell. None of the others flinched.

"Jesus save us. Prussian Guards." Ramsay stared at the magnificent formation that now opposed them. "Prussian bloody Guards."

"Prussian Guards," Flockhart confirmed. "The Kaiser has sent his finest to finish us off."

"He has." Ramsay looked behind him to what had so recently been the British front line. He saw only devastation and ruin, smoking craters marking the site of gun emplacements and dead bodies in khaki and field-grey strewn as far as the gathering dark. "They are not for us, Sergeant. I think he has sent his best to finish this war."

As Ramsay looked the sun slipped behind the western horizon and darkness crept over the world.

CHAPTER 4

FRANCE

21-22 March 1918

"If the Prussian Guards are coming, then we had better get out of here," Flockhart said. "There are hardly enough of us to stand against a group of school pupils let alone the Prussians."

"Let the bastards come," McKim muttered darkly. "They're only bloody Huns. We're the Royals. Let the bloody bastards come." He banged the butt of his rifle against the duckboards on the bottom of the trench, stamped his feet and spat on the ground.

Ramsay grinned briefly. "Good man, McKim, but there are about twelve of us left, with enough ammunition to shoot a one-legged crow, and there must be a battalion of Prussians there, plus what remains of the unit we just chased halfway to Berlin. I think the odds are stacked against us, somewhat."

"They ran very easily," McKim said. "They knew they were facing the Royals."

"Look," Flockhart pointed to the nearest of the dead Germans. The man lay on his back with his face up. "How old would you say he was?"

Ramsay glanced down. The man's face was too smooth to have ever experienced the bite of a razor; his eyes were wide, his dying terror evident. "He must be all of seventeen," he said.

"So were his chums." Flockhart indicated the heaped German dead. Young faces and immature bodies were slumped in the obscenity of death. "I doubt that any of them are twenty years old yet." He nudged the nearest man with the toe of his boot. "It looks as if the Kaiser is throwing everything he has at us this time, from the best he has to the scrapings of the schools."

Ramsay grunted. "It's worked so far. Fritz has punched a huge hole in our lines. The gunfire is miles to the rear now." He peered into the darkness of No Man's Land. "We are doing no good here. Our line has collapsed and once the Prussians realise how few there are of us they will just roll over us. As soon as it's full dark we will slip away and head for our lines." He paused for a second. "Wherever they are."

"That suits me, sir," Flockhart said. "If they leave us alone for another half hour we can slip free all the easier when night falls."

"Maybe so, Sergeant," Ramsay was less cheerful, "but if the Germans are making progress, the longer we stay here, the further through enemy-held territory we may have to travel."

He ducked as a shell burst overhead and shrapnel pattered down. Others exploded in a volley of explosions around the trench. A column of mud rose and fell leaving only the reek of lyddite and the song of a single lark. There were always larks. "They were ours," Flockhart said, "so it looks as if we've given up on this section of the line for now."

Ramsay glanced at his watch. "Half past seven," he said, "what happened to the time? No matter. We'll move in half an hour. Pass the word."

"Aye, sir." Flockhart glanced around. "Shall I try and find some scran, sir? The men have not eaten since breakfast."

"Good idea." Ramsay cursed silently at this subtle reproach of his leadership. As the officer his first priority should be the wellbeing of his soldiers. "Off you go, Flockhart."

He watched as Flockhart slipped away, his stocky figure alert yet somehow relaxed as he merged with the semi-gloom of the trenches. Ramsay touched the pistol in its holster and wondered: *Why are you not dead? Amongst all the shambles of this murderous war, why do you survive when I need you dead?*

There was no reply. There were only the usual night time sounds of the front, augmented by the sound of singing. Ramsay struggled to make out the words; he knew the tune well. Out there in the gathering gloom, a thousand voices were singing an Easter hymn: in German. Somehow he knew it was the Prussian Guards and that the monacled, shaven-headed officer was leading the chorus. Tomorrow that man would lead his men forward and there was nothing that his battered handful of Royals could do to stop them.

There were always the guns, rumbling away at Ypres to the north as they had for the past three and a half years, but apart from that there was a strange hush in the lines. The muted chatter of a distant machine gun was irrelevant, the whine of the breeze through the tangled wire a familiar melody, and the quiet murmur of the men a soothing reminder of the continuance of humanity despite the slaughter of war. Ramsay checked his periscope for the tenth time that hour. What had so recently been No Man's Land was quiet save for the writhing wounded. He saw a lone German crawling back through the wire, dragging a shattered leg with him. Somebody was sobbing, the sound so poignant with grief that Ramsay fancifully thought it was the Earth itself, crying for the folly of the Masters of Creation in thus committing collective suicide in such a long, drawn out manner. He shook himself away from such idiocy and concentrated on matters in hand. Somehow he had to get his men to safety, through an unknown number of Germans, across an unknown number of miles to reach the relative security of the British lines.

By some miracle, Flockhart had managed to locate food. Nothing grand, just cold sandwiches and hot tea, but at least the men had something inside them before the next stage of the ordeal. *Only a veteran sergeant could do that, but why did it have to be Flockhart? Could he not just die quietly and relieve me of this burden I carry?*

"Do you think Fritz has broken right through?" McKim sat in the lee of the newly rebuilt wall of sandbags, sucking on his empty pipe.

Ramsay shrugged. "I could not say, McKim, but I doubt it. We've hammered at his lines for years and he's tried ours and the French. . ." He trailed off. He was about to say he thought the war would last forever, or until every man on both sides had been killed, but no officer should voice such sentiments to a man from the ranks.

"Oh, well, we'll see soon enough." McKim glanced at the sky. "Ten minutes until full dark, I'd say. Shall I have the lads stand to?"

"No," Ramsay decided. "Let them get another few minutes rest. God alone knows what we will face out there." He checked the periscope again. "There is no movement. Fritz has other things to worry about rather than a wee handful of Royal Scots." The sound of the singing had diminished, but Ramsay knew the Prussians were still there, gathering their strength for the advance.

"Aye, sir," McKim said. He removed his pipe for a

second. "Maybe Fritzy will find out he's made a mistake then." He grinned. "Haul away, lads, we're no deid yet. Up the Royals!"

"Up the Royals." Ramsay smiled at McKim's slant on the oft-repeated saying that was so common in the streets of Edinburgh. "How long have you been in the regiment, McKim?"

"All my life, sir." McKim touched the faded medal ribbons on his breast. He took the pipe from his mouth and looked at it as if contemplating his entire past in the dark bowl. "I was always with the Royals. My father was a Colour Sergeant and I was born when the regiment was on campaign in China. . ." He tailed off and looked away as if he had released too much information.

Ramsay narrowed his eyes. As far as he knew, the Royals had last been in China in the war of 1860. If McKim had been born then, he would be 58 now; a very old soldier, yet a man who was fitter and hardier than any of the youngsters in the regiment.

McKim replaced the pipe between his tobacco-stained teeth. "My mother was a regimental wife, she just followed the drum. For all I know she was born into the strength as well. I never asked her. I think she married three sergeants in a row, maybe it was four. I called two of them father." He shrugged. "I was a barrack room bairn and the regiment brought me up."

Ramsay looked at him, noting the hard grey in the moustache and the white in his eyebrows. He had to ask. "How old did you say you are, McKim?"

"Thirty, sir," McKim said at once. He held Ramsay's eyes in an unblinking stare.

"I see." Ramsay leaned closer. "You must have been young when you won that then," he pointed to the faded medal ribbon on McKim's breast. "The South African War? If you are thirty now you must have been about 12 at the time."

McKim nodded. "Aye, sir. I lied about my age." His face remained as inscrutable as an Oriental Buddha.

"That's hard to believe." Ramsay tried to keep his face expressionless. "An honest man like you."

"Yes, sir, but I wanted to join the men you see; it was the life I grew up with." McKim looked up as a flare rose in the darkening sky; it cast a greenish glow over the trench and over every man there. "Fritz is getting restless, sir. He might be thinking of sending a fighting patrol across to visit us."

Ramsay nodded. He thought of these huge, professional Prussians pitted against his ragged handful. "It's time to move then, McKim." He passed the word softly to the men. "Take all the ammunition you can carry, walk soft and try not to talk too loudly."

The German bombardment had destroyed the communication trench so McKim climbed on to the sandbags of the rear wall and quickly rolled into the disturbed ground beyond. He vanished as silently and efficiently as any Red Indian in the Fennimore Cooper novels that Ramsay had read as a boy. "Don't let your silhouette be seen, lads. German snipers just love that." His words came as a quiet hiss through the dark.

Ramsay was last to go, ushering the slowest of the men over. He frowned as Flockhart turned back. "Where do you think you are going, Sergeant?"

Flockhart glanced over his shoulder. "I'm going to leave old Fritz a present, sir." He slipped a primed grenade under a dead German body. "Remind him that we'll be back," he said. He had a last word to the sole remaining, grievously wounded Royal; the other had died during the night.

"Good luck, Sergeant," the man whispered. "Leave me a rifle and I'll take one with me."

"You lie quiet, lad, and let Fritzy look after you. You'll be fine." Flockhart patted the man on the arm and looked up, his eyes gleaming in the reflected light of a star shell.

Ramsay jerked a thumb in the direction of the British lines. "Right, Flockhart. Now come along, man."

Only descending flares provided light as Ramsay slipped over the ravaged ground behind what had once been the British front line. He followed in the wake of his own men, allowing McKim to find the safest route through the tangle of trenches and shell craters. Once or twice men gave a curse or an exclamation of disgust as they encountered the mangled remains of soldiers or horses. Twice they halted as a star shell exploded above them and slowly drifted down, they were illuminated as stark figures in a nightmare world. They moved slowly, step by careful step, a succession of frightened, determined men moving across a landscape made unfamiliar by shelling.

"Watch the rear, Flockhart," Ramsay ordered curtly, and pushed forward, past the dim figures with their shouldered rifles and steel helmets tipped forward over their eyes. They looked up as he passed, but nobody spoke. Although they were united in danger and regiment, rank divided them as surely as a bayonet parted flesh.

As it should be. I am an officer and a gentleman, they are rankers.

There were dead men here, some blasted to fragments, others huddled in tattered lumps, and a few peaceful, as if asleep. Many wore British uniforms, but there were also dead Germans here, scores of them, lying in windrows where machine guns had cut them down, in ragged groups around the rim of shell holes or singly, where they had died alone, victims of rifle or bayonet.

"Listen." McKim held up his hand. German voices echoed through the night, harsh, guttural and confident. Somebody laughed and others joined in, the noise level rising and then fading away to a low murmur.

"Bastards," a voice said in the unmistakable accent of Leith. "Dirty Hun bastards!"

"Keep the noise down, Cruickshank," Ramsay growled. He eased to the front of his men, counting them as he did so. There were fourteen left, most wounded in some way. There were bloodied bandages around heads and arms, roughly cobbled uniforms, torn tunics and anxious eyes. Fourteen, he had lost more than half his men in one day and he had not even had the time to learn their names.

What sort of officer am I? All I can do is get wounded and lead my men to defeat and slaughter.

There was a short burst of gunfire ahead, the unmistakable staccato rattle of a Lewis machine gun and the irregular bark of rifles. Ramsay held up his hand. Should he lead his men to this obvious British presence? Or should he try and avoid trouble with his battered handful of men? It could be a determined stand by a sizeable force, or even the beginning of a counter attack. However it might only be a last hopeless stand by another group of men left behind by the hasty British retreat.

McKim had no such qualms. "That could be the Royals sir," he hinted. "Are we going to help the lads?"

Ramsay looked over his men. They came close, tripping over the ragged ground as they gathered around him. They all looked at him, eyes wary in the night, hunched with weariness but their hands still gripping the rifles that were slung across their shoulders. Most carried packs, the rest had lost them in the bombardment.

"Right, men," Ramsay spoke quietly, aware his voice

76

would carry in the night. "We are heading toward that firing and let's see if we can help."

They nodded, accepting his decision without outward question. He was their officer. *I wonder what they really think. I hope they follow me after this bloody shambles.*

"Keep together, lads, don't straggle," Flockhart encouraged them. "Fritz just loves stragglers."

They bunched up, stumbling over ground that shells had blasted beyond recognition, swearing in low undertones as they moved toward the guns. They were British soldiers; it was their job to fight; gunfire meant fighting. There was really nothing more to say. Now that the decision had been made for them, the men relaxed and began to talk amongst themselves.

"Jesus Christ, Fraser. Mind yourself, can't you? You're trampling on my heels."

"Is that you, Aitken?"

"Has anybody got a light? My matches are damp."

"Here's another body. It's Blair, poor bugger, blown to blazes."

The communication trench was only a memory, blasted beyond recognition by accurate German shelling; the machine gun posts, located to provide support to the front line, were merely a succession of craters and the light artillery pieces were ripped to shreds. They stumbled over an alien landscape, cursing softly, moving cautiously, making slow progress toward the distant musketry.

"There's Major Campbell's dugout, sir." Flockhart pointed to a deeper shadow in the dimness of the night.

"Wait here," Ramsay ordered and slid down the shell-battered steps and into utter darkness. He took a box of matches from his pocket and scraped one alight, but immediately wished he had not bothered. German storm troopers must have caught the inhabitants by surprise. Major Campbell was still inside, but his lower body was shredded and another man was equally dead. Some unknown German had thrown a grenade down the steps and followed it up with a blast of bullets. The occupants had not stood a chance. The map had been ripped from the wall, the table was a memory, but the Germans had left an unopened bottle of Younger's Ale on the table. The Glenlivet bottle was broken into a thousand shards of glass.

Ramsay spent only a second shuffling through the scatter of papers on the ground. He considered looking through them, then realised that since the German advance, all the information he required would be out of date. However, there could be some information about troop formations useful to the enemy. Ramsay cursed as the match burned down to his fingers, he dropped it, lit another and bent down to set light to the nearest sheet.

"Sorry, Major," he muttered, "but I don't know what Fritz could learn from these." He gave a brief salute and waited until the flames took hold. "Rest easy, sir."

"All right, sir?" Flockhart asked; he sniffed at the smoke that had followed Ramsay up the steps and indicated the orange glow of flames.

"Major Campbell's funeral pyre," Ramsay said. "Now let's get away before Fritz sends a patrol to investigate."

They marched in the direction of the musketry, keeping quiet, holding their rifles ready; wary, scared but defiant. The firing continued, at times dying away and then increasing in volume to a frenetic crescendo. There was the barking cheer of a German charge and the firing gradually decreased, ending in a few isolated cracks and then one final shot and silence. The Royal Scots stopped moving to listen. A solitary laugh drifted through the night.

"Christ," Niven said softly. "That's they boys gone by the sound of it."

"The Huns are wiping us out," an anonymous voice sounded from the gloom. "Hell and damnation to them all!"

"They're getting us one by one," somebody replied, "one by bloody one."

"Maybe this is it," Aitken said. "Maybe this is the German push that ends the war."

"Keep your chins up, lads. Mind we're Royal Scots," McKim muttered quiet encouragement. "We'll get the bastards back, don't you fear." He raised his voice slightly. "Up the Royals, lads. Come on, up the Royals." But there were no takers until Flockhart repeated the words:

"Up the Royals, lads. Don't let the Kaiser get you down!"

There were soft growls from the men, a rattle of equipment and a half-stifled cough as one man fought the gas that had seeped into his lungs.

"Roll call, boys," Ramsay decided. They had been moving away from the burning dugout for an hour now and were beginning to straggle as the weaker and more badly wounded men lagged behind. "Gather round."

There was a shuffling of tired feet, an occasional grumbled mutter, an urgent whisper and the men circled around. They were ghosts in the shattered gloom of the battlefield, hunched men with long coats and haggard faces, part illuminated by the occasional soaring star shell.

"Take the roll, Flockhart," Ramsay did not want to admit he did not know all the men's names yet. *I should know them. They are my men. It is my duty to know the men I lead to death.*

Like the good sergeant he was, Flockhart knew every one of his soldiers. In the tense darkness of that lunar landscape, he steadily intoned all thirty names that had been under Ramsay's command, waiting after each for a response.

"Aitken . . ."

"Sir."

The voices were soft in the night, but there were far too many silences after each hopeful name. Each silence meant a death; each silence signified a grieving family somewhere in Edinburgh or the Lothians; each silence was a broken-hearted mother or wife, orphaned children and a future hacked away by shellfire or bullet.

"Beaumont . . ."

Silence.

"Arbuthnott . . ."

Silence.

"Cruickshank . . ."

"Sir!"

Oh, thank God. Thank you God for preserving a young life. Thank you for one minor mercy in this cataclysmic horror.

"Dickson . . ."

Silence. Someone coughed. Then silence again: heavy, oppressive, prickling with apprehension.

"Mackay . . ."

"Sir!"

That was a very young voice indeed.

"MacNulty . . ."

Silence.

The silences were frightening. They hung over the loose band of men as if populated by the accusing ghosts of the dead; circling them, running sharp-taloned fingers up their spines, easing memories of laughing faces and frightened faces into their brains. The silences were too loud to be ignored – they screamed an abyss of nothingness into minds incapable of adding tragic loss to their packed burden of horror and fear and guilt.

"Nixon . . ."

Silence.

Oh God; how many more of my men?

When Flockhart finished the roll there were only twelve men left. Twelve terribly fatigued men who nursed wounds and whose eyes were shaded with memory. Ramsay stood in the centre and wondered how to lift their morale. Shoulders were drooping, but was it tiredness or despair? He looked around, unable to decide.

"We'll march at night and rest during the day, lads. I am sure our lines will stiffen soon and Fritz's advance will slow up."

I am not sure of any such thing. It looks as if Fritz has broken through and smashed us all to atoms. Now they are just mopping up what remains.

"How will we get through their lines, sir?" A sensible question from Aitken, unlike his normally near frantic self.

"We will cross that bridge when we fall over it," Ramsay said. He emphasised his grin so it could be seen in the dark. "In other words, I don't know yet, but something will turn up."

As he had hoped, the frank admission brought a quiet laugh from the men, they appreciated honesty.

"Right lads, keep together and keep quiet. We will stick on the tail of the Hun. If anybody finds ammunition, let us all know. We are the Royals, Pontius Pilate's Bodyguard!"

They moved on again, slowly and quietly, stopping frequently whenever they heard German voices. Three times they came across small groups of dead men, each time a compact body of British soldiers surrounded by a scattering of Germans. On each occasion Ramsay ordered his men to rob the dead of their ammunition and bombs, and they moved on, leaving the crumpled corpses behind them.

"God rest, lads," McKim said each time, and some of the Royals murmured their own words. They marched on, grimly, into the gloom and always toward the distant grumble and flash of the guns.

An hour before dawn they were still deep in the battered maze of trenches and abandoned dugouts that had been the British support lines. They had passed scores of bodies, both British and German, and as many horses, some still kicking in their agony.

"It's not right to leave them to suffer," Aitken said, but Ramsay hardened his heart.

"Ignore them," he ordered. "We are more important than animals." He noticed Aitken hesitating. "Come on Aitken! Move!"

They pressed on, wending their way through the nightmare tangle of water-filled trenches and ripped sandbags. To the east the sky was stygian, as though the sun had no desire to open its eyes on another day of desperate pain.

"Ahead there," McKim spoke in a soft whisper. "Fritz."

Ramsay halted the men. They stopped, shoulders hunched, feet scuffing in the ankle deep mud, but they unshouldered their rifles and looked forward. They were bone-weary and afraid, but still they were soldiers, still they were Royal Scots. Ramsay could not voice his pride. These men deserved more than he could give.

He could hear the mutter of men directly across their path. "How many?"

"Not sure," McKim said. "A foraging party, I think. Do you want me to have a look?"

Ramsay considered. As the officer his place was with the bulk of the men, but he desperately wanted to prove himself now. *I am not good enough for these soldiers. I lead them to death every time.*

"I'll come as well," he decided. "Flockhart, you look after the rest of the lads." For a long moment Ramsay wondered if he should take Flockhart with him and settle matters, but reason prevailed. An experienced sergeant was priceless in the situation they were in.

You'll keep, you bastard. When the time is right I'll settle matters with you.

McKim's teeth gleamed in a grin. "Right, sir. Let's see how many Huns there are."

Ramsay nodded. He handed back the rifle he had been carrying and loosened his revolver in its holder. In situations like this, the long rifle would only be an encumbrance. He noted that McKim also discarded his rifle, but carried his bayonet and a short, viciously studded club.

"You have done this before," Ramsay accused.

Of course you have, you're a natural soldier. I wonder how many men you have killed in your time? You love this, don't you?

"Yes, sir." McKim's face was expressionless. "This way, sir." He did not duck as a distant shell exploded. "We'd best go by trench."

The trenches were shallow here, little more than muddy depressions in a grim landscape of shell holes, broken duckboards and the skeleton of an occasional tree. This had been the old Somme battlefield, ground hard-won at the cost of hundreds of thousands of lives and months of hell, given back to the Germans in a few hours. Ramsay knew he should take the lead but sense told him that McKim was the more experienced man.

As if he had read his thoughts, McKim glanced over his shoulder. "Follow me, sir, and keep your head down. There's nothing a Fritzy sniper likes better than an officer's head silhouetted against the gun flashes." He shrugged. "Not that there is much gunfire near us, sir."

The ground was saturated, chill with night and littered with the detritus of war. There was a skull, teeth grinning obscenely to the uncaring sky, a broken rifle, a litter of paper, a shell hole reeking with phosgene gas, an unexploded 5.9 inch shell half-buried in the mud, a decomposing corpse within a uniform so rotted it was impossible to tell the occupant's nationality and a dozen fresh bodies and parts of bodies, British and German, intertwined in a macabre embrace of death.

When McKim dropped to all fours Ramsay followed. There was a slight ridge ahead, rising raggedly to what had once been a stronghold until German shellfire had blasted it to a shambles. Ramsay saw a head bobbing up, another joined it, the round helmets distinctive even in the filthy dark.

"Fritz is using this as an observation post," he whispered. "He's placed a standing patrol here to watch his back." There was no need to explain so much to a ranker, but this was not a conventional situation.

"Yes, sir," McKim said. His eyes were predatory in the night and his hand strayed to his wicked bludgeon. "Orders, sir?"

He wants to kill them. His bloodlust is strong in this environment and he wants to kill every German he sees. What the hell do I do now? Destroy this post and risk alerting their companions, or slide past and risk them hearing us?

Decide. You are supposed to be an officer, remember? Come to a decision. Indecision is the worst possible fault in an officer.

"Orders, sir?" McKim repeated. His eyes glittered in the dark.

Ramsay thought rapidly. He had two distinct choices: try and go round the Germans, which meant making a long detour though this shell-battered landscape and risk being even further behind German lines, or destroy them.

"We'll get closer," he decided. "We will see how many there are."

There are bound to be more than just two. I need time and information before I decide what to do.

"Maybe best if I go myself sir?" McKim suggested. He lowered his voice slightly so Ramsay had to strain to hear him. "I was posted to the Lovat Scouts in the South African War. I know how to remain unseen."

"We'll both go," Ramsay told him.

Lovat Scouts? That meant that McKim was something of an expert in scouting and spying out the land, he would be an excellent shot as well. I must bear that in mind.

Ramsay remembered how difficult it was to man a listening post. The German soldier's nerves would be on edge, they would jump at every sound and every supposed movement in the shattered landscape around them. They would be taut, gripping their rifles ready to fire; their eyes would strain into the dark, hoping for a quiet night.

We might disappoint their hopes.

"I'll lead," he said. He was the officer, his was the position of most danger, God help him.

Ramsay dropped to his stomach, ignoring the foul water that spread its chill right through him. He moved slowly, wriggling in the deepest shadows, stopping whenever there was a noise or a breath of wind that may carry their scent toward the listening men. He had known a man, a veteran of the North West Frontier, who had been able to smell the Germans by the food they had eaten and he had no doubt that some among the Germans would be equally skilled. Three years of warfare had given him nothing but respect for the enemy. They were not monsters, just scared and very able fighting men who had every bit as much experience as the British at this type of warfare. The propagandists and newspaper columnists might sit in their comfortable offices dreaming up lies to create hatred against the enemy, but out here where it counted nobody paid much heed to that; they fought to survive, and for the regiment, the company and for the man who stood at their side. They fought because they had to, and because they hoped to get home alive far more than they hoped for a glorious victory.

Concentrate, for God's sake, or Fritz will slaughter us.

They crawled slowly from shadow to shadow, always watching the sandbagged emplacement on the ridge ahead, alert for movement or noise. When the occasional puffs of wind died, there was nothing to disguise their scent save the normal pungent stench of the battlefield, and nothing to take away any sound they made save the distant rumble of the guns. Ramsay halted twice, listening, but McKim was as silent as a shadow. He could hear a slight mumble from the front and pictured the Germans huddled in their trench, peering over the parapet through periscopes with bombs ready to hand and an assortment of lethal weapons all carefully designed to maim and kill stray British soldiers.

The sudden voice came as a challenge, the words loud but unrecognisable. Ramsay froze, hugging the ground as closely as he could. He saw McKim's eyes gleam like a predatory cat and heard the soft slither of a bayonet sliding from its scabbard. A head appeared behind the sandbagged parapet with the coal-scuttle shape of a German helmet obvious, even in the dark. A flare shot up, blue and harsh, its glare remorseless on the savaged ground.

Ramsay wondered why the German sentry could not hear the thunder of his heart as he lay under the pitiless light. He saw the shadows drift and slowly lengthen as the flare dipped downward.

There was a shout, and the crack of a rifle, followed by another and another. Ramsay tried to drag himself under the ground; something touched his arm and he started in fear, thinking he had been hit again.

"It's not us," McKim breathed across to him. "They're not shooting at us. Look!"

Ramsay realised that McKim was correct. There were five Germans in the listening post and all were firing frantically in the opposite direction. A voice floated towards them, gloating, "Got you Tommy, you ugly pig! Now you die!"

"Right, sir," McKim's voice was hard. "Now we've got them!" Without waiting for permission he rose from the ground and ran forward.

"McKim!" Ramsay's harsh whisper was lost in the night. Cursing, he jumped up and followed, holding his revolver before him and hoping the Germans were too busy firing to hear the two Royals coming from a different direction. His feet splashed in deep puddles; mud dragged at his ankles, slowing him down but he pushed on, reckless with fear and determination as he saw the small figure of McKim dance ahead of him.

McKim moved quickly but silently, keeping in a half crouch as he dodged from shadow to shadow in the wicked maze of shell holes and saps and half obliterated trenches. He did not glance back and when he was ten yards away he halted in the shelter of what had been a firing bay in a previous trench line, lifted a grenade, wrenched out the pin, poised and threw.

"McKim!" Ramsay joined him in the bay. "I gave no orders . . ."

McKim did not reply. "Two . . . three . . . four."

"What the devil . . ." Ramsay stopped as he realised McKim was timing the fuse of his grenade.

"Now!" McKim was on his feet and running a fraction of a second after the grenade exploded. Again Ramsay followed. He saw the flash of the explosion and heard screams as McKim bounded up the sandbag parapet. For one instant McKim was highlighted against the flare of the bomb; a small man with his helmet pushed forward over his face, a bayonet in his left hand and the club in his right, and then he jumped down into the observation post and was lost to sight.

With no more need for silence, Ramsay roared out "Up the Royals!" and followed the corporal. He felt an amazing freedom, as if his life no longer mattered. He had put aside his caution and was in the hands of the Gods of War; let them decide his fate. Life and death were two sides of the same ugly coin and he was part of the landscape of death.

"Up the Royals!"

The screams continued, accompanied by McKim swearing fluently. There was another yell and Ramsay vaulted the parapet. There were two Germans on the ground, one dead and the other writhing in agony from the wounds inflicted by the grenade. Another was leaning against the sandbag wall, feebly trying to remove McKim's bayonet from his abdomen. McKim was wrestling with a fourth. Before Ramsay could react he saw McKim's head come back and smash forward; the rim of his steel helmet smashed the bridge of the German's nose, breaking it in a gush of blood. The German howled and fell back, but McKim followed, using his boots fiercely and the German crumpled into a foetal ball, pleading, "Kamerad; kamerad!"

"I'll kamerad you, you dirty German bastard!" McKim lifted his club and rained a succession of blows, grunting with effort as they landed on the face and head of the cowering, screaming German soldier. Ramsay distinctly heard the sound of breaking bone.

The fifth German looked over his shoulder, mouth wide and eyes staring behind thick glasses. He was young; he could be no more than eighteen and was obviously terrified. As Ramsay stared at him, the German's nerves broke and he tried to run for the sap. Ramsay levelled his revolver and shot him, dispassionately. He saw the boy turn and shot him again, aiming for his chest. He had nothing against the German but there was no time to take prisoners with half the German army between them and safety and this man could not be allowed to go free and alert his comrades.

What a stupid excuse for a legal murder. The Germans will hear the shots and send a fighting patrol to investigate.

McKim had finished his men and was cleaning the blood from his bayonet with a piece of sacking from a sandbag. He nodded to Ramsay. "That's the way clear now, sir," he said. He slid the bayonet back into its scabbard and removed his helmet. He examined the rim critically and wiped the greasy blood from it. "A fellae from the Hairy-legged taught me that move, sir – the H. L. I. – Highland Light Infantry. They all sharpen the rim of their helmets when they go on trench raids. Fritzy doesn't like that much."

"You did not wait for orders," Ramsay began, but stopped. McKim's timing had been perfect. If he had hesitated the Germans might have stopped firing and heard them approaching. "Well done, McKim; I will recommend a medal for you when we get back to the lines."

"I was just doing my job, sir," McKim said. All the same, Ramsay thought, he looked pleased at the words.

The distinct sound of boots splashing through mud came out of the darkness. Ramsay turned and levelled his revolver while McKim lifted a German rifle and worked the bolt.

"Royal!" The challenge sounded clear in the night and McKim sighed and lowered the rifle.

"Scots!" he called back.

Flockhart led the men in. "We thought you had run into trouble," he said. He looked around the shambles that had recently been a German listening post. "Obviously we were wrong."

"We might do yet," Ramsay pointed to the dead Germans. "Their pals will be sending out a patrol to see what all the fuss was about. We'd best be on our way."

They froze as a flare hissed into the sky and exploded. The blinding white light cast stark shadows on the ground. They remained static, for to move was to invite massive retaliation from the unseen but undoubtedly watchful and vengeful, Germans. The flare remained; inviolate, immune, a star of wonder with an opposite reality to the Christian star of hope, until it slowly faded and slid to the ground.

"Right, lads, off we go and quickly, before Fritz arrives in force."

Ramsay led them at a stumbling trot, now more concerned with putting distance between his men and the destroyed listening post rather than keeping quiet or unobserved. He sensed that the small victory had restored confidence in his men; they were soldiers again, Royal Scots, rather than refugees from a defeated army. He heard McKim recount the action to Cruickshank, who grunted, "Serve the bastards right after bombing Edinburgh. They murdered my wife."

Ramsay said nothing. He knew about the zeppelin raid on Edinburgh and knew there had been a number of casualties, but he had since heard scores of men state that one or other of their relatives had been killed in that raid and claim that as some justification for their own actions.

"Royal Sco-o-ots!" somebody shouted, heedless of the need for concealment, and before Ramsay could call for silence, somebody else joined in, elongating the vowel in

"Scots" so it sounded like the blast of a horn: a challenge to the mighty German army that although they may be victorious today, not all the British were defeated and here was a force of very defiant fighting men. Shouting may have been foolish when they were surrounded by the enemy, but it was splendid for morale. The call came again and this time he joined in, blaring out his challenge to anybody who happened to be listening.

"Royal Sco-o-o-o-ots!"

"Royal Sco-o-o-o-ots!"

It was good to yell defiance to the world, to show they were undefeated and unbroken, not just by the German army but also by fate and the horror and pain and anguish and guilt that the politicians and kings and leaders had unleashed upon them, without thought or concern of the results on the millions of ordinary men and women who bore the brunt and paid the price.

"Royal Sco-o-o-o-ots!"

It was not a regimental call, not so much pride in that particular formation of the British Army to which fate had consigned their fortunes, but more a declaration of their own individuality combined with confirmation that they were united in comradeship with the human race.

The slogan ended in a wild cheer by the men, followed by near hysterical laughter, and then Ramsay ordered them to silence and increased their speed.

From somewhere in the dark came a reply. A single voice shouted, indistinct, and then others took up the call until the noise was a deep-throated chorus rolling across the confusion of mud and trenches and shattered dugouts.

"Semper Talis!" The words were clear now. "Semper Talis."

"What the hell does that mean?" Aitken asked. "Is that German?"

"It means 'Always the same'," Flockhart said quietly. "It's the motto of the Prussian Guards." He lowered his voice. "It's not bon, Aitken; it's not bon at all."

"Listen," McKim said softly, "they're singing now." He held up his hand as the words lifted until they seemed to fill the air around them. Ramsay listened too, his hands twitching at the butt of his revolver but powerless to alter the effect the singing was having on his men.

"Lieb vaterland magst ruhig sein
Lieb vaterland, magst ruhig sein
Fest steht und treu die Wacht, die Wacht am Rhein
Fest steht und true die Wacht, die Wacht am Rhein!"

The German words were powerful. Shoulders that had been squared only a few moments before were drooping now. The German words, sung in confident tones and with military precision, seemed to enter their minds and dominate.

"Does anybody speak German?" Ramsay wondered. He was strangely unsurprised when Flockhart murmured a reply.

"It's a popular German song," Flockhart said. "They sung it in the Franco-Prussian war as well. Very patriotic of them." He gave a slow translation as the Royals gathered round.

"Dear Fatherland put your mind at rest
Dear Fatherland put your mind at rest
Firm stands, and true, the Watch at the Rhine
Firm stands, and true, the Watch at the Rhine."

Flockhart stopped translating. "That must be the Prussian Guards," he said.

"Oh, aye?" McKim was first to recover. "Well, fuck them. We're the Royal Scots; come on lads, these bastards can't outfight us and I won't let them outsing us either." He faced the direction the singing had come from and began.

"Après la guerre finie,
Soldat Ecosse parti."

He stopped, "Come on lads, join in."

One by one the men joined their voices into a small chorus, infinitesimal compared to the thousand voice choir of the Prussians, but more defiant, more rousing and every bit as heartfelt.

"Mademoiselle in the family way,
Après la guerre finie."

Ramsay had heard those words sung a hundred times and knew that, if he survived, he would hear them a hundred times again, but he knew that each time he would remember this battered band of Royal Scots, standing an unknown distance behind the front line shouting their identity in tuneless contempt for the enemy. He felt a surge of pride that he had never known before as he looked over his men, and knew he would do all he could to get them back home safely.

The image came to him again. She was lying on her back in the sun-sweet field, with her hair a golden halo around her head and her breasts bare and soft and utterly alluring. He relived the scene, as he had so often before, the scent of the grass mingling with her faint perfume, the sough of the breeze in the nearby trees adding to her soft moans.

He remembered the quietness of that day, the kiss of the sun on his naked back, the sight of the grass from ground level – stalks stretching away like a miniature forest. He remembered the look in the girl's eyes, her trust and pleasure in his company.

"Shall we do that again?" she had asked and he had nodded.

"A hundred times more," he said.

"Make it a thousand times more," she had told him and put her hands around the back of his head to pull him close for a kiss.

She had tasted good. Sweet and young then, and the entire world before them with no thought of war or trouble on their horizons. Life had been good.

I'll do my best to get them all back safely. Except you, Flockhart, you vicious bastard. You must never get back.

The singing died away and the men looked at each other, grinning through their fatigue; they were soldiers immersed in one of the bloodiest wars that had ever been fought but they were still men. As Ramsay looked at them he was struck by their extreme youth. With the exception of McKim, who was an elderly man with eyes as old as time and the attitude of a teenager, Cruickshank and Blackley who were in their mid-twenties, and Flockhart, whose age was indeterminate, he doubted if any of them had reached the age of majority; most would still be in their teens. This was a war of juggernauts and mechanised murder waged by children. Gone were the days of professional long service men who could count their service in decades. These men may have been at the front for months or mere weeks, but they had probably seen more horror than most old-time soldiers had experienced in a lifetime.

"Right, lads," Ramsay said, suddenly humbled by his own men. "Let's get away from here before the Prussians send out a company to see how many of us there are."

"Let the bastards come . . ." McKim began, but Flockhart shut him up with a glare. "Don't be bloody stupid, McKim. Do as the officer says."

They moved on again, silent now as the night eased away. Ramsay listened for the sounds of Germans following them, but heard only the usual sounds of the front; the distant rumble of the guns, the closer occasional rattle of a machine gun and the low moan of wind through the wire.

The sudden staccato bark of musketry stopped them in their tracks; some of the men ducked or dived for cover. Ramsay flinched, but remained upright, he was an officer and could not be seen bobbing.

"That could be the Royals," McKim said hopefully. "Maybe we should march to the sound of the guns, sir."

"It could be Fritz fighting himself, for all we know," Ramsay said. He guessed there would be many small parties of British soldiers making their way back after being cut off by the speed of the German advance.

"McKim could be right, sir. That could be another group of our boys," Flockhart said. "Maybe we could team up with them. There's safety in numbers."

"More men might slow us down," Ramsay said. "Let them attract the Huns. We might be able to get through a gap in the lines."

Here I am again, explaining myself to the men. I should just give an order and expect it to be obeyed. I am their officer, for God's sake, not their colleague.

"Come on, keep moving."

"Bloody officer doesn't care about the lads."

"He's scared to get involved, yellow bastard."

Ramsay turned a deaf ear to the sotto voice comments. He would not be able to identify the culprits in the dark and even if he did, what could he do about it? Shoot them for mutiny? Sentence them to field punishment number one? He grunted, checked his revolver and tried to ignore the complaints. If British soldiers ever stopped grumbling there would be something seriously amiss.

They slogged on, occasionally swearing as they encountered tangles of rusty barbed wire, floundering into shell craters and halting with hammering hearts when flares threw their lurid glare onto the ground.

"Dawn's coming soon," Flockhart warned in a low tone. "And the boys are about done in."

Ramsay nodded. He had heard their breathing becoming more ragged with each passing quarter hour, and knew they were stumbling more often than they had at the beginning of the night. "We'll have to find somewhere to hide up for the day." He peered into the pre-dawn dark; the landscape was a nightmare vista of craters and abandoned strongpoints, ripped sandbags and the skeletal stumps of shattered trees.

"There are plenty shell holes," McKim suggested.

Ramsay opened his mouth to rebuke the corporal for subordination in speaking unasked, but they were at war, not on the parade ground. Instead, he said, "The boys deserve something better than that." He looked over his shoulder. "If you know of anywhere, Sergeant, let us know."

Flockhart stepped closer. "There is a ruined farmhouse about quarter of a mile away," he said. "We fought over it during the Somme offensive." He gave a small smile. "If there is anything left of it now."

Ramsay nodded. "Lead on, Sergeant MacDuff."

"Did you hear that?" came Cruickshank's voice from the darkness. "That bloody officer still doesnae ken Flockhart's name. They bloody officers are nae bloody use to anybody."

Ramsay hid his smile and said nothing. He allowed Flockhart to step ahead and followed him into the stinking dark of the night.

CHAPTER 5

23 March 1918

The remains of the farmhouse were about a hundred yards east of the road to Albert, a crumbled shell of a place with waist-high walls gaping like the stumps of rotted teeth. Flockhart marched across the shambles, his shoulders squared like the soldier he most definitely was. "I remember this well," he said, speaking almost conversationally. "We pushed the Hun out at the end of July and they came back in force that same night. It was to and fro for days." He looked at Ramsay through wary eyes. "You were at the Somme, were you not, sir?"

Ramsay nodded, unthinking. "I was over the top with the first wave," he said.

God! How well I remember that. The sheer volume of artillery was supposed to have pulverised the German positions so there was nothing left. We were told to sling our rifles, light our pipes and we could march all the way to Berlin, with any Germans that survived so demoralised by the shelling that they would be begging to surrender. Instead we marched into a blizzard of machine gun fire that decimated us before we had gone a hundred yards and cut our numbers by 75% before we even neared our first objective.

Flockhart narrowed his eyes. He looked at Ramsay musingly. "Maybe that was where I saw you before, sir. Were you with the Royals then?"

"I was," Ramsay said. "Maybe we fought together then."

For God's sake, man, don't you remember what happened? Don't you remember where we met? It was in Midlothian, miles and bloody miles away from the Somme or anywhere else in bloody France.

He pointed to the ruins and quickly changed the subject. "Is there enough room in there for all of us?"

"There are wine cellars below," Flockhart said. "We had to push out Fritz inch by inch. God, he is a tenacious bugger when he chooses." He frowned. "I am sure I know your face, sir. I don't think it was from the Somme though. I think it was before that?"

You're getting too close, Flockhart. You will never see the British lines again, that I promise.

"I was at Loos with the 11ᵗʰ battalion," Ramsay said quietly. "Not many came back."

I never reached the Front though. Dysentery.

Flockhart nodded. "That was a bad show," he agreed. He continued to study Ramsay, cocking his head to one side. "But I was not there, so I would not have seen you there, sir. No, no, it is something else, or somewhere else, if you don't mind me saying so."

"Let's get the men settled in," Ramsay said. "We can play guessing games later."

"Yes, sir." Flockhart stiffened at the implied rebuke. "Sorry, sir. I meant no disrespect."

"Of course not, Sergeant," Ramsay reminded Flockhart of their respective ranks. "Show me this sanctuary."

Ramsay examined the ruins. The highest point of the remaining walls was only shoulder height. For a moment he wondered how even those had survived. He examined the place more closely. The house was built from heavy stone, now pitted with bullet scars and blackened with the marks of grenades and shells. Ramsay looked through the gaping hole that had once been a window. The interior was a mess of mud and tangled wire, small piles of smoke-charred rubble and the debris of battle. The courtyard was square and cobbled, empty save for scattered straw. "It looks safe enough," he said and eased himself inside.

The interior smelled exactly the same as outside; lyddite and mud and the stench of the long dead. The Royals filed in one by one, holding their rifles in expectation of an attack, glancing skyward at the fading stars, listening for danger. Three of the exterior walls still stood, lower than the one by which they had entered, but a barrier between themselves and the outside world. There was a slight sense of security in here, or perhaps a sensation of claustrophobic confinement; Ramsay was not entirely sure which sensation was uppermost. He knew he would not care to be caught by the Germans in such a place, but it did supply shelter for his men and they needed that. He looked at them as they slumped in exhaustion, they were about done.

"The lads have had it," Flockhart mirrored his thoughts. "They can't go on much longer."

Whatever the dangers of remaining in such a prominent place, Ramsay knew that his men were too exhausted to continue.

"This is as good a place as any," he said. "We will keep a sentry posted in case Fritz gets too nosey." He raised his voice, "Right, lads, we'll bed down here for the day and move at dusk. If you have any iron rations left, this would be a good time to try them out."

The men filed in slowly: Niven the tram driver, Aitken

the soft-hearted man who was always first to help others, Mackay, very young, quiet and cautious, Turnbull who started at every sound and whose nerves were clearly fully stretched, Cruickshank, squat and muscular and always grousing . . . he watched his men come in. He had got to know them in the last few days and he was beginning to understand them a little; some he even liked.

"Keep silent, lads. Keep your heads down and your rifles handy. If Fritz gets nosey we will be out the back door and away."

"There's no bloody back door," Cruickshank said.

"We'll find one just for you," Flockhart told him. "Keep a civil tongue in your head, Cruickshank."

Ramsay did not make out Cruikshank's muttered reply, but Flockhart's returning snarl was testimony to its nature.

"Listen," McKim raised a hand for silence. "Can you hear that?" He cocked his head to one side, then frowned and removed his helmet, handling the sharpened steel rim with extreme care. "It's not artillery this time."

Ramsay lifted his head above the low wall. "I can't hear anything. You're imagining things, McKim."

"No I'm not, sir, with respect." McKim's furrowed his brows in thought. "It's not a sound, sir. Wait." He lay on the ground and placed his ear to the ground. "That's it, sir. It's not a sound, it's a vibration. It's like . . . there's something coming, sir. Like a railway train or . . . an army, sir."

Ramsay grunted cynically. "There are two armies nearby, McKim. Of course you will hear them."

"Yes, sir," McKim rose to his feet. "With respect, sir, I think they are closer now."

Ramsay became aware of a slight trembling under his feet. He grunted, and peered through a gap in the battered wall. The trembling increased until it resembled a machine, a constant monotonous movement that irritated the mind and shook the loose stones from the top of the wall. It gradually became more audible until it was a throbbing sound that permeated every though.

"What the hell is that?" he asked

"It's like an engine," Aitken said.

"It's marching feet," McKim said flatly. "It's thousands and thousands of marching feet."

Ramsay reached for his binoculars and cursed as he realised they were gone, lost somewhere in the frantic struggle in the trenches or in the trudging misery of the retreat. Instead he peered into the steadily decreasing dark and wished that he had not.

At first he was not sure what he saw. It seemed like a moving wall, but as he focussed into the distance he realised that he was staring at the head of a dense column of men. They were on the far side of the farmhouse, marching slowly down the road to Albert and eventually Amiens, with their boots crunching in a terrible symphony. There was a trio of officers at the head and NCOs at regular intervals at each side of the column, ensuring the men kept in step and the pace remained constant.

"Jesus," McKim breathed, "it's the whole bloody German army."

The head of the column passed them with the men marching in perfect step, looking neither to left or right as they moved in a disciplined silence.

"Is that the Prussian Guards?" Aitken asked.

"Nah, they're just Bavarian foot soldiers," Turnbull said. "The Prussians are bigger."

"They look big enough to me," Cruickshank grumbled. He hawked and spat in the direction of the Germans. "Dirty Fritzy bastards."

"Right, keep down and keep quiet," Ramsay ordered. "Let's hope they keep marching and don't send a patrol out to inspect these ruins."

"They've no reason to," Flockhart said quietly. "They think they have won the war. Why should they stop chasing us just to look at a ruin on an ancient battlefield?"

One by one the Royals sank down from the wall and stretched on the ground. In the time-honoured tradition of the British soldier they could sleep in any circumstance, and the exertions of the night and previous day had drawn heavily on their stores of stamina and endurance. Ramsay watched them for a minute and wondered if he should try to sleep. He shook his head. Despite his physical exhaustion, he knew that he would not be able to calm his mind sufficiently to sleep. He huddled in the lee of the shattered building, the dawn salmon pink with gunfire and the columns of Germans marching past in a steady stream. Ramsay thought the sound was like the drumbeats of defeat.

The marching ended, to be replaced by the sound of hooves and the grind of wheels on the pave. Ramsay watched the slow progress of ambulances and ammunition wagons and wondered what was happening at the front.

"There's plenty of them," Flockhart said. "They have been marching past for hours now."

"But the lads are still fighting." Ramsay jerked his head sideways to the constant rumble of the guns. "So Fritz has not broken through yet."

"He's doing damned well, though," McKim said. "Death and hell to every one of them." He took off his helmet and began to sharpen the rim on the rough stonework of the wall. "We'll get him back. You'll see, sir, we'll get him back." There were tears of frustration in his eyes as he watched the Germans roll past. "If we ran at them, sir, we might disrupt them. We might catch them by surprise, like we did in the trench."

"There are too many of them," Ramsay said. "We'll stick to our original plan, McKim. Sit tight here for the day and move at night for our own lines." He watched the Germans marching past as morning sunlight glinted from the never-ending rows of helmets. They seemed remorseless, a silent snake of field-grey marching in pursuit of the retreating British Army, an endless parade of polished boots rising and falling: thump, thump, thump, as if Germany was pouring out all its manpower in a final attempt to push the British army back to the Channel and an admission of defeat.

The words of that German song came back into his mind, sung with all the arrogance of impending victory:

> *"Lieb vaterland magst ruhig sein*
> *Lieb vaterland, magst ruhig sein*
> *Fest steht und treu die Wacht, die Wacht am Rhein*
> *Fest steht und true die Wacht, die Wacht am Rhein!"*

"It's as if the Somme and Paschendaele never happened." McKim shook his head in disbelief. "All those thousands of boys, lost for nothing, and now the Huns are rolling us up as if we were not there." He scraped his helmet against the stone so that sparks flew. "We'll get him back though, never you fear, sir." He ran his thumb along the rim and repeated, "Death and hell to every one of the bastards, death and hell to them."

"Death and hell indeed," Ramsay said softly. *But to whom? The German army seems to stretch forever and there are only thirteen of us here.*

Flockhart reached over as if to touch McKim's shoulder, glanced at Ramsay and dropped it again. "We could be following the German advance for days," he said, "and never catch up."

"Nobody advances that far and that fast," Ramsay tried to sound confident. "They will march beyond their supplies and have to stop to consolidate. Then Haig will counter attack and catch them on the hop." He looked directly at McKim. "We will get back to the regiment, we will get home, and we will win this war."

They lapsed into silence, listening to the marching Germans and the rumble of supply wagons and guns over the cracked pave. "You better get some rest, Sergeant. You too, McKim," Ramsay said. "I'll stay on watch."

"I am all right for a while, sir," Flockhart said.

"Get some sleep, Flockhart. That's an order," Ramsay said. *Why the hell did I say that? If he is tired, he is more likely to make a mistake and get killed. Except he might get us all killed and these men deserve better than that. Damn it!*

"I will in a minute, sir," Flockhart said. "It's not right that I should sleep while an officer is awake."

Ramsay opened his mouth but said nothing, Flockhart had made the decision he should have made for him. Let fate decide the outcome. The Germans continued to march past, rank after rank of soldiers, some silent, some talking; there was the occasional snatch of song but most of them were grim-faced and professional. Ramsay watched and said nothing. Each German soldier between him and the British lines decreased his chances of returning home. He missed Gillian, but what would she think of him if she knew the truth? *Oh God, Gill, what would you think?*

"If you don't mind me asking, sir," McKim broke the silence, "but was it the war that brought you into the army? I know you are not a regular." He placed his helmet back on his head, pushed it down firmly and fastened the chinstrap.

As he watched the German column march past, his hand reached for his rifle. Flockhart put a hand on his arm and shook his head.

"Not yet, Kenny. Our turn will come." He faced Ramsay, his eyebrows raised. "Did you volunteer, sir?"

You are still probing, Flockhart. You are suspicious now.

"Yes," Ramsay agreed. "I volunteered when the war started." He held Flockhart's eyes and tried not to blink. The days before he donned the king's uniform seemed an unreal existence. He smiled wryly at the memories. "I had to do my bit for King and country."

Flockhart barely glanced up as a heavy shell ripped overhead to explode in a dark fountain of mud a hundred yards behind them. He glanced over to McKim. "That's our boys reminding Fritz that they have not won yet."

"Maybe the gunners are going to plaster the German reinforcements!" McKim looked eager at the prospect until Ramsay reminded him, "If the artillery starts any plastering, McKim, we are directly in their line of fire. The spotters will use this ruin as a range finder and plaster us as well."

They all looked skyward and searched for any sign of British air presence, but the Royal Flying Corps was absent and the sky clear except for a trio of German fighters flying languidly toward the British lines. The white puffs of British Archie seemed innocent from down here and the Germans flew on, unconcerned and untouched until obscured by distance.

A volley of shells followed the first, smashing down around the farmhouse and the sleeping men awoke. Aitken cowered closer to the wall while most of the others simply rolled over and fell back asleep, too tired to be concerned. A second volley followed, landing a hundred yards over, and a third landed even further away. Then there was silence, and the acrid drift of lyddite in the smoke.

Flockhart continued the previous conversation as though nothing had happened, "What were you before the war started, sir?" His eyes were more than curious, they were predatory.

"Don't you know what I was?" Ramsay began, but the sound of another passing shell drowned his words and then McKim spoke quietly. "The Germans won't win."

Ramsay glanced at him. There was no false defiance, the corporal was just stating what he firmly believed to be a fact.

"Good man, McKim." He gave a bleak smile. "It's statements such as that, and men like you, that convince me Fritz won't win this war."

McKim grunted. "Have you seen those wagons rolling back, sir?" He nodded to the nearby road. "They started just as the shells came down."

Ramsay looked up. He had been too busy ducking from the British artillery shells to even notice the changes on the road. McKim was right, the German infantry were now marching on the verges beside the road. Wheeled vehicles had taken their place on the pave.

Ramsay looked at them; military wagons drawn by teams of horses. Some bore the broad red cross of ambulances, others wore plain canvas covers over the back. They moved slowly, nose to tail against the tide of the marching men and although Ramsay stretched his neck as far as it was safe without revealing himself to the nearby Germans, he could not see the tail of the convoy.

"There are a lot of them," Ramsay said.

"Aye, sir," McKim said, "and if you look at the sides, as they pass sir, you can see inside the flaps. The Huns have the covers tied down so their troops can't see inside, but they are carrying the casualties. See the blood?"

Ramsay concentrated on one wagon out of the hundreds

that were passing. He saw the dark streaks down the side and the ominous red drops that descended to the splintered stone of the pave. "Fritz may be pushing us back but he is paying a heavy price for it," he agreed.

"And he is using his best troops, too," McKim said. "That first wave was storm troopers, they were Saxons, and then we faced the Prussian Guards, and that lot that marched past were a mixture of Bavarians and Prussians. That's the reason old Fritz won't win." He produced his pipe and thrust it into his mouth. "He's gaining ground but losing his best men." He sucked on his empty pipe. "And you volunteered for all this blood and slaughter too, sir."

Once again Ramsay was aware of Flockhart's interest as the sergeant moved slightly closer. He kept his voice neutral and nodded. "I had to do my bit," he said slowly. He could sense Flockhart watching him through narrow eyes and forced a shrug. "It seemed the best thing to do at the time."

McKim gave a small smile. "Good for you, sir," he said, "I expect it all seemed like a big adventure back then."

"It did," Ramsay agreed with a smile that was hardly forced at all. "It all seems so long ago."

The memories came back of that fateful autumn day he had signed away his life for the duration of the war.

There seemed always to be a cold wind on the Dean Bridge in Edinburgh. It came from nowhere and swirled the dead leaves around their legs, flicked Gillian's dark hair across her face despite her tight hat and flapped the lapels of Ramsay's coat in a mad frenzy against his chest. He lowered his head, tucked Gillian's arm closer under the crook of his elbow and strode on, occasionally squeezing her to show his affection and pride. A group of soldiers passed them, young men talking too loudly to hide their self consciousness in their stiff new khaki.

"We must look over the parapet," Gillian decided for them. "I always look over the parapet of the Dean Bridge whenever I cross."

Ramsay smiled indulgent acceptance and allowed her to steer him to the breast-high wall. They stood there arm in arm and Gillian stretched to stare down at the Water of Leith rushing brown and creamy white between its verdant banks far below. "I always get dizzy looking at this," she said, "and I am not sure whether I want to run away and hide from the fall, or launch myself into space. It must be a form of vertigo I have."

"We'd better get back, then." Ramsay tried to usher her away from the wall but she shook off his hand and stood on tip-toes to look further over. Her head and the top half of her body stretched over the wall and she peered down and down and further down as Ramsay smiled and held on to her arm.

"Oops!" Gillian grabbed hold of her hat and giggled nervously as the wind threatened to blow it away. She looked sideways at him, her eyes bright with mischief. "Did you see that? I nearly lost my hat! Don't you wish we could fly, Douglas? Can you imagine the fun? Being like a bird and just jumping off here and soaring away?"

"You are a strange little creature," Ramsay said.

"Why thank you, sir." Gillian half-turned her head away, but Ramsay saw her smile as she returned to her scrutiny of the water far beneath. "Where are you taking me today, Douglas?"

"You'll see." Ramsay turned the small box over in his pocket. It was cool and square and so very important.

Am I doing the right thing? Am I being presumptuous?

Gillian laughed and drew back from the parapet. "All right then. Lead on MacDuff." She bumped her hip against his with a movement that could have been deliberate, but if so there was no indication as she pulled away again to a more respectable four inches.

Ramsay replaced her arm inside his and pulled her closer, but not near enough to touch. He led her off the bridge and round the corner into the terraces and crescents of the Georgian New Town.

There was a group of women clustered at the corner of Moray Place. They were talking quietly as they held their parasols against the wind and controlled the ripple of their long skirts. They all looked round as Ramsay and Gillian walked arm in arm. One broke away from the group and approached, smiling pleasantly as she hugged a handbag to her plump breasts.

She was perhaps twenty-five, with the heavy face that signified self indulgence and would certainly run to fat in later life. At present she was graceful, elegant and confident.

"Are you on leave, sir?" Her voice was educated, Morningside more than Canongate, and her eyes were friendly as they scrutinised him. *Grey eyes, quite pretty. There is potential here, for a year or two.*

Ramsay shook his head. "No, I am not."

She thinks I am in the Army. Do I look like a soldier? It must be the spread of my shoulders and my upright carriage. What fun.

"Ah," her smile broadened, "you are still waiting for your commission to come through then."

"No," Ramsay met her smile. "I am waiting for my final Law results from Edinburgh University."

Now what do you say when you know I am going to be a solicitor? Are you impressed, my fine fat lady?

The smile faded from the woman's face. "Young man," she said, "you should be thoroughly ashamed of yourself, hiding behind the pages of a book while other and better men are dying for king and country."

You pompous hussy! Young man? I doubt I am three years younger than you!

The woman reached into her handbag, produced a small white feather and, as Ramsay stood still, pinned it on the lapel of his coat. "You should be in uniform."

You besom! You pretended friendship to trap me!

As the woman stalked back to her friends, Gillian gave a little giggle. The other women were glaring at them; one woman of about forty shook her head and repeated, "You should be in uniform." She gave Gillian a look that would have frozen hell and said, "And you should be ashamed to be seen walking out with a coward, young lady."

"Come on, Gill." Ramsay took hold of Gillian's arm and strode away. He could feel the flush of blood colouring his face. After a few steps he tore the white feather from his lapel, threw it on the ground and stamped on it. The object lay there, accusing him of all the things that the women had said.

Evil besoms. I am no coward. I am trying to make something of my life and not wasting it in a silly war. They had no right to say that, women don't go to war. They don't know what it is like.

Gillian giggled again. "Temper, temper, Douglas: I have never seen you take on so! Do you know who these ladies were?" She answered her own question. "They were the League of the White Feather. They go about the city trying to shame men into joining the army."

"Well," Ramsay said as he ground the feather under his heel, "they won't shame me." He looked at Gillian and smiled. "I have other ideas for my future than finding glory in France."

Gillian's smile spread right across her face. "I wish you would tell me what they are, Douglas. Why don't you tell me?"

Ramsay listened to the echo of his footsteps from the serene grey sandstone and to the rustle of leaves from the trees in the private garden that sat secure behind its iron railings. This was Edinburgh at its best: serene; dignified, secure, home to the High Court and very much his world. This was where he belonged, not facing death and glory in some maniacal charge across foreign fields. "I'll tell you when the time is appropriate," he said.

"Oh, you are such a beast!" Gillian squeezed his arm. She looked up at him, blinking as a wisp of hair flopped across her eyes. Ramsay brushed the hair away and bent to kiss her, but she pulled away with a slight smile. "You would look so handsome in uniform, though," she said, thoughtfully. "I can see you as a dashing captain in the cavalry, charging the Germans at the head of your men."

Oh God, not you too!

Ramsay frowned. "This war will all be over by Christmas," he told her. "Neither us or France or Germany or Austria has the resources to make it last longer than that. And after all, the Kaiser is related to the king, why should we fight each other?" He shrugged.

Don't let her think such things. Take charge!

"Even if I volunteered today, I would never get near the front. By the time I am trained it would all be finished." He looked away. That was a blatant lie. He had no intention of joining the army and leaving his comfortable life behind. The very thought was terrifying.

Gillian crinkled her nose up. "Oh, Dougie! That's so disappointing." She wriggled free of his hand and moved a step away from him, pouting. "You would suit a uniform – the tight leggings, the smart jacket, the scarlet and black and gleaming brass . . ." She giggled like a schoolgirl and looked away, blushing furiously. "You have no idea what that thought is doing to me!"

You don't need a uniform for that, my girl. Wait until I get you somewhere quiet and I will redouble those feelings.

Ramsay looked at her. "You are indeed a strange little creature," he said, and the genuine affection he felt for her redoubled. She smiled up at him and poked out her little pink tongue.

Oh, dear God! Gillian. Don't do that in public, please!

He fingered the box in his pocket again, suddenly certain that he was doing the right thing. The revelation burst on him unannounced and he stopped dead in the street. He wanted this woman. He wanted to hear her musical voice with that fascinating gurgling laugh, he wanted to smell her hair, he wanted to feel her small gloved hand inside his as they walked side by side along the elegant streets of Edinburgh and he wanted her in his bed. God, how he wanted to have her in his bed.

Is this love? Is this love, this desire to investigate and examine every aspect of her? I don't only want her body. I want her mind and her sound and her soul. Oh, dear God, I have fallen in love with her.

"Shall we step along?" he asked, and she nodded.

"Where are you taking me, sir?" Gillian's chin thrust out appealingly

"To an island in the Caribbean," Ramsay kept his voice mysterious and smiled at Gillian's gasp of delight.

"The Caribbean!" There was a pause as he guided her along the Georgian terrace, and then came the inevitable and expected question, "Where is that?"

"It's not far from here," Ramsay told her seriously. "It's a very romantic haunt of pirates and smugglers and writers."

"This is a lovely area," Gillian echoed his thoughts as she rested her head on his shoulder. "I do love Edinburgh so." She looked up at him with her eyes wide and grey and smiling. "I never want to leave this city."

"Nor do I," he told her, truthfully. *Especially not to go and fight in Flanders field.*

They crossed to the elegant terrace of Heriot Row, and Ramsay guided Gillian to the private garden occupying the entire southern half of the street. He fumbled in his pocket and pulled out the key, unlocked the gate and pushed it open. It creaked slightly as he ushered her in. The autumnal tints of the spreading trees contrasted with the bright blue of the sky above while a blackbird sang melancholic and sweet. The atmosphere altered as soon as they stepped inside; seclusion and privilege surrounded them.

"This isn't the Caribbean," Gillian protested. "This is Queen Street Gardens."

Ramsay rubbed a hand up her arm. "We aren't there yet," he said. "Come on now, it's only a short step."

He led her along the ochre-red path to where the pond lay, still under its canopy of trees, the water languid, specked with fallen leaves. "Here we are," Ramsay stopped at a green-painted bench. "Sit you down now." He watched as she smoothed her skirt beneath her and folded herself onto the wooden slats. She looked up at him, eyes bright and questioning.

"Here I am, Douglas."

Ramsay stood at her side. Now the moment had come he felt nervous, yet there was no need. He had no doubts that he was correct and the recent, overwhelming surge of affection had only confirmed his decision. "Did you know that this was where Robert Louis Stevenson thought of *Treasure Island*?" He indicated the small island that sat in the middle of the pond and then nodded to the street beyond. "He used to live just over there, in Heriot Row."

"Did you bring me here to tell me that?" Gillian's eyebrows rose slightly. There was amusement in her eyes, and perhaps a touch of something else. Disappointment perhaps?

Ramsay shook his head. He realised he was just trying to delay the moment. "No, I was just explaining the Caribbean connection." He forced a smile he guessed must look like the grin on the face of a skull. He fumbled in his pocket, found the box and pulled it out. His hand was trembling so much that he nearly dropped it on the path. He knelt, hoping there were no witnesses.

Who cares about witnesses? This is one of the most important decisions of my life.

"Gillian," he opened the box and pushed it toward her. "Would you consent to become my wife?"

God that sounds clumsy!

The call of the blackbird seemed to last for an eternity as Gillian looked at him and then at the ring. Her eyes were a liquid grey and so beautiful that he wanted to just sink inside them and stay forever.

When they came, her words seemed to cut so deep into him that he gasped. "No, Douglas," she said softly. "No. I will not consent to become your wife."

What? You can't turn me down? I am Douglas Ramsay! I am set to become a successful solicitor! How dare you treat me like this, damn you!

The blackbird was still calling, but the sound was now a mockery of beauty. Ramsay felt the breath choking in his throat. "Dear God, why not? I love you, Gillian. I am on the cusp of my career. Once I pass my finals – and I will – I will be a solicitor. I already have a position in a law firm. We will have enough money to live in comfort, and . . ."

Gillian was smiling and shaking her head. She pressed a gloved finger against his lips. "Sshhhh, Douglas, dear. I know all about your attributes. I have no doubt of your love, but you see, I want a husband of whom I can be proud, and how could I be proud of a solicitor when all the brave young men are marching to war?"

I am not going to France to get killed or have my legs blown off by some German artilleryman. Not for you and not for anybody else, for God's sake. There are plenty more women who would jump at the opportunity of marrying a solicitor.

But I love you, damn it all, and I don't love anybody else.

"To war?" Still on his knees, Douglas stared at her. "You want me to be a soldier? I thought I had explained about that. This war will all be over before I'm even half-trained."

"Well then, you have nothing to lose, do you?" Gillian shifted along the seat, away from him. "You know that all three of my brothers have joined up, don't you? I don't want to be married to the only man in the family who did not do his bit." She was still smiling, but there was doubt behind the grey eyes now, and something shifting that Ramsay did not like. He did not want to think that it was contempt.

He stood up and brushed the dirt from his knees. He had never wanted this girl as badly as he did at that second.

Damn, damn, damn!

"If I agree to volunteer, will you agree to marry me?" He kept the temper from his voice and fought against the desire to throw the box and ring into the pond and stamp away in frustration and disgust.

"Certainly," Gillian said at once.

"Well then," Ramsay contemplated her. With that single dark hair still loose across her heart-shaped face, and her lips open, ready to smile or frown, she was utterly endearing. "Well then," he repeated, "in that case, I can hardly refuse."

Oh, Christ. What have I said? Please God the war is over before I get near the front.

Her smile seemed enough reward for a lifetime of soldiering. "Is that a solitaire diamond on my ring?"

*

115

"You volunteered, then?" McKim asked and Ramsay crashed back to a present consisting of mud and broken men and lyddite-tainted smoke.

"I did," he said. "Kitchener and the King could not do without me."

McKim grunted. "Of course not, sir. The army would not be the same without you. Why just the other day General Haig was saying to me . . ." He stopped talking, "Sorry, sir. No offence intended."

Flockhart continued to scrutinise him through narrow, thoughtful eyes.

He is working out where he met me before. I have to get rid of him before he remembers and murders me out of hand.

Although the German column had passed, the tramp and shudder of marching feet could still be felt, while the return convoy of ambulance wagons was never-ending. Ramsay realised that his men were all awake again and watching the road.

"Try and grab some more sleep, lads," Ramsay ordered. "Sergeant Flockhart, you take the next watch, call me at noon." Uncaring of the mud and shattered stones, he rolled on his side and closed his eyes, not expecting to sleep. The memories of Gillian and that peaceful day in Edinburgh returned and he had to fight against self-pitying tears. The halcyon days of before-the-war seemed so far away they were like a different world. He knew, somehow, that nothing would ever be the same again.

I will never be the same careless man again.

They moved an hour after dusk, slipping silently from the shelter of the shattered farm to head in the direction of the retreating British Army.

"Which way, sir?" Cruickshank asked.

"Head for the guns, Cruickshank, and keep your eyes

116

open for Fritz." The gunfire continued as a muted roar in the distance, punctuating the horizon with red and white flashes.

"The lads are still fighting, then," Flockhart said. He pointed to a new shell crater in the ground, the remains of three Germans bore testament to the accuracy of the British artillery.

"But still retreating too," McKim reminded. "This must be our biggest withdrawal since Mons." He nudged Flockhart's side. "Remember that, Flocky? When the angels came to help us? I wonder if they will come again this time."

Flockhart grunted again. "There are no such things as angels, McKim. There are no angels and there is no God. There is only hell and demons and they are all around us in this purgatory."

"We'll keep in line with the road, lads, but far enough away so the Germans won't see us." Ramsay led from the front, but he was now constantly aware of a faint prickling at the back of his neck. He knew that Flockhart was gradually working out who he was and where they had met. Once Flockhart worked that out, then there was another threat to his life and an even greater threat to his reputation and name.

"Keep the lads together, Flockhart," Ramsay ordered. He turned around and saw the compact group of Royals, with McKim slightly to one side and Flockhart in the rear. Flockhart's eyes met his and did not drop. They probed him; musing, questioning, suspicious, and Ramsay touched the butt of his pistol as a warning. Flockhart nodded but said nothing.

He must know who I am. He must have worked it out and now he'll try and kill me. I must get rid of him before we reach the British lines. There will be an opportunity somewhere. If not I will make one.

They trudged on into the dark, stumbling over loose

strands of wire, skirting the deep shell craters with their pools of gas-poisoned water, freezing with every star shell and flare and watching the intermittent flashes that lit up the horizon and revealed where the fighting front was.

"Over there, sir." McKim pointed into the dark. "If you look at the gun flashes, you will see something sticking up. It may be a village or something."

Ramsay focussed, narrowing his eyes against the sudden brilliant flashes of artillery against the dark of the night. There was something there; an oblong of greater black protruding from the chaos of the ground.

"It might be an idea to investigate," Ramsay said.

CHAPTER 6

The church tower rose above the flattened ruins of the hamlet it had once served. Without a map and with every recognisable feature of the surrounding countryside devastated by war, Ramsay had no way of knowing the name of the place.

"Do you have any idea where we are, Sergeant?"

Face him directly, alleviate any suspicion, appear as normal as possible.

Flockhart looked around and screwed up his face. "I couldn't really say, sir. There are so many wee villages around here, and all have churches." He shrugged. "I know we are somewhere east of Albert and west of Berlin."

Sarcasm? Or humour? Is Flockhart trying to show his contempt for me?

Ramsay turned away. "That was very helpful, Sergeant. How long until dawn, McKim, would you say?" Until the beginning of this retreat, Ramsay would never have dreamed of asking the opinion of a mere corporal, but the enforced close companionship had stripped away some of the elitism of rank.

"Less than an hour, sir," McKim said at once. "Then Fritz

will see us marching across his landscape as if we own the bloody place."

Ramsay listened to the sputter of a machine gun and the crackle of musketry. He estimated it to be at least three miles away, possibly further. For all their marching since the German breakthrough, they were further behind the front than they had been at the start.

"I want to get up there," he nodded to the church tower. "I want to see how far we are from our lines."

The tower loomed upward, its top lost in the already lessening dark. "Flockhart, you organise a defensive position around the base," Ramsay ordered. "If any parties of Fritz approach, destroy the bastards."

McKim grinned. "That's the spirit, sir!"

"I'm surprised the Germans have not already occupied this place, sir," Flockhart said quietly. "It will make a splendid observation post."

"So am I," Ramsay admitted quietly. "It makes me wonder just how far they have already advanced. Take McKim and six men and set up defensive positions. I will take Aitken and Turnbull with me in case of nasty surprises."

And hope to God that our side don't decide to use this place to range their artillery.

Shelling had ruined the nave of the church and brought down the roof so the interior was a heap of shattered rubble, interspersed with shards of stained glass that glittered and crunched underfoot. The disembodied head of the Madonna stared at them from the top of a shattered pew, its eyes accusing, seemingly wondering how mankind could remain this destructive and violent nearly two thousand years after her son had carried the message of peace and love. There had been a skirmish in here very recently, with three bodies among the ruins, two dressed in British khaki, the third in bloodstained field-grey.

"Check them for ammunition and food," Ramsay ordered, and lifted three clips from the nearest man. Aitken watched and then rifled the equipment of the second British corpse. Turnbull circled slowly, keeping the muzzle of his rifle pointed toward the darker areas of shadow within the ruins. Only one wall remained nearly intact, with a staircase coiling upward.

"This bugger had his iron rations intact," Aitken said. "Shall I share it with the lads?" He showed the tin of bully beef and packets of biscuits and sugar and tea that every infantryman carried as standard issue.

"There's not much to share," Ramsay said. He eyed the food. It was days since he had eaten properly and even this meagre amount made him ache for sustenance.

You are the officer. It is your duty to look to the men first and yourself last. Ignore the hunger!

"Have half, Aitken and give the rest to Turnbull; maybe the other man has anything?"

"There's nothing on him at all, sir. He must have been a right greedy bastard." Turnbull pushed away the corpse in disgust. It was significant that neither soldier searched the German. Even in death he was still the enemy.

"You two watch the flanks. If Fritz has the sense I know he has he will have his eye on this place as an observation post." Ramsay hesitated for a moment, watching as Aitken opened the bully beef with the point of his bayonet. The smell of the beef seemed to set a fire in his stomach and for one guilty second he was tempted to pull rank and demand his share.

You can't do that. You need the respect and loyalty of these men.

"Keep alert, Aitken." Ramsay turned away and tested the first step of the stairs. They were solid stone and had probably been in place for many centuries before this war had rained new powers of destruction on them. The passage of thousands of feet over hundreds of years had worn a depression in the centre of each. The step felt secure and Ramsay moved upward, tested the next and carried on. There were fixtures in the wall to which a rope handrail had presumably once been fastened, but now there was nothing except the rough stone, pockmarked where shrapnel had smashed against it.

I feel vulnerable already. If Flockhart wants to shoot me he will rarely have a better target.

Five steps, ten, and Ramsay was well above head height. The remaining external walls were low and as the grey light of dawn expanded across the eastern horizon he felt very exposed. He was a tiny moving figure against a background of slender grey stone, crawling upward step by careful step. After thirty steps he stopped. There was a gap where a blast had torn apart the stonework and left a hole of sucking nothingness.

Now what do I do? Every German in this part of France can see me if he just glances in this direction.

He looked down. Turnbull was watching him, his face white against the dark background of rubble. Aitken was sweeping the surroundings, rifle ready, watching for the Germans.

Should he go on? Ramsay looked upward, the steps continued, spiralling round and round the central stone column toward the rapidly lightening heavens above. In places the wall remained, concealing the stairs from the outside world, in other places there were huge gaps in the stonework where he would feel ridiculously exposed. Yes, he decided. He must go on. His men were watching. He reached up, grasped the next step, three levels up, and tested it for stability. It felt firm; the step was imbedded into the central column, a solid slab of sandstone that had been carved from some quarry by hand, many centuries ago.

Ramsay took a deep breath and a firm hold of the step. *Here we go, then.* He stepped into space. For a second he was suspended, hanging on by his fingernails alone as his feet scrabbled for purchase on the rounded central column. The drop seemed to be sucking at his feet, calling him down and he remembered Gillian's remarks about wanting to fly when she looked over the parapet of the Dean Bridge. That happy day seemed so long ago and far away. He pushed aside the thought, glanced down and saw Turnbull's white face still staring up at him.

He probably hopes the officer will fall. All officers are bastards, after all. I won't provide him with free entertainment.

He stretched as far as he could until he felt the skin at the tip of his fingers scraped raw, but his feet found the joints between two stones and he pushed himself upward. There was a second of panic as he hung over the edge and then he pulled himself up and stood on the step. He felt his heart pounding and blinked away the beads of sweat that had collected on his eyebrows.

The rim of the sun had eased onto the horizon during the few moments he had been scrabbling to get over the gap and Ramsay could see the entire panorama of the old Somme battlefield. It was only a few square miles of churned earth and torn landscape, yet it had been the scene of hundreds of thousands of deaths and unthinkable agony. All now wasted as the Germans had pushed the British back in a matter of a few days.

Ramsay shook away the thoughts and continued upward, still testing each step as the sun rose along with him and the view grew immense. There were gun flashes to the south and west, intermittent. Mere pinpricks that disguised the fact they were missiles of hellish destruction. He could see villages that were now mere piles of rubble and some that were virtually untouched amidst the carnage of war. There was also a band of smoke that showed where the advance had reached.

Ramsay narrowed his eyes, trying to judge where the front was now. Some miles away, that was for certain. Even as he watched there was a series of explosions, bright bursts of shells around a small village, and the wild crackle of musketry drifting on the breeze.

Amidst the scattering of villages he saw a sizeable town. That would be Albert, surely, with the church tower even taller than this one and the railhead and bustling civilian population. It looked far enough away to be secure. Ramsay wished he had a pair of binoculars, but wishing was pointless. He stepped upward, wincing as the next step crumbled beneath his feet and fragments of stone hurtled downward, turning end over end until they landed with an audible crash just a few feet from where Aitken crouched behind his levelled rifle. Ramsay saw him jump and whirl round. He did not fire and Ramsay continued.

Shellfire had damaged the upper tower and the exterior wall no longer existed. There was only the pillar around which the stairs spiralled, leading upward in a dizzy circle toward the heavens. Ramsay held on to this central pillar with his left hand as he followed the stairs – the empty space to his right sucking at him and the sun rising in crimson splendour to the east.

"Don't you love the sunshine?" She asked him after their third bout of the afternoon.

He nodded as he watched the sheen of sweat on her upper body and the light passing shadows over her stomach. She turned her head to smile at him, with teeth uneven but surprisingly white.

"My father doesn't see it much," she sounded sad. Like so many girls of her class she was emotional and volatile, quick to anger and equally quick to tears.

"Why is that?" Ramsay asked, and then cursed his own stupidity. "Of course, he works down the mines, doesn't he?"

"Yes," she said. "He's in the Lady Victoria." There was pride in her voice.

Ramsay nodded. Although his father owned shares in various mines he had no idea which one was which. He presumed that working in the Lady Victoria was a sign of prestige to this girl. "That must be interesting."

"It's bloody hard work," the girl said. "Mother has to wash him when he comes home. He sits in the tub in front of the fire all black with coal."

Ramsay hid the thrill of shock. He smiled at the thought of his elegant and graceful mother washing his father in a tub in front of the living room fire.

"Do you find that funny?" The girl struggled to sit up so Ramsay kissed her again, softly, and eased her back to the ground.

"I find you adorable," he said, and kissed her again. She responded with a will, and then slid her lips free.

"Where will we live?" she asked.

"Where do we live?" Ramsay said, "You know where we live. I live in Edinburgh and you live in Newtongrange with your father."

"I said where will *we* live," the girl repeated. "After we are married, I mean. Where will we live? Will I move into Edinburgh with you or will you come out here with us?"

Ramsay stared at her. He did not hide his amusement.

The tower was truncated; the top had been blown off so Ramsay balanced on a single, half broken step with half of Picardy unravelled before him and empty air all around. He surveyed the view. The old battlefield of the Somme spread like a plague-site; the churned and broken grave of three quarters of a million men. A sliver of cloud obscured the rising sun and the scene darkened, as if God was frowning at this insignificant man peering over the wreckage of a beautiful country. Ramsay swore and focussed toward the west, where the British lines should be.

There was the flash or artillery and the pall of smoke where guns were firing or houses burning. There was the occasional fountain of earth and mud where a shell landed, or the bright starburst of an explosion. Ramsay concentrated on searching for any sign of a British stand. He looked for a concentration of troops and shelling, or a merging of marching men. He saw a number of mobile observation balloons floating high above the tortured ground, but they were moving too slowly for him to ascertain in what direction they were headed. Far below the nearest balloon was a truck, at the head of what appeared to be a dusty snake but which would be a marching column of men, dwarfed by height and distance. They were not far from Albert. Ramsay nodded. That could be British reinforcements marching to stabilise the front. The situation was obviously improving.

The cloud passed. A thin gleam of sunlight eased onto the column.

"Oh, good God in heaven!" Ramsay focussed on the marching men. For a second he thought they were the guards, but then the sun glinted off the ranked helmets and onto the uniforms below. They were not khaki. The Germans were pushing the British back to the very gates of Albert.

If Albert falls, how much further can the Germans get? Arras? Amiens even? Dear God, if they break through they will head north and roll up our line, all the way to the Channel!

Movement caught his eye. There was a village much closer than Albert, spread on some rising ground. There were troops formed around it and the puffs of light artillery. The British were holding out, somehow. Was that a train? Ramsay nodded. Yes. So there were still transport links between that village and the British line. Perhaps it was a salient pushed in the German advance by a counter attack, or a piece of line that had refused to crumble. He needed a second pair of eyes to verify what he saw.

Who had the best eyesight? Undoubtedly that was McKim. Then the idea came to him. He had nearly fallen when he crossed that gap in the stairs. Nobody could suspect him if Flockhart fell there. The sergeant was older and had been in the line far longer; he was fatigued, worn out with the strain of constant fighting. Get rid of Flockhart – Ramsay hesitated to use the word 'murder', even to himself – and half his troubles would be gone. After that he would only have the Germans to worry about, and surviving the war.

Dear God, I would be free!

The thought was like an electric light bulb illuminating inside his head. It lifted his spirits so that he was negotiating the descent even before the plan was fully formed.

Do it! Do it now! Don't think about it. Just do it. I'll be free!

Turnbull and Aitken were still on watch, peering over the low walls, while further out, Flockhart and McKim had organised a defensive perimeter and a scatter of khaki-clad men huddled around the ruins. Ramsay waved a hand and signalled for Flockhart to come up. He watched as the sergeant handed his rifle to Niven and approached the stairs.

"Be careful, Flockhart," Ramsay shouted, loud enough for all the men to hear. "There are some missing steps, but I need your opinion on something."

Flockhart waved an acknowledgement and came up the first set of steps.

The bastard is faster and more sure-footed than I am. How can I get rid of him without the men seeing?

Ramsay waited at the top of the gap in the stairs, holding out his hand as though to help Flockhart up. The sergeant ascended without a pause until he came to the gap. "Thank you, sir," he balanced at the lip, looked for footholds and stepped into the abyss.

Ramsay stretched down, their hands met and gripped. *Now I have you! Now I can rid myself of this burden and find peace of mind. I will be free with Gillian.*

"Up you come, Flockhart!" Ramsay exerted pressure to pull Flockhart further into the gap so there could be no possibility of the sergeant taking hold of the steps. He glanced down. Most of the men were watching for any approaching Germans, but there were a few faces staring at them. Ramsay looked away.

Flockhart found a foothold and the pressure on Ramsay's hand eased slightly. He could feel Flockhart's hard fingers slipping through his and he watched the sergeant's face furrowed with concentration as he sought safety in the upper tower.

"Sir!"

Ramsay could see beads of sweat forming on Flockhart's face. He looked directly into the hard blue eyes and saw the pain and fortitude and grief there. He saw the lines deeply etched into the face he had only glimpsed once, but remembered so well.

Do you remember me now, you bastard? Do you remember where we first met? Do you remember Grace? Do you?

Flockhart's boots were slipping on the stonework. Ramsay saw his studs strike a spark that glittered momentarily and died.

"Sir!"

There was urgency in Flockhart's voice now, as he tightened his grip on Ramsay's hand.

God he's strong, but if I loosen my fingers he will fall. He will die and half my problems will be over.

Ramsay locked eyes with Flockhart, but rather than release his grip, he pulled harder. It was an instinctive movement, not one dictated by his conscious mind, and within seconds Flockhart was lying on the steps, gasping for breath.

"Thank you, sir. I thought I was gone then."

You should have been, you lucky bastard. I won't save you a second time. Oh, God, I should have let you die.

"You're all right now, Flockhart. Take your time and recover before you try any more stairs."

They moved up together, their boots ringing on the stone stairs as Ramsay cursed himself for failing to take advantage of the situation. "You saved my life, sir," Flockhart said. "I won't forget that."

"Don't be stupid, Sergeant. It was nothing."

When they reached the top of the tower the light had strengthened; the view was huge and the air clearer. They moved up more slowly now, Flockhart was obviously still a bit shaken from his near fall. He hesitated slightly when they reached the section with no outside wall, but carried on. A rising wind tugged at them, inviting them to step over to oblivion.

You might fall yet, Ramsay thought, but Flockhart continued to the topmost step and stood upright like a khaki-clad mountain goat, surveying the panorama.

"It's different from up here, sir," he said. "It all looks so small, sort of. It makes you wonder what it's all about."

"It's all about beating the Hun, Sergeant." Having saved this man's life, Ramsay was not inclined to pander to his homespun philosophy. "Now. Look over there," he indicated the village he had seen, "and tell me what you think."

Flockhart studied the terrain for some time before he gave his opinion. "I see a straggling village with a train standing at a platform about halfway between here, wherever here is, and the town of Albert. I see British soldiers in formation around the village and the Germans trying to break the line."

Ramsay nodded. "That is about what I thought, Sergeant. Anything else?"

Flockhart nodded. "Yes, sir. I can hear gunfire and see puffs of smoke as shells explode, and I see men massing to attack."

"So what would you say was happening, Sergeant?" Ramsay hoped for confirmation of his own ideas from this sensible, experienced and level-headed veteran that he hated.

Flockhart was obviously not used to having an officer ask for his opinion. He glanced at Ramsay, looked away, and looked back before he answered. "I think that we are still holding out there, sir, and Fritz is trying to push us out."

Ramsay nodded. "I agree, Flockhart. How far would you say that village was?"

Flockhart screwed up his face. "I would say three miles, sir. Four miles at the outside. Certainly no more than that."

So the Huns have advanced four miles in, what, three days? But we are still holding out.

Ramsay nodded. "Thank you, Sergeant."

Now he had a definite target. All he had to do was get his men to that village and either help the defence or jump on that train and travel back to safety.

The ugly snarl of a Mercedes engine took Ramsay by surprise. He had been concentrating on the position of the rival armies to such an extent he had neglected his own security. The plane roared past him; the great black crosses prominent on its wings and the observer staring at him from the rear cockpit.

"Sir!" Flockhart shouted his warning a moment too late.

Ramsay looked down as the plane banked to turn. The sun gleamed on the varnished wings and the almost invisible arc of the propeller. It was a Halberstadt CL II, a specialist ground attack fighter, and to judge by the direction it was travelling, the pilot intended to rid the church steeple of these impudent British soldiers.

"Come on Sergeant, get down the stairs!" Ramsay saw Flockhart glide away in front of him as if he was a ghost. He tried to hurry down the steps toward the nearest fragment of sheltering wall but the third step crumbled beneath his feet and he staggered, and for a second his head and shoulders hung over the immense fall to the ground beneath.

"Sir!" He glanced up and saw Flockhart hesitate. The sergeant had reached the sheltering wall but was looking back as if prepared to return and drag his officer to safety.

"Stay there!" Ramsay yelled as he looked down. He could see his men scurrying among the ruins. Some were pointing upwards. Turnbull was aiming his rifle at the German aircraft, Marshall was clambering onto a pile of rubble as if to get a better shot, Niven was fiddling with his magazine. Ramsay recovered his balance and rose to his feet. As if moving in slow motion he stepped carefully over the missing step and flinched at the renewed rattle of the 7.92 Spandau.

The bullets sprayed around him, hacking at the ancient stonework and creating a haze of dust into which he ducked as the Halberstadt roared past, with the pilot grinning fiercely and an array of red and black ribbons fluttering from the struts as though the aircraft was celebrating a joyous occasion rather than trying to kill two men. For a second Ramsay stared straight into the goggled eyes of the observer; they were deep brown and warm, and then the machine roared past.

The plane turned again, streamers rippling from its struts, the pilot concentrating on his controls. The observer was struggling with his Spandau, which seemed to have jammed, and Ramsay allowed himself a few seconds breathing space. He took a deep breath and ducked as the single bullet smacked into the central column a few inches above his head, and swore again.

Where the devil did that come from? God! Had German infantry arrived while I was up the tower?

Ramsay looked down and saw half a dozen men pointing rifles in his direction; his own men.

"Stop!" He waved his arms at them, coming perilously close to overbalancing on the spiral stairs. "Hold your fire!"

They could not hear him. He saw them working the bolts of their rifles, aiming and firing at the rapidly moving German aircraft and he jumped the final few steps to where a fragment of wall offered some shelter. Just as he arrived the Halberstadt roared past again, its machine gun chattering, bullets chewing at the wall and steps below.

"You bastard!" Ramsay shouted. He unholstered his pistol and fired at the aircraft, knowing that the possibility of hitting anything vulnerable was very remote. The machine roared past, and dived on the men firing at it from the ruins below.

"Come on, sir!" Flockhart was in the shelter of the wall, watching the aircraft. "Get into cover!"

Ramsay saw the machine gun firing and spurts of dust and stone rising from the church then the plane reached the limit of its dive and rose again. He saw the Royal Scots rise from cover to fire at it, and realised that Flockhart was right. He began to hurry down the steps again.

"Come on Flockhart, we'll get down as far as we can. The nearer the ground we are the better I'll like it."

"You'll get no arguments from me there, sir," Flockhart said. "This is definitely not bon!"

Ramsay heard more musketry and the snarl of the aircraft as he ran down the remaining stairs, but the wall prevented him from seeing what was happening. By the time they reached the gap in the stairs the aircraft was gone.

"I'll go first, sir," Flockhart volunteered, and stretched across the airy gap. He positioned himself and dropped the few feet to the lower steps. "It's a lot easier going down than coming up, sir," he said, but still he waited with hands outstretched for Ramsay to negotiate the yawning hole.

They gripped hands once more; this time Ramsay felt secure in Flockhart's grasp.

"There we go, sir, all safe and sound."

It was just a small run to the ground, where McKim was organising the men. "We've lost Marshall, sir," McKim reported. "That Hun caught him clean with a burst."

Ramsay grunted as he saw Marshall's body lying crumpled beside an old gravestone. "He was a steady man. I saw him firing back at the aircraft. Who was closest to him?"

He looked around the small group of Royal Scots. After days in the line and on the march they were haggard, unshaven and ragged, but their rifles were clean and their faces determined.

"Menzies and Paterson, sir," Turnbull volunteered. "They never made it out of the trenches."

"I see." Ramsay looked at Marshall again. Although he had marched with him for days, he had never spoken to him directly. Private Marshall had died alone. "Arrange for a burial, Sergeant. I don't like to think of leaving my men for the birds."

Does it matter? Once you are dead, you are dead. But it does matter to these men. They don't like to think that their bodies will be left outside to rot.

The men scraped a shallow trench and rolled Marshall inside. A burst from the German aircraft had virtually cut him in two. They piled loose earth and stones on top of the body and Flockhart thrust a stick at the head to mark the resting place.

As soon as Marshall was laid to rest the men found a sheltered corner and curled up to catch as much sleep as they could. Nobody looked at the makeshift grave; they all knew they could be next.

"How far are we from the front, sir?" McKim asked. He had taken the clip from Marshall's rifle and placed it in his pouch. He had also piled the last stone on top of Marshall's body.

"About three miles," Ramsay said. "There's a village just that distance to the west, with what seems like a marshalling yard and a stores dump . . ."

"That will be Carnoy," McKim said at once. "It's a munitions dump."

"We are holding out there," Ramsay said. "Get the men up and ready to march."

"They've marched all night and fought off that German aircraft," Flockhart reminded, "they are dropping on their feet."

"They're Royal Scots," Ramsay said flatly. "Get them ready." He jerked his head skyward. "That machine will alert his headquarters that we are here and there'll be hundreds of Huns knocking on the door in no time."

McKim grunted but raised his voice. "Right lads, we're on the move again. Up you get!"

"Bloody cold-blooded bloody officer," somebody said, as

others groaned or cursed or sighed, but they all stumbled to their feet, shouldered their rifles and waited for orders.

"We are holding out at a village called Carnoy," Ramsay told them quietly. "It's only about three miles away, but there are some Germans in the way."

McKim did not hide his grin as he worked the bolt of his rifle. "We have another score to wipe off the slate," he said and nodded to the pile of loose stones marking Marshall's grave.

"And it's near full daylight," Ramsay had no need to say that.

"We can see them all the better in the light, sir," McKim said.

"So keep together, keep your fingers on the trigger and try and keep out of trouble. If Fritz does not notice us, don't draw attention to yourselves." Ramsay checked the chambers of his revolver, snapped it shut and replaced it in its holster. "Right, lads; let's try and get back." He nodded to McKim, "You're the most experienced man here, Corporal, you are the advance guard. Don't get too far in front and don't go looking for trouble." He looked toward Flockhart but said nothing. Flockhart was smiling, but there was a question in his eyes.

I saved his life; I should have let him fall. Why did I do that? Now I have to find another opportunity. I wonder what he will do when he remembers where he first met me?

Ramsay tapped his fingers against the handle of his revolver once more. If he had to, he would use it and chance the consequences.

"Right lads, keep together now and with luck we will be back in our own lines before dark. Food, boys. We can get food!"

Naturally, it was Cruickshank who grumbled, 'It will probably be bloody iron rations, bully beef and dusty tea."

"Less of your lip, Cruickshank!" Flockhart snarled. "Just get on with it."

Used to the cover of night, Ramsay felt near naked as he marched in the growing light of day. They passed a scattering of bodies, men from various British regiments and a larger number of Germans, twisted in the grotesque attitudes of death.

"There was a stand here," Flockhart said. He indicated a group of German soldiers, all with bullet wounds across their midriff. They lay contorted in the mud. "A machine gun got that lot."

"I hope the bastards suffered," Cruickshank said and spat on the nearest enemy body.

"Enough of that!" Ramsay ordered sharply. "These were brave men doing their duty, just as we are!"

"They're bloody Huns," Cruickshank muttered. "They were murdering bloody Hun bastards."

Ramsay chose not to hear the words. He marched on, fighting the waves of tiredness that threatened to overwhelm him. With each hour that passed he was increasingly aware of the hollow complaint of his stomach. He had eaten nothing since the iron rations of the day before, and they were not designed to take a man on a forced march across enemy-held territory.

"Sir!" McKim lifted his hand in warning. "I can hear something."

"So can I," Cruickshank said, "Oh, yes. It's the bloody guns."

As Flockhart hissed Cruickshank to silence, McKim stepped to the right. "It's not that, listen. There's somebody nearby." He worked the bolt of his rifle, putting a round in the breech, ducked low, and slid twenty paces to the side. He stopped at the lip of a large shell crater. "Here we are, sir. It's a German, sir."

"A bloody Hun?" Cruickshank stepped forward, raising his rifle.

Ramsay was there first. He looked into the crater and stopped. There had been a German position here once; the remains of a section of men was scattered around like fragments of meat. There was no way of knowing how many men there had been, for now there were only pieces; heads and shattered heads, limbs and fragments of limbs mingled with shreds of unidentified meat and broken bones. In the middle of the carnage was a man. He lay on his back with both heels drumming on the ground and both fists raised above his head while he made small mewling noises.

He's only about sixteen years old, the same age as Mackay. The poor wee boy should be at school, not in this nightmare.

McKim pointed to him. "Poor bugger. He's shell shocked and no wonder with all his chums dead."

"He's a bloody Hun." Cruickshank levelled his rifle, but Ramsay knocked the barrel up.

"He's a badly wounded man," Ramsay said quietly, "and no threat to us."

"I can't see a wound," Cruickshank said sourly.

"It's there nonetheless," Ramsay told him. He hesitated for a moment. "We can't just leave him here. The fellow will die."

Cruickshank shrugged. "Let him. He's a murdering Hun."

The boy's voice raised an octave and he began to howl. His twitching increased as he lay on the ground amidst the shattered blood and bones of his erstwhile comrades.

"We can't take him with us, sir," Flockhart said quietly. "We left one of our own behind in the trenches." He lowered his voice further. "The lads are tired, sir. They're nearly too tired to sweat so they won't take kindly to carrying one of the enemy."

Ramsay considered his words. "I agree. We'll just make him as comfortable as we can and leave some sort of marker so the Germans can find him."

As Ramsay moved the shell-shocked German to a safer spot, his men gathered together the German rifles and arranged them in a pyramid at the lip of the crater.

"That will have to do," Ramsay said. He placed a German helmet on top.

"It's more than our lads got," Cruickshank said. "And a bit too much for a bloody Hun."

Ramsay grunted. The howling of the shell-shocked German was getting on his nerves. "Let's get away from here. Keep on toward Carnoy. Take the lead Flockhart."

He gave the order in as casual a tone as he could and Flockhart obeyed without comment.

Come on Fritz, shoot the bastard. I helped one of yours, so repay the favour and kill one of mine.

Every step brought them closer to the firing, the crackle of musketry and sinister chatter of machine guns became louder and more dangerous

He began to count his steps, watching the slow progress of his feet across the wasted mess of land. There were a few thistles here, protruding stubbornly from the mess of mud, and he grunted at the bitter sweet memory of home.

There had been thistles in that field as well, tall, purple-topped beauties with feathery down, swaying slightly to the gentle hiss of the breeze. She had looked at him with laughter in her eyes and a smile of kiss-shaped lips. "David," she had said, soft and sweet and low, "David. Now we will have to get married."

His laughter had died on his lips when he realised she was deadly serious. What had started as a tumble in the hay with a willing country girl had turned into something far more intense.

Enough! Stay alert. With luck I can get these men to Carnoy and join our army. Now what do I know about Carnoy? It is on the road from Albert to Peronne, about 7 miles south east of Albert and there is a railway train there. Stay alert and stay alive.

"Keep moving lads!" Ramsay said. The words were unnecessary; the Royals were plodding on without any encouragement from him. He glanced at them. Turnbull had lost the puttees from his left leg somewhere and those on his right were trailing behind him. Aitken was looking around him nervously; Niven was glowering in the direction of Carnoy with pure determination; Blackley was whistling softly between his teeth; McKim was marching as solidly as if he was twenty years old; Cruickshank was grumbling about something: these were his men and he was more proud of them than of anything else in this world.

"Sir!" Flockhart came to Ramsay at a trot. "There's something you should see." The sergeant was obviously excited. "There's a transport limber ahead! Food and ammunition!"

About to blast the man, Ramsay paused with his mouth open. Flockhart was speaking a lot of sense. "Good man. He must have taken a wrong turning in the dark. Lead on, MacDuff."

That was Gillian's expression.

He waited and sure enough, Cruickshank mumbled the expected response. "That bloody officer still doesn't know the sergeant's name."

Rather than move in a straight line, Flockhart ducked and weaved across the ground, the Royals trotting behind him, their energy restored by the prospect of food.

The limber lay on its side, the bodies of four horses a mangled mess in front and the remains of the driver lying on his back with both arms outstretched. The steel guard on his left leg was dented and his head was missing.

"A shell must have caught them," Turnbull said casually. "Permission to look inside, sir?"

"Of course, McKim, you and Cruickshank keep watch. The rest of you, see what you can find. We need food, water and ammunition."

The men descended on the wagon with a rapacity that reminded Ramsay of the tales he had heard of Wellington's army looting during the Peninsular War. They used their bayonets to rip open the stout canvas covering and dived into the interior, laughing at the prospect of loot.

There was a box of iron rations which they opened without delay. In normal circumstances the soldiers would have treated such a thing with scorn, but three days and two nights with hardly a bite had rendered them too hungry for niceties and the tinned bully beef and crack-tooth biscuits were eaten as voraciously as if they were the choicest morsel from a fashionable French restaurant.

"Chocolate!" Mackay looked terribly young as he handled the box as if it was gold. He tore open the top and delved inside, throwing bars of Fry's milk chocolate to the men with a wide grin on his face. "I've never seen so much chocolate at one time!"

"Don't eat too much or you'll get sick," Flockhart warned, but Mackay stuffed an entire bar into his mouth at the same time as he opened a second.

"Bread! Real bread!"

"Plum jam . . . what other kind of jam could there be?"

"Look! Tobacco!" Turnbull produced half a dozen tins of 'Three Nuns' tobacco. "Here you are, corporal!" He threw a tin to McKim, who caught it with practised ease.

"Thanks, Turnbull!" McKim gave a gap-toothed grin, drew his broken pipe from the top pocket of his tunic and began to stuff tobacco into the bowl. Turning away from the slight breeze, he sheltered behind the wagon and scraped flame from a match and puffed his pipe to light.

"God, that's good," he said. He looked around with the pipe thrust between his teeth. "It has been a long time since I could stand in the open and smoke a pipe without wondering if some German has me in the sights of his rifle."

Flockhart spoke without looking round, his eyes continued to scour the landscape for the enemy. "Maybe that's the silver lining in the dark cloud of the German advance – Kenny McKim can get a pipe full of baccy."

McKim's grin was far too mischievous for a man of his age. "A decent smoke makes it all worthwhile!" He blew a cloud of smoke in Flockhart's direction and chuckled. "All things come to an end, Sergeant, and Kaiser Bill is no exception. The Royals will put salt on his tail yet."

Mackay was laughing with his mouth full of chocolate while Turnbull used the tip of his bayonet to spoon plum jam into his mouth. Ramsay saw the vestiges of German blood on the blade but said nothing. Out here at the Front people did things that were unimaginable in a more ordinary situation.

"You men," Ramsay ordered, "cram your pouches with food. Take all you can. Fill the water bottles, grab ammunition, everything we can get. Move now!" He watched to see his orders were obeyed.

"Look at this, lads!" Aiken lifted a mouth organ from the ground, tapped it against his leg and began to play a jaunty tune that Ramsay did not recognise. Within seconds the men were joining in, making mouth music around half-masticated food as Flockhart kept watch and half the

German army advanced purposely on the retreating British all around them.

"Look at this, lads!" Niven lifted a small brown envelope and glanced through the contents. "Ooh, la la. Trés bon mademoiselles!"

"What? Give us a decko!" Edwards leaped over to Niven and grabbed the envelope from his hand. He shuffled through the small pile of postcards, making comments about each.

"She is nice, not that one though, She's more my type; lovely eyes . . . and what a pair she has . . ."

"Let me see!" Mackay grabbed at the postcards and they fell to the ground. In a second there were four Royals scrabbling around in the mud to salvage as many as they could.

"Enough of that!" McKim snarled. He pulled them apart. "Niven, these are yours. Mackay, you are too young to even think of women yet. What would your mother think of you looking at things like that?"

McKim held a sepia postcard of a voluptuous woman dressed in a frilly chemise that failed to cover any part of her. He smiled. The world in its wisdom thought nothing of sending Mackay to fight and kill and witness all the unbridled horror of warfare, but baulked at the thought of him looking at a semi-dressed woman.

"You should be ashamed of yourself, Mackay. If you were mine I would fetch you a good clip around the earhole, so I would." McKim shoved the boy away and winked at Flockhart.

Ramsay hid his smile as Mackay coloured and turned away. He waited until McKim was alone. "Do you have any children, McKim?" The question was genuine. The corporal had spoken so naturally to Mackay that Ramsay thought he acted more like a father than an NCO.

McKim removed the pipe from his mouth and nodded. "Oh, yes, sir. My first wife gave me two sons and a daughter and my second wife gave me another daughter." He smiled. "My lads are in the regiment – in the Middle East now. One of my girls is in service and the other is married to a sailor, God help him."

"You were married twice?" Ramsay asked.

"No, sir, three times." McKim pulled his pay book from a tunic pocket. "Here they are. Margaret, she died in India of fever. Jemima, she died in South Africa and this . . ." He produced a small photograph and kissed it fondly. "This is Janet. She is waiting for me in Edinburgh. Once I am time-expired and out of the regiment, Janet says we will open a small pub in the High Street, near the Castle, and grow pickled together." He showed Ramsay the photograph. The woman could have been in her fifties or early sixties; she stared remorselessly and nervously at the camera lens.

"Nice looking woman," Ramsay gave the stock answer. "You are a lucky man, McKim, but I can't imagine you leaving the regiment."

McKim grinned. "Nor can I, sir. When my time is up I will enlist again as I always do. I can't see myself tied down to a publican's hours!" He winked, "It keeps the missus happy, though. Gives her something to live for."

Ramsay nodded. "I see."

Aitken was still playing the mouth organ and most of the men were eating and dancing, thumping their feet up and down in a release of tension as they chanted words that may or may not have been related to the music. Ramsay was tempted to break them up, but he allowed the fun to continue; the men had been through a rough time and needed a few moments of pleasure before they continued with the march to whatever horror lay ahead.

"Here's ammunition," Turnbull said. He passed out a box of 303 clips. "And there's plenty more where that came from. There are bandoliers as well."

"Bring them out, Turnbull," Ramsay ordered. "Everybody refill your ammunition pouches and get a bandolier or two. If we are going through the Hun lines we will have to fight."

"Things are looking up, sir," Flockhart said. "Food, ammunition and our boys holding back the advance. Up the Royals!"

Ramsay heard musketry in the distance and the chattering of machine guns. There was still a battle going on; the British were still holding out at Carnoy, although how he was going to get his men through the German positions was a mystery that remained to be resolved.

"Begging your pardon, sir," McKim asked, "but are you a married man?"

There was the scent of the grass again and Grace lying on her back with those wondrous blue eyes. Her statement hung in the air, a tantalising thought that surrounded him with amusement.

"Marry you?" He had laughed then, at the ridiculous idea. "How on earth could I marry you?"

Her expression had altered from contented adoration to disbelief within the space of a few seconds.

"But David, we have to get married after what we have just done." Her voice had the musical cadences of Midlothian, combined with the grit of the mines. "Mrs David Napier. I want to be Mrs David Napier."

Ramsay held her eyes as he shook his head. "After what we have just done?" He mocked her. "We passed a pleasurable hour or two rollicking in the hay, Grace my darling. That is all we have done."

Grace shook her head as her eyes filled. "But you must marry me, you must!" Belatedly, she covered herself up. She pulled down her skirt and dragged her shawl over her upper body.

"Why on earth must I do that?" Ramsay remained where he was, smiling down at her.

"Because you've seen me and you've been intimate with me!" She crossed her legs in sudden embarrassment and raised her voice to a wail. "And I might have a baby!" Grace fairly howled out the words.

"So you might," Ramsay reached down and lifted his trousers. He brushed a few blades of grass from them and casually hauled them on before fastening the buttons of the fly. "But on the other hand, you might not, and I certainly am not going to marry you for such a trivial reason." He adjusted his braces and lifted his jacket. "The idea is ridiculous, given our respective positions." He leaned closer. "I think you should find yourself a man of your own type, Grace, and quickly, just in case I have honoured you with a bastard."

He looked down as Grace let out a howl of protest and tried to step away, but she dived sideways and clung to his leg.

"No, David. Please, no. Don't say that!"

Ramsay lifted his leg and shook it, but when Grace only tightened her grip he reached down, grabbed her hair and pulled her head backwards until she screamed and let go.

"Get off me, you hussie! Get off!" Ramsay grabbed his boots and strode away, flattening the long grass as he did so. At the edge of the field he stopped, sat on the five-barred gate and was pulling on his boots when the man appeared.

"Are you a married man?" McKim asked again.

About to blast him for his impertinence, Ramsay shook

his head instead. "No, McKim. I am engaged, but we are not tying the knot until after the war."

McKim smiled. "It's good to have somebody waiting for you, sir. Knowing that there is somebody that cares whether you live or die, it makes all this . . ." He waved his hand aimlessly at the wreckage around them. "It makes it all mean something, somehow." He sucked on his pipe again and stuffed tobacco into the bowl with a calloused thumb. "But if you don't mind me saying, sir, most women would prefer not to wait that long to get married. I mean, sir, we are at war and things happen."

Ramsay stood up and retrieved a packet of army issue biscuits. The men were beginning to settle down now so he gave orders for them to start a small fire, brew up some tea and rustle up hot food.

I should be more in control here, but they need some time before we enter the town. God alone knows how we can get past Fritz, or how many of us make it.

"You mean I may get killed, McKim."

"Yes, sir. And leave your lady without the memory of a marriage."

"And have her wearing widow's weeds before she has even reached twenty one." Ramsay kept his voice neutral. "I think not."

Did I make the correct decision when I said we would not marry until after the war? I did not wish to burden Gillian with a child, but perhaps she would want a child of mine?

"Char up!" Turnbull called out cheerfully and the men clustered around, as happy and unconcerned as if they were in Edinburgh Castle. The tea was only lukewarm but it was wet and welcome.

"Can't beat a cup of char," Blackley said. He had the deep tan of tropical service on his face and the slight sing-song accent of a man who had spent time in India. Four wound stripes gleamed golden on his sleeve.

Ramsay had taken only a single sip of his tea when Flockhart slipped up to him.

"Fritz, sir. Coming this way, lots of them."

CHAPTER SEVEN

24 March 1918

"Get your gear, men. We're pulling out! Turnbull, douse that fire. McKim, take two men and act as rearguard." Ramsay acted instinctively as he poured out orders. "Show me where they are, Flockhart."

In peacetime the ridge would have been almost invisible, but when all Europe was aflame, every scrap of land in the combat zone was used for military purposes. The ridge shielded an area of dead ground in which the transport limber had been wrecked. Flockhart inched to the summit, ensuring that his head was not highlighted on the skyline.

"Over there, sir, coming fast."

The German formation was around half a mile away, marching in a close formation across the landscape with no thought of breaking step for any obstacle that may have been in their path. As usual, there were officers in front and NCOs at the flanks.

"They *are* coming fast," Ramsay agreed. He glanced over his shoulder. The Royals were about ready. McKim had them in hand, joking and rebuking in equal measure as he checked their ammunition, water bottles and food.

"It's our old friends, sir," Flockhart said, "the Prussian Guards."

"It's time we were gone, then," Ramsay slid down the side of the ridge even as he spoke. "Come on, lads, the Prussians are coming."

"Not a-bloody-gain," Cruickshank mumbled. "Bloody Prussians, it's about time somebody shot the buggers."

"You do it then, Cruickshank," Flockhart suggested. "There are thousands of them."

"Quick march, lads, get those feet moving!" Ramsay decided on his route, aiming at a 45 degree angle, away from the advancing Germans. "McKim, keep a sharp lookout there, in case they have men out in front."

"Yes, sir." McKim hefted his rifle.

"Go on Kimmy, ambush the bastards," Cruickshank said quietly. "Maybe you can kill the lot of them."

"Keep quiet and keep moving," Flockhart ordered. "Save your breath, we'll need it."

"Aye," Niven said. "Them Prussian bastards never give up. They will march on and on until they reach Paris."

"Or until they are all killed," Cruickshank said.

McKim grunted and shouldered his rifle. "You're lucky it's only the Huns. If that had been the Boers we would have been diced and sliced by now. Those boys could ride!"

"Save your breath for marching!" Flockhart ordered and the men fell silent, save for an occasional grunt of effort or muted curse if they stumbled on the uneven ground.

Ramsay glanced up, three aircraft made pretty patterns in the clear sky. They were too high for him to discern whether they were friend or foe, but the last thing he wanted was to be caught in the open by a German machine.

"Keep moving, boys!"

"What the hell else does he think we're doing?" Cruickshank muttered, but put his head down and pushed on.

The musketry around Carnoy was nonstop, and every step brought them closer.

The ground was open here, a level plain that sloped slowly down towards the village. Ramsay looked ahead. He could see Carnoy plainly now, with a line of makeshift trenches in front and the occasional bobbing heads of the defenders.

"Sir," Turnbull was at his elbow, "Corporal McKim sent me, sir. He says that the Prussians have altered direction."

McKim was correct. Ramsay lay prone behind a mound of ripped sandbags and watched as the Prussians changed direction on the march, as efficiently as if they were on the parade ground. The column opened out until it was sixteen abreast; then thirty two, sixty four and finally it was around a hundred men abreast and still marching toward Carnoy.

"These boys are good," Flockhart said.

"Bloody parade ground soldiers." McKim spat on the ground, but Ramsay noticed the intent expression on his face and wondered if the corporal was working out the best way to defeat the military machine known as the Prussian Guards.

The Prussians marched on, now moving in waves with each man a precise distance from his neighbour and each wave twenty paces behind the one in front.

"They are going to take Carnoy," Flockhart said quietly. "These lads won't let anything stop them. They'll keep going like a steamroller."

Ramsay said nothing. He could only watch as the Prussians marched on, inexorably, until the officer in front stopped for a moment. He turned around, shouted an order and the line behind him halted immediately, as did the following lines.

"What's happening? Have they seen us?" McKim levelled his rifle.

Ramsay pushed the barrel down. "Rest easy McKim, even if they had seen us, they would not stop. Look where they are."

The Hauptmann had halted at the rim of the crater

where the Royals had erected the triangle of rifles. Ramsay watched as he slipped down and gestured to some of his men to follow. Within a few moments the Prussians had lifted the shell shocked young soldier and two men were carrying him back through their own lines.

For one moment the officer turned towards him and Ramsay saw him clearly. The officer was tall and broad-shouldered, as would be expected of any Prussian Guardsman, but as a stray shaft of sunlight caught the man's face and reflected on a monocle Ramsay recognised him. This was the same Hauptmann he had faced in the trenches.

Ramsay watched as he reformed his men and continued the advance. This was not at all the typical Prussian officer that the propaganda messages depicted; this man had halted an advance specifically to help a wounded man – an act of compassion that Ramsay had never seen any officer, British or German, perform before.

The Prussian advance continued as though the incident had never happened, but Ramsay had seen a different side to the enemy, and he wondered at the shape of this new animal that national politics dictated that he must fight.

I would like to meet that man after the war. As Kipling said, 'You're a better man than I am, Gungha Din.'

"Orders, sir?" Flockhart asked. "Shall we continue to the village?" He nodded toward the Germans. "We might get there before that lot, but I think they would be hard on our tail, sir."

"Carry on, Sergeant. Double."

The Royals increased their pace as they tried to keep ahead of the Prussians. Ramsay led from the front, while Flockhart was in the rear to shepherd any stragglers and McKim, the oldest man there by at least twenty years, acted as a sheepdog, circling the men while still watching for any Germans.

As they got closer to Carnoy, there were more Germans and Ramsay had to alter his route to skirt round gun emplacements and an encampment of hospital tents.

"Just like ours, sir," McKim said with some surprise. "I have never seen a German hospital before."

There was a steady trickle of stretcher bearers carrying men in, with some walking wounded and others supported by their comrades. Ambulances left at regular intervals, presumably taking the more serious cases to hospitals behind the lines.

"Fritz may be driving us back sir, but he is still paying the price." Flockhart said. "This push may cost him more than it costs us in the long run." He shrugged. "If we keep withdrawing and keep killing him, he'll have nobody left to fight with."

Ramsay grunted. "Best leave the high strategy to General Haig, Sergeant. I am sure he knows more about it than you or I do." He looked toward the tented hospital, where a Red Cross flag hung limp in the breezeless air. "I am not saying that you are wrong, though. We are making him pay for his attacks."

They skirted around the hospital, keeping well clear of the corrugated track along which the stretcher bearers struggled, and kept marching toward Carnoy.

Ramsay felt an uneasy prickle on his spine and flinched; he knew that feeling well. It was a warning of danger and instinctively he knew that it was not the Germans this time. When he looked over his shoulder, Flockhart was watching him, shaking his head as if he was unsure where he had seen him before.

The man was shorter than Ramsay, and perhaps ten years older, with the broad shoulders and weak legs common to a man who spent his working life crouched in a tiny space, hacking at a seam of coal. Blue scars on his face and hands told their own story of accident and danger.

"Good morning," the coal miner said politely. His eyes were curious as they scrutinised Ramsay but he recognised a gentleman and did not enquire further.

"Morning," Ramsay replied. He made to move past the miner.

"It's a fine day." The miner leaned against the gate, pulled out a pipe and began to stuff tobacco into the bowl.

"Yes." Ramsay tapped his walking stick on the gate. His bootlace was not tied properly so he knelt down.

"David! David Napier! You can't leave me!" Grace's clear young voice cut across the air like a knife.

The miner looked into the field where Grace was pushing through the long grass. "Grace? Is that you?"

Ramsay cursed inwardly. It was just his luck that he should meet somebody who knew the troublesome girl, but he supposed that in a tight knit mining community such things were more likely than not. He nodded to the miner, tied his lace, swung his stick as a statement of intent and stepped away from the gate.

"Just a minute." Perhaps the miner was respectful of a gentleman, but he was obviously not inclined to be intimidated by one. He placed a hard hand on Ramsay's arm. "Is that you Grace is talking to?"

"Get your hand off me, fellow! What the devil do you think you're playing at?" Ramsay tried to shake himself free but the man's grip tightened.

"Grace?" The man raised his voice in a shout. "Over at the gate!"

Grace ran over to them. She had pulled her clothes together but had not fastened them properly and her hair was tousled and drifted across her face.

"Rab? I didn't know you knew David."

"We've just met." The miner did not release Ramsay's arm. "What the hell have you been doing Grace Flockhart? As if I have to ask!"

"David has to marry me now," Grace said at once. "He has taken liberties with me and now I'll have a baby."

Ramsay struggled in Rab's grip. He thought quickly. This miner was unbelievably strong and probably well used to brawling. It would be unseemly for a gentleman to indulge in fisticuffs, and might result in a court case and public exposure, as well as an undignified defeat.

"We will make a fine baby together," Ramsay drawled the words. "So if your friend Rab – Robert is it? – unhands me, we can plan for the future." He gave Grace the full force of his most charming smile.

"Oh, David!" Grace stopped crying. "I thought you were running away from me!"

"Good God, no! Why ever would I do that? I was just going for a quiet smoke to plan our next step." Ramsay patted her arm fondly. "Come, Grace, and you and I will talk about our life."

There were many more German formations now, some resting in encampments small and large, others preparing to move forward. There were ammunition limbers and store dumps, water carts and artillery emplacements, strings of mules and detachments of men carrying wire and other equipment and everywhere the infantry, marching or standing smoking.

"Plenty of Fritzes here," McKim said. "I didn't know there were so many Fritzes in the world."

Flockhart smiled. "Aye, the Kaiser is trying to make sure of winning the war before the Yanks get in. He's defeated the Russians and now he thinks he can beat us."

"No bloody chance," McKim said. "We're not bloody Ruskis."

"Fritz!" McKim hissed the warning to Ramsay.

The German voice floated across to Ramsay, the words harsh. Ramsay looked around. The ground was open here, with no cover into which they could duck. They had to run, fight or try to make themselves invisible. Running was hardly an option with so many Germans in the area and for the same reason fighting was hardly an option.

Make a decision!

"Down lads, form a circle," Ramsay said quietly. He did not need to say more as his veteran soldiers dropped to the ground and lay in a circle, feet almost touching feet as they faced outward, ready to face any German force but hoping they did not have to.

They lay still, waiting, as the German voice sounded again. Ramsay slid the revolver from his holster, cocked it and looked out. In lying down the Royals had rendered themselves less visible, but they had also cut their own arc of vision. He could see little except a slight ridge topped by ripped sandbags, a broken traversor mat and a broken fascine, left over from some abortive tank attack at the time of the Somme battle.

A quick glance reassured him that his men were in position, rifles ready, bayonets loose in their scabbards, eyes probing, watchful, waiting for discovery.

The German voices came closer. There were about a dozen of them, men talking amongst themselves with casual camaraderie. Ramsay saw one round helmet appear at the periphery of his vision. The man was walking away from Carnoy, he was laughing and his rifle was slung over his shoulder as if he had no immediate intention of using it. As Ramsay watched, a second German came into view, walking with his head down and a bandage across his forehead.

Ramsay sensed a slight movement and glanced to his right. Cruickshank was settling down for a shot, having slid his rifle forward and was peering into the sights.

"Easy, Cruickshank. One shot and all the Huns in Hunland will be down upon us."

The German voices grew louder as more appeared until there were fifty men, sixty, a hundred, shambling back from the front. Some were lightly wounded, some smoked pipes or cigarettes and few were paying attention as they passed only a few yards from the British positions.

"Easy, lads," Flockhart muttered. "Keep your nerve." He had his forefinger curled around the trigger of his rifle, moving the barrel slightly to aim at whichever German soldier came into his line of vision.

The Germans crowded around the Royals position and Ramsay visualised what would happen if one of them noticed the prone British soldiers. The Royals would have the advantage of surprise, so the initial conflict would go their way as they opened fire on the unsuspecting Germans. That would be the first stage, but Fritz was a tough fighter and would soon recover and then there could only be one outcome. The advantage of numbers would tell and the Royals would soon be overrun, with death and wounds or imprisonment the only possible outcome. *How would Gillian take that? She would mourn, but she is a beautiful woman and would soon find somebody* else.

The thought of Gillian in somebody else's arms caused a shiver to run the length of Ramsay's spine. He visualised the scene. Gillian laughing as a shadowy man held her. The man's arms were around her waist and his hands were exploring the length of her body, travelling north and south. She was laughing, revelling in his touch. Then he turned around and it was Flockhart who was with Gillian, taunting him, taking sweet revenge for that occasion so long ago . . .

Ramsay shook himself back to the present. He saw the Germans file past, talking, grumbling, singing. One man had a harmonica and played a melancholic air; his helmet was pushed well back on his head and blonde hair flopped over his face.

Ramsay tightened his grip on the butt of his revolver and slid his finger around the trigger; the steel felt cold to his touch.

One more ounce of pressure and I could kill that man. I would have helped win the war. I would have killed another German soldier.

The thoughts ran through Ramsay's mind, tripping over themselves in the confusion of his brain. He took a deep breath, realised he was shaking with tension and eased off the pressure slightly. The blonde German walked on, the notes of his harmonica following until they faded away.

"They've gone," Mackay said. He was white under the grime that covered his face, and his voice cracked with the strain.

"There will be others," Ramsay said. "McKim, have a decko and see if the coast is clear."

McKim nodded and slid away, belly down on the mud as he followed the line of a long abandoned sap before emerging into the open land beyond. Only then did Ramsay realise that the musketry had risen to a crescendo, and then faded away, dying into a number of isolated rifle shots, a sudden burst of machine gun fire then silence. The smell of smoke drifted to him.

"Sir, the Huns are in Carnoy." McKim spoke in an urgent whisper. "It looks as if they've taken the place."

CHAPTER EIGHT

24-25 March 1918

McKim was correct. Ramsay crested the ridge overlooking the village and looked down. He could see grey uniforms everywhere and the distinctive disciplined formation of the Prussian Guards marching down what he presumed was the main street.

"Look," Ramsay pointed, "all the Germans are at the opposite side of the village from the train. It's still standing in the station." He grinned as a sudden crazy idea came to him. "If we only had a train driver we could capture that train and ride it all the way back to our own lines: what an adventure that would be!"

Already Ramsay could see his name in the papers: *British Officer breaks through German lines in train. King awards him the Victoria Cross.*

Now that would impress Gillian if anything could.

"Niven!" he called the private to him as the idea formed in his head. "You were a tram driver you said."

"Yes, sir," Niven agreed.

"Do you think you could drive a train?" Ramsay pointed to Carnoy. "That train there?"

"Jesus." Niven breathed out slowly. "Sorry, sir. I mean,

that's an interesting plan. You mean to drive it away right under the noses of the Germans?"

"That's exactly what I mean, Niven. Could you drive it?"

Niven shook his head. "I don't rightly know, sir. A tram is very different from a train . . ."

"I realise that, Niven, but you are the best man we have for the job. Are you game?" Ramsay said sharply, "Come on, man! Give me an answer so we can act before the Germans wake up to the fact that it's there."

"I could try, sir," Niven said. 'It has steam up already, I see . . ."

"Good man," Ramsay interrupted him. He raised his voice. "Right, lads. We are going into Carnoy and if things go well we are going home in style. Put a bullet up the spout, ensure your magazines are fully charged and follow me."

Once the decision had been made, Ramsay felt a new thrill of excitement. He felt that he had been skulking around, hiding from the Germans, ever since the collapse of the British front line. Now he was going to lead his men straight through the advancing Germans and into a French village to grab a train and drive it towards God only knew where. The feeling of reckless devilment gripped him and for a second he wished he had a piper with him.

"Right, lads. Keep together, avoid trouble if you can but if Fritz gets in our way, bloody destroy him!"

That raised a cheer, as he had expected, and when Ramsay stood up straight and began a quick march toward Carnoy, the men fell in step behind him and followed without question.

The Germans had entered at the south of the village, so Ramsay headed for the north, moving as quickly as he could. As they neared the outlying houses he saw a scattering of dead and wounded men on the ground, and a few dazed-looking German infantrymen.

"Ignore them," Ramsay ordered as Cruickshank lifted his rifle. "Push on." He increased their speed so they were moving at a trot, passing larger formations of Germans who looked bewildered at the sight of a group of khaki-clad men running past them from behind their own lines.

"Keep moving. Don't stop for anybody." Ramsay increased his speed until he was almost running. As they got closer to Carnoy the number of German casualties increased; they passed a long row of bodies, obviously caught by a machine gun, and then a group that a shell had butchered, and all around and in between were individuals and small groups of men in a hundred obscene positions of death.

The old British positions came into view – sandbagged trenches that had been hastily dug and even more hastily fortified; farm houses and cottages made into strongpoints, machine gun nests marked by piles of shining brass cartridge cases, light artillery emplacements and supply depots.

There were British casualties now, less than the Germans but still in significant numbers.

"Too many of our lads here," McKim said. "Too bloody many."

"Not bon," Niven said. "Not bloody bon at all."

"Over there, sir." Flockhart had dropped to a crouch behind a scatter of sandbags. The others followed him, rifles at the ready. They were on the village side of the defence line, with an area of open ground between them and the cover of the buildings. There was a scattering of dead bodies on the ground, but for some reason the Germans had ignored this section of the line and there were none of the enemy present. Ramsay eyed the distance his men had to cover and wondered if he had brought them so far, only to fail at this hurdle.

"What do you think, Sergeant? Can we make it?" It went

against the grain to ask a sergeant for his opinion, but Ramsay knew it was only common sense to use the experience of a veteran.

Flockhart scrutinised the open ground. "It's about eighty yards sir and no cover, save for that broken cart." He nodded to a farm cart from which one wheel had been broken so it lay on its side, tangled with the remains of a disembowelled horse. "We will be lucky to get halfway without attracting attention, that's for sure."

Ramsay nodded. "Well, Flockhart, we're not going back."

The Prussians were already tidying up the defences, lifting sandbags, checking for discarded weapons and organising burial parties for the dead. Although they had recently seen action, they appeared immaculate and utterly professional.

"We have to try," Ramsay decided. "But we won't go all at once. Keep low and move one at a time," Ramsay ordered. "The rest will provide covering fire if needed. You first, McKim."

Ramsay slid behind the meagre shelter of a waist-high sandbag wall and held his pistol ready as he watched the Prussians at work.

"Efficient buggers aren't they, sir?" Flockhart lay on the bottom of the makeshift trench with his rifle ready.

"So it seems, Sergeant."

One by one the Royals slipped out of what little cover they had concealed themselves in and made a lunging run across the open ground towards the first houses of the village. Ramsay watched, counting his men. He knew them all, by name and personality, and now he felt true responsibility toward them.

These are my men. I want to get them back. I want to prove that I am a good officer after all.

Ramsay glanced over the men at his side. They were

watching the Prussians, aiming through the sights of their rifles. They looked calm, if nervous.

Good lads, my lads.

Niven was next to attempt the run. Flockhart tapped his shoulder and nodded toward Carnoy. "Off you go, boy. Low and fast. Take care because we need you."

Niven gave a brief, nervous grin, touched the collar of his tunic and stepped out from cover.

You take care, Niven. We need you most of all.

Ramsay looked over his men again. He focussed on Flockhart.

You too, you bastard. You are one of my men too. I want you dead and out of the way, but paradoxically I want to get through with all my men.

Niven had reached the shelter of the cart and rolled behind the single wheel.

"They're moving," Flockhart hissed. "The Prussians are moving."

The nearest Prussians were edging closer. They had reached the last traverse in the trench before Ramsay's position and were only about two hundred yards away. Ramsay admired their efficiency, but also thanked God that they were so intent on discipline that not one of them stopped working to look around. If they had they could hardly have missed the handful of khaki-clad Royals who crouched behind pitifully inadequate shelter.

"Five men left to cross," Ramsay said. "Keep an eye on them, Flockhart."

"Yes, sir." Flockhart had not moved a fraction. "Niven's on his feet again."

How did he see that without moving? It must be some special skill that sergeants possess.

Niven left the cover of the cart and ran toward the

buildings. When he took a single glance behind him, Ramsay waved him urgently on. *Move Niven! Move!*

Turning away, Niven put down his head and raced for the first of the cottages. They were low walled and roofless, damaged by the shelling, but in better condition than most of the villages in the battle area, which proved that the fighting here had not been as intense as in other places. Even after their stand, the British retreat had been precipitous compared to the usual stubborn, yard by yard withdrawals of either army.

We're being caned. The Germans really have us on the run, but in this case it may turn out to our advantage if we can capture that train. And if we can keep Niven alive.

Ramsay watched as McKim half stood to usher Niven into the relative safety of the village. For a second both were highlighted against a smoke-dark background and then they were gone.

"Next man," Ramsay ordered. "Turnbull, off you go."

Turnbull and Aitken rose; both men moved off, hesitated and returned.

Jesus! Somebody move!

"Turnbull, you go. Aitken, wait until he is safe." Ramsay kept his voice level and quiet.

Four to go –Turnbull, Aitken, Flockhart and myself. I have to be last, the position of most danger. That is my duty and obligation as an officer.

Turnbull followed Niven's path, jinking across the ground in a crouch with his rifle at the trail. He glanced at the cart but did not stop and raced over to McKim at the cottage without hesitation.

"Good man. Now you, Aitken." Ramsay spoke without looking round. The Prussians had stepped closer in their methodical cleansing of the trench. He could make out every detail of the nearest man; tall and dark-haired, he was joking as he worked, swinging sandbags back onto the trench wall with scarcely a pause.

Ramsay realised there had been no response. "Aitken! Move, man!" He glanced over his shoulder. Aitken was clutching the ground with both hands, shaking his head. "No, sir, I can't go!"

Oh God! His mind's broken. What shall I do now? There is nothing about this in the officer's training manual.

"You must," Ramsay began, and looked helplessly at Flockhart for support.

"Bloody get going, Aitken, if you want to see your sweetheart again!" Flockhart did not move from his position. "Jenny needs you, Jim. You won't get to her unless you get to that train. Just think of Jenny, Jim."

Come on, Aitken. Move, man. For the love of God, move before the Germans see us!

Ramsay looked from Aitken to Flockhart and over to the Prussians. Aitken had altered his position. He was sitting up now, with his head above the sandbags and the distinctive shape of his British helmet clear for any half-sensible observer to see.

All it needs is for one German to look up now and we are all dead men. Move Aitken! Please move!

"There she is!" Flockhart said quietly. "She's over by that house, Jim. Jenny's there now, waiting for you."

"Jenny?" Aitken spoke in a conversational tone, his Edinburgh accent carrying easily across the ground.

God! These Prussians must be deaf as well as efficient.

"Where's Jenny?" Aitken raised his voice. "Jenny?"

"Over there, by the houses," Flockhart said. "She said you have to go over and see her. She said you have to keep quiet in case you wake the bairn."

"Is wee Davie there too?" Aitken stood upright until Ramsay hauled him back down.

"Keep quiet you fool!" Ramsay hissed. "Wee Davie's sleeping! It's past his bed time."

"You get over to Jenny now," Flockhart's voice was quiet, persuasive. "Get over there, Jimmy. Hurry, man, before she thinks you're not coming and goes away."

Ramsay saw McKim peering toward them, obviously wondering what had gone wrong. He saw the dark-haired Prussian take another few steps forward; he was at the last traverse, once he turned that corner he could not fail to see the British soldiers.

"I'm going to see Jenny," Aitken said. He stood up and ran forward with his mouth open. For a moment Ramsay thought he was going to shout out Jenny's name, but he kept quiet and some strange soldier's instinct compelled him to weave and bob as he ran. Ramsay saw him reach the shelter of the cart, but rather than stop, he passed right by, on the side nearest to the Prussians.

The shout was loud and in German, as the dark-haired Prussian looked up at exactly the wrong moment.

"They've seen him," Flockhart said. "Permission to fire, sir?"

No. Hold your fire, they might concentrate on Aitken and miss us!

"Yes, fire away. Give Aitken as much cover as you can." Ramsay lifted his revolver and fired three quick shots, but Flockhart had already squeezed his trigger. He must have had the Prussian in his sights all the time, for the bullet took the man full in the forehead. The force snapped back his head and threw him against the back wall of the trench.

Ramsay saw Aitken hesitate, then fall, just as McKim thrust up his head and fired toward the Prussians.

"Here!" Flockhart fired away the clip from his rifle, rammed in another and threw a grenade along the trench. "Share that!" He ducked away from the explosion.

"Come on, Flockhart. Time we were gone." Ramsay hauled himself out of the cover of the sandbags. "Come on, man!"

Flockhart was a second behind him, and together they ran toward the shelter of the cart. Ramsay heard a fusillade of shots behind him; he heard shouts in German and McKim's raucous war cry. "Up the Royals! Royal Scots! Death and hell to you all!"

Something struck him a massive blow on the left foot and he yelled and fell down.

"Are you all right, sir?" Flockhart loomed over him, his face anxious.

"Get on!" Ramsay shouted instinctively. "Get to the houses and get away! Don't bother about me!" He rolled over, desperately trying to avoid the bullets that whined around him. "Run, man!"

He could see heads bobbing up along the rim of the German trenches, he could see rifles pointing toward him. Flockhart still hesitated. Ramsay tried to rise, there was no pain. He looked down and saw that the heel of his boot had been shot off, but there was no blood and no pain, only a tremendous numbness. He rose, put his foot on the ground and began to run.

"Come on, Flockhart!"

McKim and the others were firing like madmen and bullets flew in a frenzied crossfire. The cart was only a few yards away and Ramsay dived behind it. He lay there, panting, beside Flockhart as German bullets thudded into the body of the cart and spat splinters of wood all around them.

Ramsay emptied his revolver in the direction of the Prussians, and thrust cartridges into the chambers.

I could shoot him here and now and nobody would know. It would be the easiest thing in the world.

For a second temptation almost overcame him. Ramsay altered his position behind the cart and allowed his revolver to fall slightly until the muzzle was pointing towards the sergeant's side.

All I have to do is squeeze the trigger. A slight pressure and it would all be over and that worry would be gone for good. Just a slight pressure . . .

"Are you wounded, sir?" Flockhart asked.

Ramsay shook his head. "No. They shot the heel off my boot, but I'm unhurt. How is Aitken?"

"Still alive," Flockhart said. "He's moving, but I think he's in a bad way."

They looked at the private. He lay curled in a ball, a few yards between the cart and the Prussians. Although bullets smacked into the ground all around him, no more hit him, but his tunic was deeply stained and blood pooled around him.

Somebody shouted an order from the German trench and their firing halted immediately. "Stop firing, boys," Ramsay ordered and an uneasy silence descended. The stink of lyddite filled the air.

Aitken moaned, the sound loud in the hush. Ramsay looked at Flockhart.

"What the hell is Fritz playing at?" Flockhart wondered.

It's that Hauptmann with the monocle. He is giving us a chance to rescue Aitken. Oh, God in heaven. Do I take it? I have to, I am the officer.

"You stay here, Flockhart. If I am shot, leave us both and make for the rest. Try and get them home."

"Sir? What are you going to do . . . ?"

Taking a deep breath, Ramsay stood erect. He tensed,

expecting a volley of shots from the German lines, but the silence continued. He stepped forward, hearing his own breath harsh and brittle. Aitken was moving, shifting in the agony of his wound.

Aware that every eye would be on him, Ramsay knelt beside the wounded man. "How are you doing, Aitken?"

The eyes that turned on him were liquid with pain. "Jenny?"

"Not Jenny, Jim. It's Lieutenant Ramsay. How are you, son?"

Son? Aitken was the same age as he was.

"Where's Jenny?" Aitken tried to sit up, gasped in pain and sank back down again. "It hurts, Jenny. It hurts sore."

"You rest easy, son, and we'll get you home." Ramsay crouched down at Aitken's side. "Let's have a look at you." It was surreal, tending to a wounded man in full sight of an unknown number of German soldiers, knowing that there would be scores if not hundreds of rifles pointing at him and that every second he spent here was jeopardising his chances of escape.

What do I do? Leave a wounded man to the mercy of the Germans, or risk having the rest of my men killed or captured?

Ramsay looked up. Flockhart was staring at him as if it was the first time he had ever seen him. There was a strange expression on his face, recognition perhaps.

Somebody spoke on the German side. The words were unintelligible, but Ramsay recognised the meaning. He was being asked to get a move on. The tall German Hauptmann rose calmly from the trench; the low sun reflected from the monocle of Ramsay's old adversary. The German raised a hand in salutation and held up three fingers.

He is giving us three minutes grace before the war starts

again. Sir, you are a gentleman and it is a privilege to fight against you.

"Come on, Aitken," Ramsay raised his voice. "Flockhart, give a hand here, would you?"

The sergeant emerged slowly, still holding his rifle. A single shot sounded from the German trench and a fountain of dirt erupted immediately in front of Flockhart.

"Dirty Hun bastards!" McKim's voice came a second before the crack of his rifle, but Ramsay was nearly as quick.

"Cease fire! Stop firing!" He faced Flockhart. "Sergeant, shoulder your rifle. That was a warning shot!" He lowered his voice. "If they meant to kill you they would have."

With obvious reluctance, Flockhart lowered his rifle and slung it over his shoulder.

"Now help me lift Aitken." Ramsay put a hand under Aitken's left arm and lifted. Flockhart did the same to his right and together they hauled him upright.

McKim was watching from the shelter of the cottages. He had seen the byplay with Flockhart and had balanced his rifle over his shoulder. The other Royals were equally unprepared for the sharp outbreak of musketry.

"Jesus!" Flockhart yelled as one of the Royals fell and the others dived back behind the shelter of the cottage walls. "The bastards were fooling us!"

I did not expect that. I thought my German friend would keep his word.

Ramsay began to run, dragging Aitken as best he could. He felt the shock of the bullet and looked down. Aitken's head lolled onto his shoulder and fresh blood spurted from his mouth.

"He's gone," Flockhart said. "Drop him and run, sir."

Flockhart was correct. A German bullet had slammed into Aitken's back and exited from his chest. He had died instantly. Ramsay released his grip on Aitken's arm and fled for the cottages.

Bullets were kicking up the ground and McKim had organised a defence. The Royals were returning fire, working the bolts of their rifles and firing as fast as they could. Ramsay ducked as a bullet whined over his head, and then vaulted the low wall, all that remained of the nearest cottage. McKim nodded to him; he still clenched the broken pipe between his teeth.

"Bloody Bavarians," he said and slammed another bullet into the breach of his rifle, took quick aim and fired again.

"They're Prussians," Ramsay said. He saw Flockhart lying panting in the shelter of the wall, loading his rifle; Turnbull was prone, firing through a gap in the stones; young Mackay was crouching and crying, but still firing as best he could.

"Not the boys in the trench. It was the other lot that started firing at you," McKim spoke around his pipe and nodded his head to the right. "They arrived just as you and Sergeant Flockhart lifted Aitken."

For some reason Ramsay felt a surge of relief. He had not wanted to think that his Prussian enemy had broken his unspoken word.

The Bavarians were on their left flank. They were moving cautiously, firing fast but with a lack of accuracy that caused Ramsay to believe they were raw troops rather than veteran Prussians.

"How's Jim . . . Aitken?" McKim spoke without relaxing his concentration. "There's one Hun who won't make it back to Bavaria." He worked the bolt and fired again, releasing the fifteen aimed rounds a minute that he had been trained to do. "And there's another. Death and hell to all of them, death and bloody hell."

"Aitken did not make it," Ramsay said.

McKim grunted, aimed and fired three shots in quick succession. "Death and hell, you Bavarian bastards. He was a good lad, was Aitken, another good man gone."

Ramsay looked around, The Royals were loading and firing, but there was a company of Bavarians opposing them and now the Prussians were also firing. He checked who had fallen: Benson was lying still with a neat bullet hole in his head.

Ten men left now.

"Time to get our train," Ramsay squeezed off a volley of shots from his revolver. "There will be hundreds of Fritzses here shortly. McKim, you take Niven and two men and head for the station. Flockhart, you and I and Turnbull are the rearguard." He waited until the Royals were prepared. "Right, on the count of three: One, two, three!"

He fired again, alongside Turnbull and Flockhart, aiming and firing as fast as they could, trying to keep the Bavarians and Prussians quiet as McKim led his men away.

The cottages were at the end of a short street that stretched toward the main square of the village. McKim led his men into the next cottage along and set them into defensive positions.

"Ready, sir!"

The firing increased and a group of Bavarians rushed forward, but the concentrated fire of the Royals accounted for five of them and the others threw themselves onto the ground or ran back to the shelter of the trenches.

"Up the Royals!" McKim yelled.

"Follow me, lads!" Ramsay rose, jumped over the wall at the back of the cottage and dashed up the street to the next in the row. The studs on his boots struck sparks from the cobbled ground and he slid sideways, nearly fell, but recovered his balance in time to lunge through the low doorway of the cottage.

"Here they come again." Flockhart was a few seconds behind him. He looked over his shoulder as Turnbull tripped over the uneven ground and staggered through the door. "The Prussians are on the move."

"Not far to the train," Ramsay could see past the line of cottages to where the train sat, isolated and miraculously untouched. "It's only a few hundred yards."

"And there are only a few hundred Huns trying to stop us getting there," Flockhart said. He aimed and fired. "I can't see us getting out of this, sir."

Ramsay raised his voice, "Flockhart! Take Turnbull and Niven and get to that train. Get it moving. We will cover you. Once it's travelling, you and Turnbull will cover us." He ducked as a bullet smashed into the wall and sprayed splinters of stone in his face. "Jesus!"

"Are you all right, sir?" Flockhart sounded concerned.

"Yes, keep firing!"

The Prussians were advancing in three long regular lines, immaculately spaced and with the monocled Hauptmann leading from the front.

I can't shoot that man, nor can I order my men not to shoot him. He will have to take his chance with the rest of them.

For an instant Ramsay's eyes met those of the German officer. Neither acknowledged the other, but Ramsay thought he detected a tacit understanding. He raised his revolver high and pointed it toward the German. The German did not flinch, but marched on expressionless. Ramsay lifted his arm high and slowly and deliberately swung his arm round to the right, far from the officer, and fired a single round.

"Five rounds rapid, lads!"

The Royals responded with a will, thrusting the barrels of their rifles toward the Prussians and opening fire.

"Shoot them flat, lads!" *But not that officer, he is a true gentleman.*

"Death and hell!" McKim gave his inevitable slogan, "death and hell to youse all!"

The concentrated rifle fire took a heavy toll on the Prussians as they marched across the open ground and bodies began to pile up. Ramsay spotted some Prussians ducking behind the cart and he fired in that direction.

"Bomb the bastards out!" McKim yelled and young Mackay threw a grenade that exploded in a shower of splinters a few yards above the men cowering behind the cart. There was a chorus of screams and yells and the Prussians fell back, carrying their wounded with them.

"Cease fire!" Ramsay ordered. "Give them time to get the injured away."

"For God's sake! We may as well take them tea and biscuits," Cruickshank grumbled. "They're the bloody enemy." But he lowered his rifle and the Germans retired in peace.

"Next house, boys, and then we dash for the train."

Without waiting for the Prussians to reach the shelter of their trenches, Ramsay led the Royals out of the cottage and towards the next. Once he was outside the shelter of the walls he again experienced that familiar feeling of vulnerability. He could sense the Bavarians and Prussians aiming at him but tried to ignore the crackle of musketry and the crash and ping of bullets on the road and against the buildings.

The door of the next cottage was closed and Ramsay had to boot it open and dive inside, his men following him in a pell mell scurry. Mackay was giggling as his nerves got the better of him, but McKim pushed him roughly inside. "Get in there, boy and don't dawdle!"

Bullets hammered against the far wall as Ramsay kicked the door shut.

"That's the way, sir. They'll never get through that," Cruickshank said. He ducked as shots crashed through the window, smashing the last remaining pane of glass. "Go on, Fritz, ruin the woman's house."

"Any sign of the Prussians?" Ramsay tried to peer through the window. Now that they were further up the street, their view of the open space was limited.

What do we do now? Keep moving from house to house or make one long run to the train?

A long whistle helped make his decision.

"That's the steam whistle," McKim said. "Niven's telling us that he's all ready to move."

Ramsay nodded. "On the count of three, break out and run for the train. Don't stop for any wounded, don't stop for anybody or anything. One, two, three!"

He was first into the street, hearing the mad hammer of his heart that seemed to complement the incessant crack of rifles. He heard a yell behind him as somebody was hit, flinched as a bullet ripped through the leg of his trousers, heard a long drawn out scream and saw the train ahead of him.

It was three carriages long, with the engine at the front and a closed guard's carriage at the rear. He could see Niven in the driver's cab and Flockhart at his side, while Turnbull leaned out of a window, shooting down the street. Sparks and splinters of steel and wood showed where bullets were clashing against the bodywork.

The carriage doors hung open as Niven sounded the whistle again; white steam shrouded the train, acting as a temporary smokescreen. The Royals scrambled on board, fingers and feet scrabbling for purchase. German bullets crashed and whined and smashed the remaining windows.

"Are we all on?" Ramsay looked down the road; there was one crumpled khaki body. Mackay had not made it. He looked very small lying in the devastated street. "Get moving, Niven. Get this train moving!"

"Come on lads!" McKim roared. "Last train to Waverley Station!"

Flockhart flinched at the words and jerked his head round to look directly at Ramsay.

The words had acted as a trigger.

CHAPTER NINE

25 March 1918

"Last train to Waverley Station! Last train to Waverley!" The stentorian roar of the station master echoed across the double tracks of Newtongrange Railway Station. As always, the platform was filled.

There were miners' wives returning home from trips to Edinburgh or Dalkeith, self-important managers and clerks, a handful of gentlemen and their ladies trying to pretend they were of a different breed, and the ubiquitous travelling salesmen who spent half their lives at small railway stations as they scraped a precarious living from the pennies of the poor. Sprinkled among the hard-faced miners and busy women was a scattering of soldiers in khaki, one sporting a bandaged head and carrying the unmistakable air of a veteran, but the rest were eager young men on their first leave of their training.

Ramsay felt Gilllian's hand slide inside his and he squeezed his reassurance. "Soon be home now," he told her.

Steam from the engine filled the station, channelled by the high banking at the rear of the platforms, to cover the milling passengers. A crowd of bare-footed children ran past, laughing, as their mother shouted after them.

"I would like children," Gillian said, and smiled as Ramsay stiffened. She patted his arm. "It's all right, Douglas. Not for a few years yet."

"Not for many years yet." Ramsay felt her hand slide away from his. "But we will have them," he added. Her hand returned, the gloved fingers pressing for entrance to the security of his palm.

"Three children at least" Gillian pressed her advantage. "Two girls and a boy."

"Two boys and a girl," Ramsay corrected.

As a press of people emerged from the train, Ramsay and Gillian walked quickly along the length of the platform. "The first class compartment must be here somewhere," Ramsay said. "Let's get away from these peasants."

"Don't be so disparaging, Douglas," Gillian rebuked him. "These men work hard." She looked around at the raucous crowd pushing and shoving their way on and off the train. "They are a bit shabby though, aren't they? They could have made at least a little effort before they left their hovels."

Ramsay laughed and stepped aside to let an elderly woman squeeze past. "I will be glad to return to Edinburgh but Father insisted that I view the family mines at least once every year. I don't know why. He is only a minority shareholder."

"You will be going alone next year," Gillian said and stopped short. "Sorry, Douglas. I forgot for a second."

"Next year I will be a soldier in France, or dead." Ramsay decided he could add drama to the situation. He shook his hand free. *Try for sympathy; it might gain you something.*

"Or the war could be over and you could be back home and married," Gillian neatly countered his argument. She grabbed his hand back. "Now stop your complaining and take me home. I have had enough of coal mines, numbered rows of brick cottages and coal dust at the back of my throat."

Ramsay smiled. "So have I. Here is what they laughingly call the first class carriage." He turned the handle, pulled open the door and offered his arm to help Gillian up.

"Hey, you!" The voice was rough and aggressive. Ramsay paused with his hand in Gillian's and a smile frozen on his face. Two men were on the platform, distinct from the crowd only because of their obvious anger. One wore khaki and bore the stripes of a corporal on his sleeve; the other had the flat cap and heavy boots of a working man. When Ramsay looked at him, he recognised the man he had seen at the gate just a year previously: Rab.

"That's the fellow, Jamie!" Rab pointed to Ramsay. "That's Napier. That's the man who knocked up your sister!"

Oh, God. I thought that incident was long dead and forgotten.

"Are these men addressing you, Douglas?" There was curiosity in Gillian's voice. "He certainly pointed to you, but he called you Napier."

"I don't think so," Ramsay said. He handed her up inside the carriage with more force than he had intended. "Come on Gill, let's get inside."

Rab and the soldier pushed through the crowd as Ramsay turned to follow Gillian.

"Not so fast, you bastard. Napier, we want a word with you!"

"Last train for Waverley!" The station master roared above the hubbub of the crowd. "All aboard who's going aboard!"

Ramsay slammed the carriage door shut behind him. Neither James nor the corporal flinched at the bang. James grabbed hold of the handle, but the station master shook his head.

"This is a first class carriage, Tommy. Soldiers travel third class." He shoved the soldier's hand off the handle and blew a long blast on his whistle as the train emitted another spurt of steam.

Ramsay guided Gillian across the corridor and into a compartment where two occupants looked up without interest. The man returned to the scrutiny of his newspaper while his female companion turned her face to the window.

"Sit here, Gill." Ramsay waited until Gillian had taken her seat before slouching in the corner furthest from the window. The train began to roll away from the platform. He took a deep breath.

It is over. I escaped. Another year without discovery.

The rapping at the window was urgent and loud.

"These men seem keen to see you, Douglas," Gillian pointed out. "I think they may be tenants of your father." She nudged him with a sharp elbow. "The least you could do is acknowledge them, Douglas!"

The men were at the window closest to the platform, running alongside the train as it gathered speed.

"They must have missed the train," the man with the newspaper sounded amused.

"They are desperate to see you, Douglas," Gillian said. "Are you sure you don't know them?"

Rab looked directly at him and shouted, but the words were lost as the train emitted another shrill whistle. As the train picked up speed he fell behind. Younger and fitter, the corporal took his place at the window. He took hold of the sill and clung on by his fingertips as he opened his mouth.

"I'm James Flockhart! Remember my name, you bastard! Wherever you hide, I will find you!"

Gillian watched as Flockhart's grip on the window slipped and he tumbled down. The train rattled on its journey to Edinburgh and left him behind.

"He must have mistaken you for somebody else," she said.

Slightly shaken by the experience, Ramsay nodded. "That must be it. He thought I was somebody called Napier."

The woman at the opposite window gave a slight smile. "He was probably drunk," she said. "Soldiers are often drunk."

Her husband looked up from his newspaper. "That's the only reason they join the army," he said. "They give them too much nowadays."

Ramsay held Flockhart's gaze for only a fraction of a second as the memories sped through his mind.

Does he know now? Did McKim's shout trigger the memories?

Flockhart dropped his eyes. "Here come the Huns," he shouted above the rattle of the train and the incessant crackle of musketry. "Hundreds of them!" He raised his eyes and stared at Ramsay for a second too long, his eyes narrow and calculating.

Oh God, it's out at last. He has remembered where he saw me.

Ramsay flinched as a volley of bullets shattered the window into a thousand pieces and shards of glass imploded toward him. He thrust through his revolver and fired at the Prussians, but did not see any fall.

The train picked up speed, but the Germans were running toward it, some with rifles at the charge, others with rifles at the trail. The monacled Hauptmann was in front, giving rapid orders that resulted in a section of men sprinting forward as the others gave covering fire.

"Come on, Niven!" Turnbull yelled. "Fritz is catching us."

"Death and hell to you!" McKim smashed the glass of

his window with the butt of his rifle then leaned out. He fired, worked the bolt of his rifle and fired again, shooting a Prussian each time. "Death and hell!"

The train picked up speed but Niven raised his voice, "I need a fireman. I need fuel!"

I did not think of that. Damn!

"Turnbull, go forward and help Niven!" Ramsay yelled. "Move, man!"

A long line of Germans followed the train, the slowest already giving up. Two hundred yards in the rear, a line of kneeling riflemen rained constant fire on the train.

"Where's my fireman?" Niven's roar was desperate. "We're losing pressure!"

"Turnbull! Get forward!" Ramsay withdrew from the window, just as a bullet skimmed through. He felt a hammer blow on his head and was thrown backward across the carriage.

I've been shot. The Huns have shot me again.

Ramsay tried to focus but the carriage spun before his eyes. The seats and door and ceiling were intermixed into a confusion of images that made no sense at all. He extended his arm, grabbed hold of something solid and attempted to pull himself upright but his hand had no strength and he slumped back down.

This is serious. I am dead.

There were sounds he could not recognise and sensations he could not name. Somebody was moaning; somebody else was shouting "death and hell"; somebody was leaning over him.

That will be Mother, surely, come to ensure I am all right.

"Mother? I'm very hot, is the fire on?"

His mother was holding him in hands far too rough; he tried to pull away but lacked the strength. "Leave me, let me alone."

"Death and hell to you all!"

There must be workmen in the house, nothing else could account for that incessant loud banging as they used their hammers on his head.

"Leave me alone. Mother, do the workmen have to make such an infernal noise?"

"Sir, sir, are you all right?" The face that loomed over him was certainly not his mother; it was dirty and she had never sported a five day growth of beard like that. Nor had her dress been stained yellow and green with lyddite fumes.

"Of course I'm not all right! I've been shot, damn it!" Ramsay took hold of the hand that Flockhart proffered and hauled himself upright. He staggered as the train bounced across points. He blinked as something blocked his vision, and passed a hand across his forehead. It came away sticky and red with blood. "God . . ."

Flockhart looked closer. "It looks like a bullet has scored your head, sir. There's lots of blood but I don't think it's serious."

Why me? Why not me? I get wounded every time I come to the front.

"Here, sir. Try this." Flockhart handed over a handkerchief.

"Thank you, Sergeant." Ramsay wiped away the worst of the blood from his forehead and eyebrows. More followed in a steady flow, but he probed upward until he found the wound and pressed the handkerchief firmly down. He gasped at the pain but applied pressure until the flow of blood eased.

"It is just a graze," he said.

That will be a fine scar to show to Gillian when her hero comes marching home from the war.

Fighting against the hammering pain in his head, Ramsay took a deep breath and tried to focus on his surroundings. The train was slowing down. He looked out of the window.

They had left the station and were in open countryside, still scarred by war but not as mutilated as most he had passed through. There was something burning on the horizon, he could see huge flames and a pall of dark smoke rising. He could no longer see the Germans, although the occasional crash of a striking bullet told him they had not forgotten about the impudent Royals in their midst.

"Find out why we are slowing down," he ordered. "Tell Niven to keep moving no matter what. The greater distance we can put between ourselves and the Prussians, the better."

"Yes, sir." For a moment something flickered behind Flockhart's eyes, but he nodded and moved forward from the compartment.

He knows; I am sure he knows who I am; how the hell do I get out of this mess?

Ramsay tried to follow Flockhart but his knees buckled and he crashed to the floor. He lay there for a moment as the carriage spun around him, then pushed himself back upright, clinging to the seats for support. This train lacked the corridors he knew so well and was composed of open plan carriages, with seats each side of a central aisle. He staggered to the front and opened the door that connected to the guard's van.

The van was crammed with bags and baggage, boxes and all the paraphernalia of a retreating army. Ramsay ignored it all as he pushed forward to the far end, where a wooden door allowed him access to the tender and the engine itself. He had been aware of the sound of firing for some time but now it increased to a non-stop rattle of musketry. He pushed open the carriage door.

The sudden blast of air nearly knocked him off the step but also cleared his head. Turnbull was firing, his nerves under control and his face set, Cruickshank was sheltering as he tried to clear a jam. Edwards was lying back with blood on his face, Blackley was shovelling coal as Niven stared forward along the track as if he had been a train driver all his life.

"Sir!" Flockhart pointed to the left.

A battery of field guns was wheeling around to face the train. The drivers lashed their horses unmercifully as the sun flashed from burnished metal. It was a gloriously military sight; lovely for civilians to watch but so dangerous in the reality of battle.

"Not bon!" Cruickshank shouted, "Not bloody bon at all."

"Shoot the gunners," Ramsay shouted, and winced in pain as Turnbull fired only a few inches from his ear. "Everyone concentrate on the gunners. Niven, can't you get this train to move faster? My granny could walk faster than this and she's been dead for years!"

The Royals opened rapid fire, leaning out of the glassless windows as the train rolled along the track. Ramsay saw some of the gunners fall, but the others continued their work and as the train approached a broad bend he found himself staring down the black muzzles of the guns.

"Here we go!" Flockhart said quietly. He lifted his rifle, took careful aim and fired. One of the gunners fell. "That's one less anyway, but their guns are bigger than ours."

"Here comes the receipt." Cruickshank ducked as all six guns opened up at once.

Ramsay stood transfixed as he saw the guns leap back with the recoil. He did not see the rush of shot, but saw the results as the ground erupted a good three hundred yards to the right, beyond the train.

Flockhart fired again, and McKim followed suit. A curtain of falling earth from the explosions prevented Ramsay from seeing the result.

"Get shovelling, Blackley!" Ramsay shouted. "Niven, get as much speed as you can from this train!" He looked around, as far as he could see there was no cover as the line crossed the open countryside of Picardy.

"Do you think we will make Albert?" McKim asked, just as the guns fired again.

The Germans had corrected their aim. The explosions fell either side of the train, spreading shrapnel and stones across the track and shattering the last remaining carriage windows. The shock jolted the train sideways, first one direction and then the other, until it righted itself and Niven steered it around the wide curve.

"They're firing again." Flockhart worked his bolt and shot at the artillery. "Missed!"

"Here it comes!" McKim said.

Ramsay ducked involuntarily as the shells burst. He only saw two explosions, but felt the results of at least one more as the train heeled to one side and rocks and shrapnel tore into the bodywork of the carriage. One shard of metal ripped through the seat beside which he stood, emerging sharp and wicked, inches from his hand.

"Jesus!" somebody blasphemed as the train juddered sideways. Men and loose fittings were thrown across the carriage; a discarded rifle clattered along the slanted floor, Turnbull rolled past him, swearing wildly and he put out a hand to help.

"We're going over," McKim yelled.

"Hold on lads," Flockhart roared and then there was pandemonium as the carriages crashed onto their side and scraped and crashed along the tracks. Ramsay tried to grab hold of a seat for support but it was torn loose of its mountings and he was thrown the length of the carriage amidst a jumble of men and fittings, broken glass and equipment. For a moment it seemed that the whole world was in confusion as the carriage crashed onto the ground with a litter of seats, men and equipment falling on top of him, and then he lay still, with a crushing weight on top of him and pain in his head and his left leg.

Ramsay gradually became aware of his surroundings. There was a cacophony of noises; groaning and cursing, the hiss of escaping steam and a crackling he could not identify. He tried to make sense of the various sounds.

"Get off me for Christ's sake, Turnbull."

"Has anybody seen my rifle? Where's my rifle?"

"I can't see. Oh, God, I can't see!"

"Hurry, lads, before the boiler blows!"

"Bloody Fritzes. Bloody, bloody Fritzes!"

Ramsay 's vision was obscured by blood dripping from his reopened head wound, he tried to raise a hand to clear his eyes but something held him trapped and he could not move.

"Sergeant Flockhart? McKim? Are you there?"

His voice was lost in the general hubbub. The crackling sound was growing stronger and he coughed.

God. That's smoke. The train is on fire!

"Flockhart, get the men out of here before we all burn to death!" Again he tried to move but with no success. Another drift of smoke swept over him and he coughed again, harder. "Is anybody there?"

Other men were shouting and Ramsay took a deep breath that contained as much smoke as oxygen.

Don't panic, think what is best to do. You are an officer and a gentleman, it is your place to lead and show an example. Check if you can move all your limbs.

Ramsay tried his feet, left and then right. Nothing.

Am I paralysed? Oh God what a way to die, burned to death in a train in France.

His right arm was trapped, but he could move his left slightly. He concentrated, tried to block out all extraneous sounds and the increasing smell of smoke. He shifted his arm from side to side, felt something solid and pushed hard. It moved a little and he had more space.

"Flockhart!" Ramsay yelled.

Now he could move his arm as far as his shoulder and he inched his arm up. There was a rattling sound and something rolled heavily onto his legs, but his left arm was free. Ramsay wiped the blood from his eyes. He opened them and saw a scene of utter chaos. The carriage lay on its side: all the chairs were piled up, together with what appeared to be pieces of the body of the train and a number of khaki-clad corpses. The smoke was not as thick as he had thought; blue and evil, it slid in from the left, where the engine should have been.

There were two heavy seats on top of him and a section of what had once been the roof of the carriage. Ramsay shoved at the nearest chair and wriggled free. He stood in a half crouch and examined himself for injuries, but save for bruises, cuts and grazes he was unscathed.

"Is that you, sir?" As usual, McKim had his stub of a pipe in his mouth as he picked his way through the mess. "Fritz got us proper that time," he said casually, "but we'd better get out before the boiler blows."

He kicked at the nearest man. "Come on, Cruickshank. You're not hurt. It's just a scratch."

"Get up, lads, and get outside," Ramsay took over. He checked the two remaining men. Edwards was dead, his head almost severed, but Turnbull was alive although he nursed a broken wrist. "Outside, lads. Come on now!"

Ramsay led the way by climbing out of the far window, which was now facing the sky, and helped Turnbull up. It was the work of a moment to slide down to the ground and assess the damage.

A shell had hit the track immediately in front of the engine. Niven had not had a chance to stop and had driven right into the explosion. The engine had crashed into the shell crater and the carriages had derailed one after the other. They lay on their side like a metallic snake – orange-red flames surging from the engine and lightening up the rapidly darkening landscape.

"Have you seen Sergeant Flockhart?" Ramsay asked and one by one the men shook their heads.

"I think he was in the engine with Niven," Turnbull said. McKim had fixed him with a temporary splint and sling and he nursed his arm, in obvious pain.

"McKim, you gather the rest of the men. I'll check the engine." Ramsay moved forward, occasionally stopping to clear blood from his eyes.

"Be careful, sir! If that engine blows. . ." There was no need for McKim to complete his sentence. A boiler explosion would be just as lethal as the German artillery.

Flowers of flames surrounded the engine and licked at the spilled coal of the upended tender. Ramsay saw Niven lying on his back, pinned under the body of the engine. He was immobile, with his arms outspread. Blackley was a few yards away from the engine, groaning.

"Blackley," Ramsay knelt at his side. "Can you move?"

Blackley looked up and nodded. "Only winded," he gasped. "I was thrown clear. How's Niven?"

"Dead." Ramsay said shortly. "Have you seen Sergeant Flockhart?"

Blackley shook his head. "Not since the shelling began," he said.

Free. I am free of him. The Germans have done it for me.

Ramsay tried to hide the immense relief that came over him. He had lived with the fear of discovery for so long that it had become part of him, but now he no longer had that worry. He was free. Only the Germans remained as a threat.

"Back to the train, Blackley," Ramsay said. "Let's get out of here before Fritz comes to see what remains."

McKim had gathered the Royals together. They stood beside the train, most nursing wounds and only two still carrying their rifles. Ramsay counted them:

"Me, McKim, Blackley, Turnbull, Cruickshank." Only five men left. "Right, lads. Let's move out of here." He led the way, heading into the dark for what he hoped was the British lines, as the flames spread across the train and leaped up to the sky. "Come on lads. Toute-de-suite."

There were flames on the horizon. Ramsay was not sure what was burning, but it was large, lighting up the horizon to the south.

"We have not stopped Fritz yet, then," McKim said. He had retained his rifle and ignored the cut that dripped blood from his right arm as he walked.

"It doesn't look like it," Ramsay said. He could hear the growl of guns and see intermittent flashes on the horizon. "We are still fighting though. It looks like the line is at Albert now." That was a guess, but as an officer he liked to appear omnipotent.

"Is that where we are headed then?" McKim asked. He stumbled over a high tussock of grass, looked down, cursed and continued.

"That's the plan," Ramsay said. He had no plan at all, except to get as far from the train as possible. The Germans would be clustering there in minutes.

"The lads need a rest," McKim reminded. "They have been going non-stop."

"We will rest when it's safe," Ramsay said. He looked behind him. The burning train dominated the night, the flames soaring skyward as a warning to everyone within a ten mile diameter of the further destructive cost of this war.

"We'll march for another hour, then rest for four and continue," Ramsay decided. "Head for the guns."

"Which bloody guns?" Cruickshank grumbled, "There are guns everywhere."

"Mind your lip, Cruickshank," McKim stopped Ramsay from having to explain further. At that moment he felt that if he had to make another decision his brain would explode.

They halted in the lee of a small group of shell-blasted trees, with the light from the burning train on one horizon and the intermittent flash of shellfire on the other.

"What date is it, sir?" McKim asked.

Ramsay tried to work it out but shook his head. "I don't know, Corporal. We seem to have been retreating for days." Once again he cursed his loose tongue.

I am getting too familiar with these men. I should learn to keep more distance between us, but that is not easy when we share the same shell hole and use the same latrine.

Ramsay wondered what the lack of expression on McKim's face meant; was he sneering at him? Was he wondering why he was only a lieutenant after all his experience at the front?

"Try and get some sleep," Ramsay said curtly. "I'll take first watch."

God knows, I can't sleep anyway.

He watched as the Royals slumped onto the ground around the base of the trees. After the fire they were smoke-stained as well as unshaven and ragged, and all were carrying a number of minor wounds and cuts, some of which were already showing signs of gas gangrene from the contaminated shell holes they had negotiated.

There are not many of us left now. Once again I've let my men down and got them killed.

Stripped of their bark by shrapnel and explosive, the trees pointed stark fingers skyward to an unforgiving God. They provided scant shelter in the shattered landscape, but they were a focal point, a reminder of earlier times when fields were green and soil was a promise of future life, not a sanctuary from death or hideous disfigurement.

As she stood under the branches of the tall elm tree, she was beautiful. There was no other word to describe Gillian. With her long coat almost touching the short grass and her bonnet tight around her heart-shaped face, she was a picture of female perfection.

She greeted him with open arms and soft lips. A year earlier such a display of affection would have brought disapproving frowns from the righteous and the respectable, but after twelve months of war people were used to women greeting their soldier men. What was once reserved only for the lower classes was now acceptable for gentlemen and ladies; certain proprieties had been put aside, at least for the duration of the war.

"Your last leave before you are off to the front, my Hector." Gillian did not release him, but whispered the words in his ear. "We must make it memorable."

Ramsay pulled her even closer, seeking comfort in the proximity of her body, rather than mere sexual desire. He did not want to go to France. He wanted to stay here in Edinburgh and live a quiet life among the papers and deeds and legal terminology for which he had been trained. He looked around. Princes Street Gardens spread on either side, the lawns not quite as immaculate as they were in peacetime and the late summer flowers losing their fire to the cool onslaught of autumn. He was desperate to remain.

"You look so smart," Gillian pulled back and examined him. "You suit uniform, you know. Maybe you should remain a soldier even after the war is won." Her eyes were gentle, but also urgent with an emotion he had never thought to see in her. "Just think of all the places we could visit!"

Ramsay said nothing, but his mind intoned the words: Mons, Loos, Le Cateau; Ypres. Death and horror awaited him in a thousand different forms and shapes.

"Imagine it, Douglas. We could be posted to Poona and live in a hill station with ten servants to do our bidding!" A smile curved Gillian's lips at the thought of having people to bow to her and follow her every command. "Our babies would have Indian nannies, Douglas. I would have tea with the Colonel's lady and you could hunt tigers."

No fighting in your army then, Douglas thought bitterly. He heard a bugle's insistent call from the castle above and shivered at the martial sound. God, but he hated the army and military life! Maybe some miracle would end the war before he reached the front; maybe the next push would break through the German lines. Maybe . . .

Gillian's eyes were bright. She ran her hand down his chest, allowing her fingers to play with his brass buttons. "You've lost weight Douglas, but it is all muscle now." She pushed her open hand against his chest, her tongue protruded from her mouth for just a fraction of a second. "My, I bet you are strong now."

"Strong enough," Ramsay said. He remembered the tales he had been told of Mons, the Germans advancing in uncountable hordes. 'We shot them and shot them,' the veterans had said, 'but they just kept coming. They were like machines.'

"We might be sent to Egypt," Gillian said breathlessly. She patted him, panting slightly. "We could see the pyramids

192

and the sphinx, watch the sun rise over the desert and ride camels beside the Nile. How romantic!" Her eyes were wide. She stepped back slightly. "Oh, Douglas, what a wonderful life we could have. You could be the Colonel of the regiment and lead your men into battle . . ."

"And get my head blown off, like as not," Ramsay said, but Gillian did not hear or chose to ignore him.

"You would be a hero. I know you would be brave as a lion and win a whole uniform full of medals." She intertwined her hands with his. "You could rise to be a general like Kitchener." She pulled him close again and kissed him openly, despite the two elderly ladies who sat on a bench within a few yards of them.

Her lips were soft, but Ramsay was not prepared for the quick flicker of her tongue into his mouth.

"Gillian!" If any of his other girls had acted like that he would have been delighted, but Gillian was to be his wife. He expected certain standards of decorum from her, especially in douce Edinburgh.

"I do wish they had kept scarlet uniforms," Gillian said. "You are smart, but khaki is so drab compared to scarlet. Full dress is so much more becoming when it is bright, don't you think?"

Ramsay tried to imagine a scarlet-clad regiment in one of the trenches he had heard so much about. "I'll pass your idea onto the King next time we meet," he said.

"Will you meet the King?" Gillian asked and then gave him a playful slap. "You are teasing me."

They walked hand in hand along the winding paths of the garden, the rock of the castle frowning on one side as a reminder of Ramsay's military future, and the bustle and trams of Princes Street on the other, taunting him with his civilian past. Gillian moved closer, bumped her hip against his and giggled. "Father is away on business," she said artlessly. "We have the house to ourselves."

Ramsay thought for a moment. "Your maid will be there," he said, "If your mother still keeps a maid."

"She does, but I could send Isobel to her mother's. With both her brothers at the war, Isobel would be pleased to go home for a while." Gillian bumped hips again. "We could have the entire house to ourselves, Doug, including the bedrooms . . ."

"Best not, I think," Ramsay said. "It would not be proper."

"Proper!" Gillian's hand tightened around his for a moment, then slackened and she slid it free. "Since when did propriety concern you, Douglas?"

Ramsay said nothing, but lengthened his stride and walked on so that Gillian had to hurry to catch up with him. She walked at his side for a few moments and then slipped her hand inside his again.

"You are very quiet, Douglas," Gillian said as they stopped to admire the ornate fountain. "Are you all right?" She paused for a significant moment. "Don't you like me anymore?" She put her right hand on his face and turned it towards her. "Am I no longer good enough for you, now that you are a commissioned officer? You were keen enough before!"

What's happened to me? I have changed! Gillian is offering herself to me on a plate and I'm turning her down. What have I become? I'm in love. The previous women were unimportant, all of them: Mary, Georgina, Lucia and the others, even Grace. They did not matter but Gillian does.

He shook his head at her troubled eyes. "You are far too good for me, Gillian, but I am about to go to war. I may not come back. I do not wish to leave you with something you may regret, especially since I would not be in a position to rectify matters."

"You mean I may fall pregnant." Gillian surprised him with her bluntness. "Well, Douglas Ramsay, I would not object to that in the slightest. Many ladies . . ." she emphasised the word, "are bearing children just now, even though their men are at the war."

"I will not leave you a pregnant widow, or even worse, a pregnant and unmarried woman," Ramsay proved he could be every bit as frank. "Once this war nonsense is finished and we have kicked the Kaiser back to Berlin, then I will make you my wife and we can have as many babies as you like."

God! I mean that! I want to father this woman's children.

Gillian stepped back and shook her head. "You're a strange man, Douglas Ramsay. Nearly everybody I know warned me against you. They told me you were a bounder, a womaniser and a cad, but I knew there was more to you than that." She held up her hand as Ramsay opened his mouth to speak. "No! Don't try and deny all the other women you've known. I don't care and I don't want to know. All I want is your assurance that they are in the past, and that I am the only one now."

"You are. Of course you are," Ramsay said.

Gillian touched her fingers to his lips. "Then that's all that needs to be said about the matter. The past is dead and never to be mentioned again. It is only our future that matters."

Grace: I must tell you about Grace in case there is trouble in the future. You must know that side of me if we are to be a proper man and wife.

"Now, you will have heard how some women allow their men some latitude when they are at war." Gillian's smile faded. "I am not of that persuasion, Douglas. I will be faithful to you and I expect you to do the same."

"I will," Douglas said.

I mean that. I genuinely do.

Gillian's smile returned. "I have heard all about the French girls and their tricks to entice men, and I want you to promise that you will have nothing to do with them." Her smile remained, but there were shadows in her eyes. "Go on, promise!"

Ramsay remembered the medical officer's lectures about venereal diseases and the horrors they could inflict on his body. "I promise," he said quietly, and smiled. "Cross my heart and hope to die."

Gillian seemed satisfied. "Then there is nothing more to be said."

There was never any pretence with the Prussian Guards. When they attacked, they did so in style and with effect. When they defended, they did so with great resolution and a stubbornness that ended only with death. When they marched they were erect and solid. They were marching now; rank after rank of tall men in long grey coats, each with his rifle held at precisely the same angle over his shoulder. They appeared out of the dusk and headed west, toward the constantly retreating British lines.

Ramsay had watched them march past for ten long minutes before he realised the time and shook McKim awake.

"Keep the boys quiet," Ramsay said. "Fritz is moving again."

McKim wriggled forward. "Heading to Albert," he said. "They have never been so far forward before."

"And we have never been so far back," Ramsay scanned the shadowy figures passing him in a steady stream. "Once these Prussian lads are past we will get moving again. With luck we can overtake them and get into Albert before they do."

McKim removed the broken pipe from the corner of his mouth. "They might stop for the night, sir."

"They might," Ramsay said. He watched as the last of the Prussians marched past, two immensely broad-shouldered NCOs acting as rear markers.

The Hauptmann with the monocle is not there. Maybe he has been killed.

"Shall I get the lads up, sir?"

Ramsay looked over the few men who remained. They lay around the trees in various positions. Cruickshank's hands were curled around his rifle while Turnbull was curled in a foetal position, cradling his broken wrist. "Yes, we have to get moving."

They waded the River Ancre without difficulty, although as the smallest man there, McKim had some trouble keeping his head above water, but once on the far side they slowed down.

The gunfire was so incessant that Ramsay barely noticed it, but despite obvious resistance, the German advance showed no sign of slowing. Once again Ramsay kept his small command parallel to the Bapaume road that ran right through Albert, and they saw the constant flow of traffic moving in both direction. Reinforcements and replacements marched or rode towards the front, alongside ammunition wagons, guns and supplies, while ambulances rolled eastward, together with an occasional batch of dejected British prisoners.

Twice they heard sudden outbursts of firing and guessed that the British were offering stiffer resistance, but on each occasion the firing died away. The German columns slowed or temporarily halted, only to start again, rolling inexorably westward. As the horse-drawn transports passed the infantry, soldiers shouted greetings and waved their hands and rifles.

They are confident now. They think they are winning the war. Maybe they are.

They passed small groups of dead; the British wore full packs and lay in clusters or extended lines, where they had charged forward.

"Bloody Fritzes are still pushing us back," Cruickshank said. "That's day after day now and we are still running like bloody rabbits."

"At least they died fighting," McKim said. "God rest you, lads."

"Much bloody good it did," Cruickshank said, and they trudged on wearily and with hope diminishing with every yard they covered.

A marching column of infantry split to either side of the pave when a staff car snarled forward, its headlights gleaming yellow in the fading light.

"Bloody red tabs. The Hun variety is just as bad as ours." Cruickshank hefted the rifle on his shoulder.

"Save your breath." McKim looked at Ramsay. "I wish Flockhart was still with us, sir."

I wish they were all still with us: Mackay and Buchanan and Aitken and Edwards and Niven and all the rest. What a terrible waste of good men.

"Well he's not, McKim, and there's nothing that we can do about it now. Keep marching."

"They're after Albert," Cruickshank said. "They're after the Golden Virgin."

Ramsay said nothing. An officer did not exchange small talk with his men, it was bad for discipline. Cruickshank was right. The Germans hoped to capture Albert. He remembered the bustle of the town just a few days ago when he was on his way to the Front, and wondered how it was that so important a centre, with so many men, could possibly be in danger from the German advance. If they were successful in taking Albert, what was next? Amiens?

"Something's happened," McKim said. "Listen."

"Wait, lads. Halt just now." Ramsay put a hand on McKim's arm. "What is it, corporal?"

"The Huns have halted."

McKim was right. The constant thump of boots had fallen silent and there was no sound of grinding wheels.

"They've stopped," McKim said. "May I have permission to have a decko, sir?" He threw a very rare salute.

"Take care," Ramsay nodded, and McKim slipped away into the dark. Ramsay listened to the sounds of the night. A German voice barked a guttural order. There was soft German singing and somebody played a plaintive tune on a melodeon until another harsh order silenced both.

"Keep your rifles ready, lads. Fritz might send out patrols."

Musketry sounded ahead, joined by the chatter of a machine gun, and then silence. A flare slid skyward to the west, hung like a suspended floodlight and slowly descended. Darkness returned and with it the spatter of rifles as nervous owners targeted imaginary enemies in the night.

A single shot sounded, close to, and the yell of a challenge. Another shot, a third and then silence.

McKim? Have the Germans shot McKim?

A shell whizzed down to explode a few yards from the road. For an instant the explosion silhouetted the traffic on the road; a string of supply wagons was motionless along the centre of the road. The horses stood with their heads bowed as they rested from their life of toil. Around the wagons, spread in regular lines and lying in neat groups, were German infantry.

When the light died the darkness was stygian: thick and threatening and pregnant with menace.

Ramsay blinked to try and recapture some of the night vision that the shell had shattered. He peered toward the road and hoped the Germans would stay put. He glanced behind them, where their train still smouldered red on the horizon. One fire among many.

That's where Flockhart died; that's where I regained my freedom from worry. That's where I lost more of my men. That was the last train to Waverley Station.

A flare burst overhead, revealing a change in the landscape. The road narrowed as it squeezed between a thick hedge and a steep embankment. It would be a perfect place for an ambush. If he commanded the defence of Albert, he would place a Vickers machine gun there and delay the Germans for hours. The Germans knew their stuff: that would be why they halted.

The thought hit him like a douche of cold water. With the British in full retreat, the war might not last long. If he was to walk up to the nearest German and surrender, he could sit in comfort until peace came and then get back to Gillian and the sane life of an Edinburgh solicitor.

I would survive. I have done my bit for King and country now, surely. I have killed my quota of Germans and led my men to the best of my meagre ability. I am no soldier; I never wanted to be a soldier; they can't expect me to do any more, please God, they can't expect more from me.

Ramsay sat down and leaned against the bole of a tree, slumped forward and buried his face in cupped hands.

How much longer will this nightmare last? How many more days will I wake up shaking and bathed in sweat, how many more days will I spend pretending to be brave so my men do not realise I am quaking in terror; how many more nights will I close my eyes praying not be killed in the fearful hours of darkness. Every time I light a cigar I flinch in case a sniper is peering at me down the barrel of a rifle; every time I drop my trousers in the latrine I pray not to be wounded or killed in that most undignified of positions; I pray not to be emasculated by shot or shell, or hideously disfigured so that Gillian recoils from me in horror.

How much longer; oh, God, how much longer can I take this, before my mind breaks like Aitken's or that young German soldier, and I lie gibbering in an endless nightmare that is no worse than this reality?

"The whole bloody German army has stopped." McKim appeared out of the darkness, unseen and unheard. "There is no movement as far as I can see. The advance has stopped."

"Or maybe we have stopped it," Cruickshank said.

"Maybe we have," Turnbull said.

"Are you all right, sir?" McKim sat beside him. His eyes were concerned, more like a father to a son than an NCO to an officer, but suddenly Ramsay did not care. McKim was a good man; he would be a good man in any society and class.

"I'm just a bit tired, Corporal," Ramsay said. "Thank you."

This is our chance; we can get back to our own lines. Surrender? Not a bloody chance; I will get my men home safe and get back to Gillian as a hero officer and not as a coward. She would not know, but I would.

Ramsay raised his voice. "Right, lads. Fritz has stopped for the night. We won't. We will get past him and march right into Albert. General Gough seems to have halted the German advance so hopefully the line has stabilised now."

CHAPTER TEN

ALBERT

26 March 1918

There was no barbed wire, no series of trenches, not even a proper sequence of outposts and strong points. After three and a half years of static warfare the front had opened up into a war of fluid movement, but rather than the British pushing eastward for Berlin, they were running westward, leaving a trail of discarded equipment, abandoned wagons and broken men and horses behind them.

"Halt!" The challenge was abrupt and unexpected. Ramsay stopped at once.

"Who the hell are you?" The accent was English, coarse and flat.

"Lieutenant Douglas Ramsay, 20th Royal Scots, and don't you know to salute when you address an officer? And you call me sir!" He barked the words instinctively although he felt like weeping at the sound of a British voice again, after so many days wandering behind German lines.

"Oh. Sorry, sir." The Englishman did not sound sorry. "I was not sure who you were. You came in from the German side."

Ramsay did not respond, the man was merely a private. "Where is your officer?"

The Englishman shrugged. "I don't know, sir. Most of the unit pulled out earlier today and left a few of us as rearguard. As soon as orders come we are moving too."

"Where is your sergeant, then?" Ramsay said. "Or whoever is in charge."

The Englishman snorted. "Christ knows where anybody is, or who's in charge now."

"You say sir when addressing an officer," McKim snarled, "and stand to attention, you slovenly creature! What kind of soldier are you?"

"Sorry, sir." The Englishman stiffened to attention.

"Are you saying the army is not going to try and defend Albert?" Ramsay asked.

As if a mere private soldier would know. Pull yourself together, man!

"I don't think so, sir."

"Carry on then, private," Ramsay ordered. He hid his bitter disappointment. He had hoped to find an organised defence, with a proper military hierarchy, and instead he had walked into chaos and confusion. The world he had known for the past three and a half years had turned upside down.

"There's no front line here," McKim said. He hefted his rifle, checked the magazine and worked the bolt. "There is nothing to hold on to and Fritz is going to walk right in." He glanced at Ramsay, "Unless you organise a defence, sir?"

Ramsay felt the fear return at this new responsibility McKim expected him to assume.

Oh, God, no. I can't! I am not a real soldier. I am just here to keep Gillian happy.

"If that Durham is there, there might be others, sir. You can gather them all together and stop the Fritzes. They won't be expecting anything . . ." He looked up with hope bright in his dirty face.

An hour ago I was contemplating surrendering and spending a peaceful duration, now I am being persuaded to organise the defence of Albert against half the German army. Trust McKim to know exactly what regiment that private was from.

But what a thought; what would Gillian think if I went back as the man who held Albert and stopped the German advance?

Ramsay nodded. "Let's show them what Royal Scots can do, McKim." Despite his tiredness he smiled at the expression on the corporal's face. "See how many men you can gather; I don't care what unit they are from, just bring them together. Start with that Durham."

Ramsay remembered Albert as a bustling transit town, damaged by German shelling but still functioning, with busy shops and a population confident that the British Army could protect them from the German hordes. Now he saw a town in terror. Lamps lit the night time streets and people were packing up their belongings and loading them onto carts, horses or mules.

"I have never seen such fear," Turnbull said. "These poor people are terrified of the Huns."

We have let them down. We came with our guns and our arrogance and our confidence that the great British Empire could defend the citizens of Albert and all of France from the rapacious hordes of Prussia. Instead here we are, running like khaki rabbits and not even attempting to defend these poor people. Imagine if this was Edinburgh and the Hun was at the gate with their rape and pillage and slaughter; how would I feel?

What if Gillian was waiting helpless for Fritz with his usual Hun frightfulness?

Ramsay saw an old woman stumbling up the street with all the worldly possessions she could carry balanced in her frail arms. He saw entire families crowding onto carts piled high with furniture, bags and baggage, children crying as their mothers held them tight and their fathers led the horse. He saw women gathered in corners, weeping in despair and fear at the prospect of German occupation. He saw an ancient man with a long moustache standing in his doorway, weeping uncontrollably and knew the sad reality of war.

"Jesus," Cruickshank breathed out as he loosened his bayonet in its scabbard, "these poor bastards."

"Is this the defence line, sir?" The speaker was a small man in the uniform of the Army Service Corps.

Ramsay nodded, wearily at first and then grimly as his resolution strengthened. "Yes. This is where we will make our stand. You are ASC?"

The small man nodded. "Yes, sir." He was around fifty, his steep helmet lying low on his head. He threw a crooked salute that would have disgraced a schoolboy. "878, Private Timms, sir."

"Have you seen much action?"

"Not yet, sir. Everybody thought I was too old and unfit." The man stood as erect as he could.

Good God. He's a bald old man with bad eyesight, but he is volunteering to stay and fight while others run.

"Good man, Timms, you'll do. Let's see how many more men we can find and we'll give old Fritz a fright, eh?"

Timms smiled and immediately attempted to look martial and tough, an image he promptly spoiled by almost dropping his rifle.

Ramsay ignored the racket of the fleeing evacuees as he tried to work out some sort of defensive plan. He had a tiny force of men and only a few weapons, while there was an entire army of efficient Germans waiting to occupy Albert as soon as their commander gave the order.

When will they come? When would I come? Just before dawn so the advancing men have the advantage of growing light.

"I found these lads doing nothing, sir," McKim encouraged three unshaven privates forward with the point of his bayonet. "They claim that their regiment left them behind and they have been searching for another unit to join."

The men shambled to attention in front of Ramsay. In the dark he could not make out the insignia on their uniforms.

"Welcome to the new front line, lads." He was not sure he had managed to keep the irony from his voice. He jerked his thumb in an eastward direction. "Fritz is coming from out there," he nodded to the town, "and he wants to take Albert. We are going to stop him."

None of his new recruits looked particularly enthusiastic at the prospect.

"You men have the chance to make history if you stand firm and do your duty." Ramsay looked for signs of agreement on their faces, but they merely looked sullen. "What are your names?"

There was a few moments' silence then the nearest man muttered: "Smith, sir, 456."

"Jones, sir, 768"

A longer pause and then, "Perkins, sir, 973."

That last name could have been genuine but Ramsay suspected that the others were not.

Are these men deserters? Or men who were genuinely left behind and are so demoralised that they just hoped to surrender. I was thinking that myself not long ago. Are we so close to defeat that we are willing to give up?

"We have a chance to dent the German advance boys! You could help win the war."

There was still no response so Ramsay sharpened his tone. "I expect you to fight. Dig yourself a trench and fortify it with sandbags. God knows there are plenty lying around. Carry on."

Ramsay acknowledged their too-brief salutes and paced where he intended to make his stand. He had no barbed wire, only a handful of tired men and no heavy armament to stop half the German army.

"I know you bastards were ready to desert or surrender," he heard McKim's snarl through the gloom. "Well, I've been around too long to let that happen. I am Corporal McKim of the Royal Scots, First of Foot, right of the line and pride of the British Army. Remember the name. If any of you run from here I will hunt you down and shoot you like a dog!"

Ramsay hid his smile. Maybe the Germans were making huge inroads, but as long as the British army had men such as McKim, there was hope. The Prussian Guards might kill him eventually, but they would never defeat him.

More men came in through the night. They arrived in ones and twos, a couple of cooks, a beribboned veteran with a fierce moustache who almost rivalled Cruickshank for truculence, a duo of bewildered storemen and three men that McKim winkled out of an estaminet.

"Here are three drunken sods for you, sir. Some sort of fusiliers I think, but not the best sort." McKim pushed them forward. "Stand to attention you miserable bastards! That's a real officer you are addressing, not some dugout king!"

Ramsay appreciated the implied compliment. A dugout king was an officer who stayed out of danger; McKim was quietly telling him that he was now recognised as a fighting man.

Dear God, I am accepted. The old veteran thinks I am of some use.

"You three, get sober and get digging. We have a town to defend."

Turnbull unearthed two more volunteers, men who had been left behind when the bulk of the army retreated and he ushered them to Ramsay.

"Here we are sir; two more rifles."

The men stared at Ramsay as if he were some sort of ogre until McKim roared at them to stand to attention and "at least try to look like soldiers and not tailor's dummies wearing dirty khaki!"

Ramsay smiled. "Don't mind him, lads. He's a corporal, he can't speak without shouting and he can't shout without an insult. It's a gift that all corporals are born with."

The two relaxed slightly but still stared wide-eyed at him.

"So what unit did you lads belong to?"

One wore spectacles with thick lenses; the other was about three stone underweight and stood with a permanent stoop.

"We are shoemakers, sir," the spectacled man stuttered, "but we want to help stop the Germans."

"Shoemakers," Cruikshank said in the background. "Jesus help us – shoemakers. I bet Kaiser Bill is shaking in his boots."

"Well, a shoemaker can shoot as straight as anybody else." Ramsay did not smile. "Welcome aboard, lads. Corporal McKim will find you shovels and you can start to dig a trench. You will do fine."

As the hands on his watch gradually circled toward dawn, the train still burned toward Carnoy and stars appeared in the sky. Ramsay heard a drift of singing from the German positions. He recognised the song that the Prussian Guards had regaled them with a few days earlier.

"Shall we sing back, sir?" McKim asked. "We can let them know the Royals are still here."

"No!" Ramsay said firmly. "We want them to think that the place is undefended. There are so few of us that our only advantage is surprise."

As more men joined Ramsay's force he had created a defensive line about two hundred yards long, only a fraction of the perimeter of Albert, but hopefully long enough to at least stall the German advance.

We cannot possibly halt them, but if we delay them for only an hour or so, we might give our army time to form a better defence.

Ramsay checked his watch. Four in the morning and dawn was pink in the east. Dew formed on the grass in front of the makeshift trenches, pale-glittering in the starlight.

"Stand to, boys. They might probe with a raiding party." He watched as his warriors - reluctant, eager or resigned - woke up, stretched, yawned and took up their positions. One by one rifles protruded, ready to greet the Germans with at least a show of resistance.

He paced the length of his front. His flanks were based on two solid houses, both of which he had tried to form into strongpoints by sandbagging the windows and doors and placing determined men inside. With no machine guns they would have to rely on their personal weapons, but massed musketry had scared the Germans at Mons, and might work again.

Unfortunately I don't have a mass of men, and certainly not of the superb quality that we had at Mons. Oh, for a hundred of the Old Contemptibles! I would flatten the front ranks of the Prussians.

He looked at his hodgepodge collection of drunks, cooks, clerks and laggards. It was hardly an inspiring sight, despite the thin scattering of his own Royals and the few veterans McKim had managed to scrape up from the depths of Albert.

Timms was scowling fiercely at the slowly rising sun, with his helmet pushed well over his face and his bayonet fixed and ready.

"Are you fully loaded, Timms?" Ramsay asked kindly and Timms nodded.

"Yes, sir. I am ready for them."

"Good man. That's the spirit." Ramsay thought of the tall, broad and highly trained Prussian Guards who were probably already assembling a couple of miles away and hid his fear. Timms had all the guts in the world, but he would need much more to stand a chance against the military machine that was the German army. In the last sixty years the Prussians had swept aside the Danes, Austrians, French and Russians, as well as flattening all opposition in Africa in their march to a world power. Now it was Britain's turn to face them.

And what do we have in opposition? Private Albert Timms, never having fired a gun in anger, with shaking hands and a shrapnel helmet two sizes too large for his head. God save us all.

"Plenty food at least." McKim joined him in his tour of the trenches, handing out French bread and glasses of wine. "There's no rum, boys but vin blank is bon, eh?" He was smiling and as jaunty as ever, his broken pipe emitting aromatic smoke and sandbag-sacking protecting the bolt of his rifle.

And then we have McKim.

The men did not object to wine and when the veterans began to brew up tea, Ramsay said nothing. Whatever aided morale could only be helpful when they faced impossible odds.

McKim stiffened slightly. "Fritz is singing," he said softly. "He must think he has won the war."

The sound filled the pinking sky; the same deep-throated

210

melody they had heard before as a thousand Prussians boasted of their love for their fatherland.

"Musical buggers aren't they, sir?" McKim sucked at his pipe.

"They are," Ramsay agreed. "Good soldiers, too."

McKim considered. "Not bad," he conceded, "but a bit limited. They are efficient at this sort of warfare. If we faced them on the veldt we would run rings round them."

Ramsay smiled. "I am sure we would, McKim, and once this war is won we can return to the old days."

Ramsay looked around. Their train was still glowing red but the dawn was stronger now, streaking the eastern sky with bands of ochre red. A wind ruffled the grass and carried a whiff of smoke and the distinctive sour aroma created by tens of thousands of men living without proper sanitary facilities.

"They will be coming soon then," McKim said calmly. He took the pipe from his mouth and added more tobacco to the bowl. "Well, death and hell to them all."

"Death and hell to them," Ramsay echoed. He checked that his revolver was fully loaded. "Good luck, McKim. If anybody gets through this, it will be you." He surprised himself and held out his hand.

McKim hesitated and then tentatively accepted the handshake. His hands were surprisingly small, but hard as granite callused along the base of the fingers. They shook gingerly and then both tightened their grip in an act of mutual respect.

"Good luck, sir," McKim said.

The Prussians came just as the first low rays of the sun crested the eastern horizon. Ramsay blinked and tried to shield his eyes.

Clever buggers, the Hun. We are half-blinded by the sun.

He saw movement ahead and readied his revolver. He had expected the Prussians to come in their long, extended lines that only death stopped, but instead there were a few scattered parties of men, walking cautiously over the sloping ground as they approached the shattered town of Albert.

"Scouts," he said. "Keep low and don't fire. There are only a few of them. McKim, once they have passed us, take two men and deal with them. Quietly."

"Prisoners, sir?" McKim drew his smoke-blackened bayonet from its scabbard. The sight carried so much menace that Ramsay almost felt sorry for the German infantry.

The German scouts were within a few yards when Timms opened fire. "There they are!" He shouted, "I see them, sir! It's the Germans!"

The scouts dropped immediately and Ramsay cursed. His plan had depended on the discipline inherent in regular or at least experienced troops, but most of his tiny command was neither. Once the first shot was fired there was no point in remaining quiet.

"Fire, lads! Shoot them flat!"

It was easy to distinguish the steady, rapid fire of the veterans from the staccato fusillade from the inexperienced, but the combined result knocked down half a dozen of the scouts and sent the rest scurrying for shelter.

"Cease fire!" Ramsay ordered. *No sense in letting Fritz know exactly how many of us there are.*

"McKim, if you see movement, shoot. The rest of you, all of you, including you Timms, hold your fire until I give a direct order."

The artillery fire began five minutes later, a short, intensive bombardment from light guns that landed mainly behind Ramsay's position and added to the devastation of the town. And then the infantry came in.

They advanced in long lines with bayonets fixed, tall men silhouetted against the rising sun, a light rolling barrage flattening everything in front of them. Ramsay kept his men down until the shellfire had stopped and then watched the infantry advance.

"Saxons, I think," McKim said casually as he aimed. "Or maybe Wurtenbergians. They're not Prussians at any rate."

"Hold your fire," Ramsay ordered. The Germans were quarter of a mile away and walking rapidly. The first line was extending to overlap their position.

Damn! I can't do anything about it. Keep calm. Do as much damage as we can and see what transpires.

"Hold your fire!" he repeated.

The Germans were four hundred yards away now and still approaching steadily. Ramsay could make out the features of individuals; he could see the officers marching in front and the NCOs at regular intervals keeping the line precise.

They were three hundred yards away now – about five hundred German infantry against his twenty-two scattered and half-trained men.

Two hundred and fifty yards and still they came. McKim had ignored the officers and had his rifle pointed firmly at one of the senior NCOs. As an old soldier he knew that they were the backbone of any military formation. Officers could come and go, but sergeants were the lifeblood, the soul and the experience of any army. Kill them and the officers were left with nobody to translate their orders to the private soldiers.

Two hundred yards. *Oh, God. I will have to give the order soon.*

McKim glanced at him. His finger was curled around the trigger, already white under the pressure.

One hundred and fifty yards. Even his most inexperienced men could not miss at this range.

Ramsay stood up so he could clearly be seen. "Fire!"

He pointed his revolver at the mass of Germans and squeezed the trigger as the British opened up. The initial volley was ragged, but it still tore holes in the German line. As the firing continued, the veterans made the most of the close range and the element of surprise, firing their fifteen aimed shots a minute and the enemy fell in droves. Ramsay distinctly heard the German officers shouting orders. He aimed at the closest and fired: two, three, four shots. The man turned around, a look of surprise on his face, then he crumpled and fell.

Ramsay reloaded as his men fired, worked their bolts and fired again. He heard Timms shouting and McKim giving his habitual slogan of "Death and hell to you" as he fired. He saw the leading German line falter, lifted his revolver and aimed at the next German officer. Something tugged at the skirts of his coat, but he ignored it and fired until that officer fell, then looked for his next target.

"They're running!" Timms sounded excited. "We've beat the Germans!" He hauled himself out of his trench and took a few steps forward until McKim grabbed hold of his collar and threw him back.

"Get back in there, you bloody idiot!"

"Keep firing!" Ramsay emptied his revolver. "The more we kill the less likely they are to return."

His scratch force responded with a will, knocking down another dozen Germans before Ramsay called a halt. "Withdraw to the shelter of the town, lads. Fritz won't be pleased at us."

He left the details to McKim, who responded as though withdrawing a tiny rag-tag bunch of soldiers only half a mile away from a huge German army was something he did every week. The shells began to land before the men were all clear and Timms screamed in sudden fear.

"Run, Timms!" McKim shouted, "Don't mind the shine!"

The shells landed in groups of six, plastering the positions the British had so recently vacated, throwing up great columns of mud and soil and the remains of sandbags.

The lyddite fumes had not yet cleared when the German infantry came again.

"That's not the Saxons this time," McKim said quietly. "That's the bloody Prussians."

"Get back in line, boys, and bowl them over!" Ramsay led the men back to their old positions. A couple of stray shells exploded and a machine gun began its insistent chatter, spraying the line of defences so that now his men had to throw themselves behind the meagre cover left by the bombardment.

The Prussians advanced faster than their predecessors – two long lines of tall men carrying fixed bayonets and led by the usual quota of brave officers.

"This lot won't be stopped by a few casualties," McKim commented.

"Maybe not, but we'll send as many to hell as we can." Ramsay said. He felt a new sort of madness, a crazed desire to stop the Prussians by any means he could.

"Come on, Fritz! Come on! Die for your Kaiser! Up the Royals!"

Ramsay stepped forward from the trenches and opened fire. He heard himself cheering as he faced the still-distant Prussians. "Come on you Prussian bastards! Come and face the Royals!"

The words were unheard amidst the growing crackle of musketry as the defenders opened fire and the Prussians continued to advance. They seemed huge in the morning light, rank after rank moving inexorably in an impersonal advance, covering the ground with methodical skill.

"Death and hell to you!" McKim was shouting, but his firing was unhurried, professional as he aimed each shot.

"Oh, God! Oh, God, there's thousands of them!" That was an English voice. One of the shoemakers perhaps, but its owner was still firing, still keeping his position despite the danger.

"Get back in cover, sir!" McKim was beside him. "We need you alive!"

Sanity returned as Ramsay realised what he was doing. He was standing a full two yards in front of the British position in full view of the Prussians, a lone officer with a pistol, facing hundreds of enemy infantry.

What would Gillian think of me if she saw me? Would she think I am her Hector, a hero of antiquity?

"Get back, you bloody fool!" McKim made no secret of his feelings. "You're an officer, not a bloody recruit looking for a medal! You'll catch a bullet sure as death!" The corporal stopped firing for a moment to grab Ramsay's tunic and haul him back to the meagre shelter of the sandbags.

Putting a hand on an officer is probably against Kings Regulations. I could have him court martialled for that . . .

"Thanks, McKim," Ramsay said. A machine gun opened up and bullets sprayed the front of the British positions. Somewhere on his left a man screamed, high-pitched and agonised.

"Keep firing boys! Send them back!"

There were gaps in the German lines, but they kept advancing. The officers gave an order and they quickened their pace from a fast walk to a trot and then lowered their bayonets and began to charge.

"We can't stop them! Run boys!"

Ramsay looked along the line. The man who had called himself Smith had left his position and was backing away.

He dropped his rifle, turned and began to run, screaming as his panic overcame him. One of his companions, the man named Jones, quickly followed.

"Smith! Get back in line!" McKim whirled round and aimed his rifle at the fleeing man.

"Leave him, McKim. Let him go!" Ramsay understood McKim's reasoning, for panic could easily spread and Smith and Jones' example might lead to a mass exodus. "Concentrate on the Germans. Those men are not worth your attention."

The Prussians were about seventy yards away and coming fast despite the gaps in their ranks. Ramsay estimated that there were three hundred in the front line alone. He glanced along the defensive line. He had twenty men, about half of whom were front line soldiers.

Do we fight to the death or retreat? The boys are shaky already.

The decision was taken from him as Turnbull shouted, "They're behind us! We're outflanked!"

Prussians were pouring in either side of Ramsay's small group, some stopping to kneel and fire, others advancing at speed, their long bayonets snaking forward.

Ramsay had no time to give the order. His line collapsed as his mix of deserters, shoemakers and odds and sods broke and ran. Only the Royals remained, together with Timms, who was still firing when Ramsay gave the order to retire to the village.

"But we can beat them!" Timms screamed.

"Come on, you stupid bastard!" McKim grabbed his collar and hauled him back.

Ramsay left three dead behind, including the moustached veteran who was slouched over a sandbag, still facing the enemy.

"Back to the houses, lads," Ramsay ordered.

I have ordered more retreats than advances, yet again.

"We held them for a few minutes at least," he shouted, but McKim corrected him.

"We held them for more than an hour sir; that's more than the generals could do."

"Do you know Albert, McKim?" Ramsay stopped to fire three shots at the advancing Prussians. None took effect. The Prussians on the flanks joined those who had been in the frontal attack. They stopped to dress their lines.

"Yes, sir," McKim said. "I have been here before."

"Can you guide us through the streets?" Ramsay reloaded as he moved. His men were scattered, the Royals a compact group and most of the others running ahead.

I should call them back, but for what purpose? Let them go; they did their bit.

"Yes, sir. Are we leaving Albert now?" McKim shoved a magazine into his rifle and ducked as Prussian bullets gouged holes in the wall immediately behind him.

"As fast as we can, McKim," Ramsay said.

McKim nodded and shoved his pipe back in his mouth. "This way lads. We'll leave by the Amiens Road. If any Huns get in the way we'll send the bastards to hell!"

The Germans were close behind them as McKim led the British in a crazy race over the cobbled streets of Albert. The Cathedral tower still stood, but the Virgin and Child, the symbol that had withstood a hundred German bombardments, was down now, felled by a British shell. The figure lay in Cathedral Square, its gold face battered and still somehow accusing as Ramsay ran past.

"Nothing much left here," said McKim. Artillery had pounded the buildings surrounding the square to piles of rubble. A few civilians remained, cowering for shelter as the

Germans poured in and the last of the British stragglers ran for their lives.

Their boots crunched over sacred mosaics and more pedestrian fragments of brick and stone, scraps of paper littered the streets and the smoke of a score of fires drifted between the buildings.

"Over there!" Turnbull ran awkwardly, still cradling his broken wrist, but he managed to indicate the junction of the Amiens Road and the Millencourt Road. A shell had blasted open the ground and the main town drains were exposed, seeping noxious fumes into a place already made filthy by lyddite and rubble and the ugly hint of gas. "Germans!"

Ramsay saw the distinctive round helmets of German infantry amongst the rubble; they swarmed forward bravely, dozens, scores of them. Their long bayonets caught the morning sun and their faces were set and determined and grim as they advanced along the Millencourt Road, the officer in front holding a pistol and roaring orders.

"There's more, sir." McKim pointed behind them, along the Amiens Road. A long column of Prussians were approaching, shoulder to shoulder across half the width of the street, marching in utter silence except for the steady crunch of their boots. "And there." Cruickshank aimed and fired, worked the bolt of his rifle and fired again. "There are hundreds of the woman-murdering bastards!"

"They're ahead too," McKim said. "They're everywhere, sir." His voice was calm as he stopped running and stood in the doorway of a house, chewing on his pipe.

Is this it? Is this the end of our war?

Ramsay called his men to a halt. They gathered around him, some panting, some clearly scared, Cruickshank as truculent as ever. He looked around. German soldiers were in every direction, marching, running, laughing, joking. The enemy had taken Albert and were celebrating their triumph.

"Where to, sir?" McKim was kneeling behind a pile of rubble with his rifle at the ready. "Where to?"

Where to? We are surrounded by thousands of Huns for God's sake. There is nowhere left to go. I don't want to surrender now. I want to get back to the British lines.

"Where shall we go, sir?"

"Where shall we go, David?" Grace was smiling as she asked the question. There was such hope in her eyes that Ramsay almost felt affection for her. "Where shall we get married? Your church or mine?"

She patted his arm and moved closer as they walked through the sun-blessed field towards the cool water of the South Esk.

Ramsay shook his head and wondered if he could just push her away and make a run for it, but with Rab acting as chaperone only a few yards behind, he did not think he would get far. "I think your church would be best, Grace."

He tried to imagine Grace meeting his family or standing at the altar of St Andrews and St George's in George Street, with the elite of Edinburgh gathered all around. She would be in her shabby best, completely overawed by the educated voices and intelligent conversation of judges and advocates and businessmen; she would also be plump and pregnant and a figure of veiled contempt. As would he of course; men of the Ramsay family simply did not mix with mining stock from Midlothian.

"My church?" Grace was obviously thrilled at his answer. "Would your family come out here for the wedding? We could gather in father's house before and maybe the men could meet in the Miner's Institute afterwards."

Ramsay shuddered. He had no idea what the Miner's Institute was, but he imagined it to be some drink-sodden den where flat-capped miners downed pints of sour beer before going home to kick their wives. "That sounds delightful," he told her.

"This is Trotter's Bridge," Grace told him as they stood at the parapet of a low bridge with the water churning creamy brown beneath them. "It is my favourite spot in all the world. I often come here to think. We can bring our children here, even if we live in Edinburgh." She pronounced it "Edinbury" and gave a little frown at the same time. "I'll miss my mother but I dare say I'll get used to living in the city. Will your mother talk to me?"

That last question was fired at him out of the blue and suddenly Ramsay realised that Grace was not quite the simpleton he had imagined her to be. She was just as aware of their class differences as he was.

Grace continued: "My father won't talk much to you. He will see you as a 'toonie' and won't think much of a man who doesn't work with his hands."

The contempt would be two-sided then; miner to solicitor as well as solicitor to miner.

"We will not be welcomed in either family, David," Grace surprised him further with her acumen. "So where will we go, David? We can go to Newtongrange and be shunned by my family or go to Edinburgh to be ignored by yours." She perched her plump little bottom on the parapet of the bridge and faced him squarely, "Or we can go somewhere new that is just for us – you and me and our family. Where will we go?"

Ramsay made his decision. With the Germans all around, there was no choice.

"We don't go anywhere, lads. This is it I'm afraid. We dig in and stay right here."

They looked at him, Cruickshank with his hatred of everything German, McKim with his decades of military experience, Turnbull with his injuries and all the newcomers, cooks, shoemakers and sundry hangers-on. They had all depended on him to lead them and he had led them to ultimate defeat.

"This is as far as we go." Ramsay looked around. The street was a shambles of ruined houses and shell craters, and a single house set back from the road. He looked closely at the house: it had restricted access so it would be difficult for the Germans to approach without being seen

That will do.

The nearest German was about a hundred yards away, fast approaching with only a few shattered shops between them. "At Waterloo and Omdurman we formed a square, here we will do the same. Form all round positions and we will hold out at long as our ammunition lasts and then we try and break out if we can or . . ."

"Or we surrender?" Cruickshank slid his bayonet from its scabbard and clicked it into place. "No bloody surrender, sir. I'm not surrendering to the Huns."

McKim grinned, moved the broken pipe from his mouth and nodded. "I've been in four wars and God alone knows how many actions, sir. I've fought Boers, Germans, Pathans, and hunted dacoits in Burma. I have never surrendered in my life and I don't intend to start now. As Cruickshank says – no bloody surrender." He raised his voice in a roar that carried across the street and must have been heard by every German within two hundred yards. "Up the Royals! Royal Sco-o-o-o-ots!"

"Enough!" Ramsay cut short McKim's rousing slogans. He pointed to the house. "In there, lads, and hold out."

They scurried in, pushing at each other to kick down the

door and rush inside. Timms hovered outside, pointing his rifle in the general direction of the Prussian Guards.

"Get in, Timms. What the hell are you waiting for?"

"After you, sir," Timms said, probably the most surprising thing that Ramsay had ever heard on a battlefield in his life. "It's not polite to enter in front of an officer and a gentleman."

Ramsay grabbed hold of the collar of his tunic and physically shoved him through the broken door. "In you get, you bloody idiot! This is no time for politeness!"

The interior of the house had been partially cleared by the owners, but there was still furniture and some household possessions. Ramsay took a quick look around. "You two, close the door and barricade it with the table. Cruickshank, shoot any Fritz who even looks at us. McKim, take six men upstairs and keep the front clear. Let's make a nuisance of ourselves as long as we can."

They smashed the remaining panes of the windows with rifle butts, dragged the furniture across as additional protection and settled into position.

Every minute Fritz grants us makes us stronger, but where the hell are they? They know we are here, they should be swarming all over us by now.

Ramsay checked his watch: midday. They had been in the house for a full five minutes and still not a single shot had been fired at them. There was a great deal of noise outside; singing and shouting and the sound of breaking glass, but the shooting had ended, save for the occasional British shell bursting within the town. Ramsay stood beside the window and cautiously looked outside. His view was restricted, but there were no Germans in the small alley that led to their house.

"McKim!" Ramsay shouted, "What's happening up there?"

"Fritz is having a party, sir," came McKim's reply. "He's looting everything in sight."

Ramsay mounted the narrow wooden stairs two at a time. Even on the upper floor his view was restricted, he saw only a small section of the Amiens Road, and a dozen German soldiers looting a shop.

"I've never known that before," he said to McKim. "What has happened to the famous German discipline?"

McKim took the pipe from his mouth. "In my youth," he said, and he smiled faintly, as if reliving an experience from a very long time ago, "the boys still wore red coats, and we were notorious for drunken brawls. On weekends, or before a regiment was posted abroad, garrison towns lived in fear of mobs of Tommies on the batter.   Now . . . ?" He shrugged and replaced the pipe. "We are soft as shit, sir. There's hardly a peep out of us when we have leave, but I think the old spirit is still there, somewhere."

Ramsay waited. He guessed that McKim had not yet reached the point of his story.

"I think the Germans are like that. They have a reputation for fearsome discipline that makes them scared to act in case the officers hammer them. They must have lost tens of thousands of men in their advance. We've seen the ambulances remember, and now they have come to a town of temptation." He shrugged. "Their discipline has collapsed."

Ramsay nodded. "You look after the house, McKim. I am going out to see what is happening. Fritz should have attacked us a long time ago."

"You can't go alone, sir!" McKim put a hand on his sleeve and withdrew it immediately. "Sorry, sir!"

"I'll go alone."

Who else could I take? The only man here I could trust is McKim himself and somebody has to take care of things here. Turnbull is injured, Cruickshank is on a hair trigger and could erupt at any time and the rest simply lack the experience.

It was easier to slide out of a window than to unblock the door and once in the street Ramsay moved into the side to try and merge with the shadows.

He moved slowly, aware that he had only his wits and a revolver to pit against thousands of trained and dangerous German soldiers. He could hear the sounds of breaking glass and of laughter. Somebody was singing, but not the usual German martial song; it was more raucous, higher – a drinking song.

He moved into the Amiens Road, slid into the shelter of a deep doorway and stopped.

Good God! Is this the fearsome German army?

The whole street was in chaos. Soldiers from half a dozen different German units were roaming around, laden with items looted from shops and houses. One man was wearing a woman's dress and giggling drunkenly; another had smashed the neck of a champagne bottle and was swallowing the contents in huge gulps; a third had dragged a chest of drawers into the street and was systematically emptying them one by one.

The more Ramsay looked, the more chaos he could see. A group of Bavarians sat cross-legged around a table, laughing as they wolfed down bread and what looked like old cheese. A mob of Saxons, led by a fierce-looking sergeant, passed around a bottle of brandy, taking a swallow each and singing songs. There were a number of young private soldiers sprawled in various positions along the street, drunk, fatigued or having just decided that they needed a break from the business of killing and being killed.

The German Army has broken down. If only I had sufficient

*men I could counter attack now and push them right back to
their starting line*

Ramsay heard the snarl of a motor vehicle and shrunk
further into the doorway. He took the revolver from its
holster and waited. That was a lighter sound than a lorry, it
had sounded like a car.

*Only staff officers drive cars. If the German higher
command is coming here, they must think that this area is
secure.*

Ramsay inched forward with his revolver extended. He
saw the staff car drive into the Amiens Road and halt. The
driver got out, stepped to the rear and opened the door. Three
tall men, obviously high-ranking officers by their splendid
uniforms and mud-free boots, emerged and looked at the
shambolic scenes around them.

*Oh, God. You boys are in trouble. Do the Germans still
have the firing squad for neglect of duty and looting? If so,
there will be many customers later when this lot get arrested.*

The staff officers looked around them and then had a
hurried conversation. Ramsay expected an explosion of
wrath, but instead they ignored the scattered soldiers and
dashed into the nearest shop, to emerge a few moments later
laden with bottles and fancy foodstuff.

Dear God! Even the staff are at it!

While one officer opened the boot, the other two ran back
and forward to the shops, bringing out a selection of items,
from bottles of wine to fripperies for their female friends.

Ramsay holstered his pistol and withdrew slowly, then
hurried back to the house.

"Out, lads. Out you come. We're getting out of Albert."

McKim raised his eyebrows but said nothing.

"The Germans are looting Albert from Monday to
Christmas. Even the staff are going crazy. The advance has
stalled and we can get away."

226

McKim was too experienced to rush into danger. He sent Cruickshank and a Durham man named Hedge to guard either end of the alley while he organised the removal of the remainder of the men.

"Don't dawdle!" Now that he was committed, Ramsay was anxious to get away before the German officers took control of their infantry and the advance continued. He shoved Timms forward, "Come on, keep moving. Keep your heads down, try and keep out of sight and move as fast as you can. And keep your rifles ready!"

Ramsay led them at a steady trot, keeping behind houses as much as possible and dropping low whenever a party of German soldiers appeared.

"They must be blind today," Timms said, "we've passed dozens of them." He crouched behind a shattered wall a dozen yards from the Amiens Road and indicated a group of grey-clad soldiers who laughed around a barrel of cognac.

"They're not blind," McKim told him, "but they are preoccupied."

Timms looked blank. "What do you mean? Preoccupied with what?" He struggled to find a more comfortable position.

McKim pushed him further down. "Keep your bloody head down, Timms! Do you know Kipling?"

"Kipling? What's he got to do with anything?" Timms obediently put his head down, but left a leg trailing.

McKim pushed that down as well. "Don't make it easy for Fritz, Timmy. There's nothing their snipers like more than a nice juicy target." He waited until Timms had settled down. "Kipling wrote about loot, Timms, loot. That's what the Huns are after."

"Could we not booby trap something and kill some of them?"

"You bloodthirsty bastard," McKim shook his head. "And you look so innocent, too!"

"The street ahead is clear," Ramsay said. "We can make it to that estaminet across the road, it will hold us all. McKim, you take the rearguard and send me the boys over in groups of three."

The estaminet sat in the middle of a short street of five or six houses. Shellfire had shattered the window and blown in the door, but the Germans had not found it yet. Ramsay estimated the distance as twenty yards, across a cobbled street littered with debris and two dead civilians. The day was bright, with the sun not long past its zenith so there were few shadows for shelter. It all depended whether the Germans were looking in his direction or not.

"Cruickshank, keep me covered."

Once again Ramsay felt that surge of insanity. There was a part of him that welcomed this encounter with danger, this pitting himself against the professionalism of the German army. It was a new sensation with which he was not yet fully comfortable, but it excited him in some unfathomable way.

He grinned. "Good luck, McKim," and stepped into the road.

His boots clattered on the cobbles, raising echoes in the bright street. He moved quickly, counting his steps; twelve, fourteen, eighteen and he was at the door of the estaminet. He dived in. If any German had seen him, they had not reacted.

McKim was watching from a shaded doorway. He looked as efficient as any Prussian. Ramsay waved and a moment later two British soldiers dashed across. The sound of their studded boots on the cobbles sounded like cymbals crashing to Ramsay, but they also crossed without trouble and he began to breathe more easily.

He signalled for the next group and watched as the two

shoemakers and Turnbull left the shelter for the perils of the road. Turnbull ran awkwardly, his rifle in his left hand and his right bouncing in its sling, but he was still faster than the shoemakers, who hesitated halfway. The smaller man stopped to peer up the street.

"Come on man!" Ramsay signalled urgently to him. "Get over here!"

The shoemaker looked at him uncertainly, and then decided to obey. He ran across in an ungainly fashion and entered the estaminet slowly.

"Keep out of the way," Ramsay ordered, "and see if you can find some food in here, the boys need to keep their strength up."

The British crossed in pairs and threes; McKim was the last man over. His pipe was still firmly clenched between his teeth when he entered the estaminet.

"That was easy enough, sir," he said. "Old Fritz is far too busy robbing Albert blind. It's as if he has not seen food for years, the way he's carrying on."

Ramsay nodded. He did not really care how long the Germans had been without food; he only cared that they would concentrate on other things while he led his men out of Albert.

"We are not far from the edge of town," Ramsay said. "So maybe another couple of hops would see us safe."

Safe! We are in the middle of the worst war the world has ever known, with millions of men killed and wounded. There is nothing and nobody safe here.

But I am safer now; Flockhart is dead. I only have to survive this war and life will be sweet, whoever wins.

Ramsay checked the road outside the estaminet. He could hear the Germans singing and shouting but there were none in sight from this spot. He estimated that it was about two hundred yards to the edge of town and then there was open countryside stretching up to a ridge. If the British high command had any sense that ridge was where they would make their stand.

When the Germans left Albert they would have to advance up the slope to face the British, who would have all the advantage of height. Ramsay grimaced; he remembered how hard it had been to move up towards the German positions at the Somme. Now it would be the German's turn to try that particular nightmare.

"Next step, boys, is diagonal, up the street and to the end house," Ramsay indicated the building he had in mind. "From there we should be able to leave the town and hot-foot it up the ridge to our own lines." He ducked as a shell landed in the town behind him. The crash shook the estaminet and a few tiles slipped from the roof to shatter amidst the general debris in the street.

"I see it." McKim had not flinched. "The house with the open door?"

"That's the one." Ramsay ducked again as a trio of shells exploded near the town centre; tall towers of smoke and pieces of rubble rose skyward, the fragments descending and the smoke gradually dispersing in the breeze.

"We'll use the same system," Ramsay said. "I'll go first and ensure it's safe and you send the boys over in small groups." He looked up as a 5.9 inch exploded high above. "We'd better hurry. Our own lot seem to be angry with Albert."

McKim smiled and sang softly:

"Après la guerre finie
Soldat Ecosse parti
Mademoiselle in the family way"

He shrugged. "The war will be over by Christmas, sir, and then we can all go home."

A few weeks back Ramsay would have torn to shreds any ranker who dared be so familiar with him. Now he smiled back. "Let's hope so, McKim; let's hope so."

He surveyed the ground he had to cross. About forty yards this time and over open ground, but the end result would be worth the effort and danger. He took a deep breath, opened the door and stepped out.

Once again he experienced the feeling of exhilaration and heightened fear that jangled all his nerve endings. He was almost tempted to stop in the middle of the road and look around him, but common sense drove him forward, one long stride after another. There was the familiar whoosh of a large calibre shell passing overhead, but he was experienced enough to know that the shell would explode well beyond him so he did not look up.

Thirty yards to go. The cobbles were uneven under his feet; he spotted a child's doll lying on its back. Some small person would be crying sore at its loss. That's if it was still alive; children were so vulnerable even in peacetime.

She was blooming, carrying the new child within her, smiling to everybody as she walked between the uniform streets of brick houses. Ramsay watched her for a full five minutes before he let his presence be known.

"Grace," he said, and saw the genuine pleasure cross her face. If only circumstances were different, he thought, he might be quite attracted to this girl. She was pretty enough, in a plump and coarse way, and he would have no problems with her faithfulness. Grace was as straightforward a girl as he had ever met. Even as things were, he quite liked her at times, despite her obvious shortcomings and the difference in their social status. He *quite* liked her, no more than that.

"I do love you so," Grace told him, openly and loudly in

the middle of the street, to the obvious amusement of the passers by. Not that they mattered, of course. They were merely colliers and their women, or people associated with the mines in some way or another. They were so far beneath him that they barely registered in his mind.

"I love you too," he lied. He linked his arm with hers and walked with her along the main street of Newtongrange, with its many domestic chimneys belching smoke and the gas works chimney and the pit head of the Lady Victoria Colliery dominating everything.

"I thought you might be here sooner." Grace was not complaining, Ramsay knew. She was only voicing whatever ideas ran through her mind at that instant. He did not expect she had developed her mental powers sufficiently to control the space between thoughts and voice.

"I got here as quickly as I could," Ramsay said. They stopped outside the Dean Tavern and he contemplated taking her inside. Were women permitted entry to such places?

"When will you take me to meet your family, David?" Grace asked bluntly.

Ramsay had expected that question. "My father is in India," he lied easily, "and my mother does not keep well at all. I do not think she could cope with the shock of me being engaged to wed."

"You mean she would disapprove of you being engaged to a miner's daughter and not some Edinburgh girl."

"You are my choice," he told her and pulled her towards him.

A light rain pressed the smoke down on the streets so every breath inhaled miniscule particles of soot and every inch of his clothing was contaminated and dirty within minutes. Ramsay looked around at the men and women who lived in this environment every moment of their lives, as their parents and grandparents had before them. He expected to see depression and dejection, shuffling people pressed down by their lives but instead he saw hard pride and a tight-knit community.

A group of men passed him, three generations walking together and all dressed the same in broad flat bonnets, their Saturday afternoon second best. They looked at him with disapproval but said nothing.

"What is wrong with them?" Ramsay asked.

"They wonder why we are not yet married," Grace told him.

Ramsay hid his smile. He had not thought of Midlothian miners as being particularly moral people.

"You are surprised," Grace read him far too easily. She wrestled free of his arm. "You think we are all savages here, like Africans or Eskimos!"

Ramsay shook his head. "I never thought anything of the sort . . ."

The group of miners had halted and were listening. The oldest of them stepped closer and beckoned the others to join him.

"Don't deny it!" Grace's quick temper was gathering quite a crowd of onlookers as a pair of be-shawled women joined the men. They folded their arms and glowered at Ramsay as if he was their mortal enemy. Grace thrust her face forward and into his. "You think you're too good for the likes of us."

The crowd growled, obviously in full support of Grace. One woman pointed to Ramsay's suit. "Look at him, all toffed up as if he owns the place."

"Toonies. They should stay in Edinbury!" her friend agreed.

"Well, you're not better than we are!" Grace had worked herself into a passion now. "You are no better than the rest

233

of us." She patted her swollen belly. "And our baby will be from Nitten, not Edinbury!"

The crowd was larger now. About a dozen strong, they formed a semi-circle a few yards from the pair, openly staring and making derogatory comments.

"I hope you'll make Grace a respectable woman, you!" The older woman pointed at Ramsay.

"We've heard all about you, David Napier!"

Ramsay looked around. *What on earth am I doing mixing with this type of person? I am from a respectable family, for goodness sake. I am of a higher breed.*

"Go on, get away!" Grace shoved him and he staggered. "We don't need you anymore. My baby and me will do just fine without the likes of you."

"He'll need a father," one of the women shouted. "He'll be a bastard else."

"I will marry you," Ramsay said quietly. He knew it was the right thing to do, but at the same time he knew he was condemning both himself and Grace to a lifetime of unhappiness.

"No you bloody won't!" Grace screamed. "I'd rather have my child a bastard than be married to one."

"I will marry you," Ramsay repeated. He thought of decades trapped with this bundle of volatility, of badly cooked meals and neighbours in cloth caps and the constant grit of smoke in his lungs. No, he would not sacrifice everything because of a few moments' pleasure. "But we will live in Edinburgh."

She slapped him then, a wild swinging blow that caught him by surprise and echoed around the narrow street. "There! That's for you!"

Ramsay instinctively put a hand to his face and stepped back. "What was that for?"

Strangely, the blow had altered the opinion of the crowd. "Hit her back," two of the men shouted, "hit the bitch."

"I will marry you," Ramsay said for the third time.

Grace shook her head. "I don't want my baby growing up with folk like you," she said. He saw the tears bright in her eyes and, despite himself, he reached out for her, but she pushed him away, turned and ran up the street in a rustle of skirts.

"Let her go, man!" the youngest of the miners advised. "Grace Flockhart was always a flirt."

"You're better without her," another miner said. "You offered, she refused. Run while you have the chance."

One of the women stepped forward. Hardship and work had aged her, but there was warm light behind her eyes. "If you want her, son, then go after her. If you don't, you'll never get her back."

Ramsay nodded. Knowing it would only bring him trouble, knowing that they could never forge a happy marriage, knowing his family would disown them both, he shouted, "Grace!" and followed, striding down the street. "It's my baby too!"

Another shell crashed down somewhere in the town, but Ramsay barely heard it as he reached the building. The door gaped open and the interior was dark. He plunged inside, gasping with the strain of his passage across, and had a quick look around.

There was a very small hallway with doors leading to what had been a living room and a bedroom, both now stripped of everything but the largest items of furniture. His men would be cramped inside, but safer than on the street and closer to the outskirts. It would do as a temporary refuge. Ramsay signalled to McKim to send them over and watched for any Germans.

Shells came over in ones and twos, a desultory bombardment that had only nuisance value. He watched as two men left the estaminet; Turnbull and Timms, running in a zig-zag pattern to confuse any enemy snipers. McKim and Cruickshank were on guard, their rifles moving as they scanned the street. Ramsay started as there was movement at the far end of the street.

The German soldiers arrived just as Timms reached the centre of the road.

Oh, God! I knew it was too good to last.

Ramsay crouched in the doorway and aimed his revolver. Out of the corner of his eye he saw McKim readying his rifle, but there was no need. These Germans were no threat. He watched them stagger up the street, one carrying what looked like a bolt of cloth and a pile of women's clothing and the other with a wine bottle seemingly permanently attached to his lips.

"McKim!" Ramsay spoke in a whisper that could not possibly carry the distance. "Don't fire!"

Perhaps the force of his thoughts conveyed the message, or maybe McKim was too experienced to draw attention to himself, but he restrained himself. Timms and Turnbull clattered into the house and Ramsay ordered them into the front room.

"In there and keep quiet," he said.

Now what? Do we wait until the road is clear of Germans? Or trust to blind luck?

We can't stop. We must keep on.

"McKim!" he hissed. "Send the next bunch over."

McKim acknowledged with a wave of his hand. Ramsay waited, hearing the thunder of his heart. The two Germans were still reeling along at the far end of the street. The man with the bottle was singing, the words slurred and the tune indecipherable, the other was swaying from side to side under the weight of his burden.

The shoemakers were next. They scurried across the road in panic, one looking over his shoulder at the two Germans as though petrified.

"Move!" McKim encouraged them. "Don't bloody stop!"

Ramsay stepped on to the street and waved them in. "Come on lads!"

They ran in, grinning as if they had performed a meritorious feat that deserved a reward.

"Into the back room and keep out of trouble!" Ramsay checked the street again. The more sober of the two Germans had dropped some of his loot and was trying to pick them up. The breeze had blown a long dress closer to the estaminet. McKim had withdrawn inside the doorway and was watching events.

Ramsay heard the sound he had been dreading: the distinct bark of a German officer giving an order. It was loud and clear across the babbling roar of undisciplined looting.

Oh, Jesus. Somebody is taking command out there. I have to take a risk.

Ramsay raised his voice to ensure it was heard. "Come on McKim! Never mind the German drunkard, get the men across!"

McKim looked across for a second, nodded and spoke over his shoulder. Four men came this time, running with rifles at the trail and without looking back.

Neither of the Germans paid any attention; one was too drunk and the other was wrestling with the woman's dress.

All four men got across within seconds and Ramsay thrust them inside the house. "Come on, McKim," he said and realised that the woman's dress had floated against the door of the estaminet. The German was following, his face screwed in concentration at the thought of losing his prize.

The German officer was shouting again and Ramsay heard the drumbeat of marching men. There was some disciplined force in Albert now.

Ramsay stood in front of the house. "Come on, McKim," he shouted. "Get the men across and let's get out of here!"

The German had lifted the dress; he looked up as a press of British soldiers erupted from the estaminet. He dropped all his loot and tried to unsling the rifle from his shoulder, but McKim was quicker. Before the German had swung the rifle round, McKim had slid his bayonet into the man's throat and sliced. The German died instantly, without uttering a sound, and McKim lowered him to the ground.

"Come on!" Ramsay yelled, as some of his men hesitated, whether to help McKim or out of shock, he didn't know. He noticed that McKim was counting the men and then the corporal returned inside the estaminet. "McKim! Come on!"

The sound of marching was distinct now. Ramsay expected to see German soldiers come around the corner into the street at any minute. "McKim!"

Another shell exploded overhead, scattering shrapnel around. One stray fragment bounced from the cobbles and grazed the leg of the drunken German, who jerked away in pain. He looked up, saw the mob of British soldiers and yanked his rifle round to fire. Ramsay aimed but hesitated, unwilling to squeeze the trigger in case the noise alerted the approaching Germans, but as the soldier pulled the rifle to his shoulder he knew he had no choice.

He aimed and fired, once, twice, three times. The noise of the shots echoed around the narrow street. The German soldier screamed as at least one bullet hit him. He looked directly at Ramsay and lifted his rifle higher. Ramsay took deliberate aim and fired again. He saw the German's head jerk back and the man slumped down; his rifle fell to the ground with a clatter.

Please God the Germans don't notice that in the general noise.

The whole affair had taken less than ten seconds; the bulk of the British soldiers were still crossing the road. Some had halted when Ramsay fired.

"Don't stop!" Ramsay yelled. He waved his hands. "Come on! Move it!"

The sound of marching was louder now; the tramp of feet dominating Albert.

Where the hell is McKim?

"McKim! Come on, man!"

McKim appeared at the doorway of the estaminet, he was dragging one of the English soldiers behind him. "Come on, you drunken bastard!"

Ramsay looked at the men behind him: eighteen of them, from veterans to cooks and store men, all dependent on him to get away. He looked at McKim, an elderly, experienced corporal trying to save a soldier who had obviously succumbed to the temptation of the estaminet.

"McKim! Leave him! Fritz is coming!"

As Ramsay shouted, he saw two German soldiers turn the corner of the street. Unlike the previous two, these were sober and carried their rifles ready to use. They saw McKim immediately and shouted a challenge.

Ramsay fired, but he had no idea where his shots went. "McKim! Drop him and run!" He shouted into the house, "Fritz is here! Out, lads, and head for our own lines!"

The Germans dropped to their knees and fired. One shot thudded into the door at Ramsay's head, but McKim had dropped his burden and snapped a shot in return. More Germans had filed into the road, they took up firing positions as the hammer of Ramsay's revolver clicked on an empty chamber.

He swore and reached for more cartridges. "McKim!"

Cruickshank was firing, snarling as he advanced toward the Germans. "Come on, you bastards! Come out and fight, you woman-murdering Hun bastards!"

Timms joined him, firing and advancing as McKim ran across the road to join them. The Germans had halted to form a disciplined line; more joined them; thirty tall men wearing round helmets on their heads and boots that still shone.

"Bloody Prussian Guards," McKim said.

Prussian Guards. Who else but the Prussians would keep their discipline when the rest of their army was dissolving into a rabble?

The Prussians were advancing slowly, one group moving forward as the others gave covering fire. He saw one drop as Timms, or more likely Cruickshank, found his mark, but they were getting too close.

"Cruickshank, Timms, get out of that." He saw McKim bang himself into the shelter of a doorway and fire two shots. At that range a marksman such as him did not miss and the two foremost Prussians dropped. The rest continued as if nothing happened.

Ramsay glanced behind him. Most of his men had left the house and were vanishing around the corner of the street. "Timms, Cruickshank, McKim. Come on!" He pushed in the last of his cartridges and fired a single shot in the direction of the Prussians just as the officer appeared.

As before, their eyes met immediately. The Prussian looked as immaculate as he had in their previous encounters, tall and smart and very much in command. Ramsay mentally contrasted his own appearance: unshaven, with his khaki coat cut off at the knees, torn and stained with mud and lyddite, his boots carrying mud an inch thick and dried blood crusted from the crown of his head to his chin. But he was still here and still fighting.

"Up the Royals!" McKim gave his unique perspective on the appearance of the officer. "Death and hell to all of you!" He snapped off another shot, worked the bolt of his rifle and withdrew.

Ramsay and the Prussian officer continued to stare at each other for what seemed like an age but in reality was probably only a few seconds. For some reason, Ramsay straightened to attention and saluted, the Prussian did the same and for an instant he felt a renewed bond with this enemy who had fought in the same actions as he had, yet was on a different side of the war.

"Sir!" Cruickshank was at his side, loading as he spoke. "They're coming again!"

These few words shattered the connection. Ramsay's loyalty was to his men, as the unknown Prussian's was to the soldiers who wore his uniform.

"Get out of this street," he shouted and fired a single shot in the direction of the Prussians.

It was as if his life had been in temporary suspension, but now things were back to their normal speed as the Prussians advanced toward him and McKim knelt a yard away, firing rapidly.

A bullet crashed against the wall, a foot from his face, spraying him with chips of stone. Another ricocheted at his feet.

Time to go.

"Come on lads." He led the way around the corner to see the rest of his men in a loose group, some running, some walking back and one or two waiting in doorways with their rifles ready.

This is no good, most of these men are only half-trained.

"Right, lads. Form into two groups. One group withdraws while the other supports them and then swap over." He let

McKim attend to the details; corporals did that sort of thing far more efficiently than he could ever do.

"Not bloody bon, boys!" McKim said cheerfully. "Follow my lead."

This street was short and relatively undamaged. Some of the houses had holes in their roofs where shells had gone through, and one was on fire. At the far end there was a single farmhouse behind a protective wall and beyond that Ramsay could see fields, rising to the ridge that overlooked the town. There was certainly movement on that ridge, he hoped it was the British Army preparing a defensive line that would halt this German advance once and for all.

Just one more push and they would be through and in open countryside. Just one more effort from his exhausted, filthy, battling Royals and the collection of odds, sods and bottle washers he had picked up en route and he was home free and without Flockhart to worry about.

Gillian will have heard about the German advance. She will be worried about me. She will be waiting and now I can meet her without fear and with a clear conscience. I have proved myself. I am fit to be an officer, I am fit to be with these men.

"Keep moving now. McKim, take your boys to the end of the street and cover us."

Ramsay took up position behind a fallen chimney stack and looked over his men. He did not know all their names, but McKim had left him Cruickshank and Timms among the varied others.

"Keep up a steady fire, boys. Keep the Prussians back until McKim's lads get clear up the road."

He heard the German officer giving orders and wished he could speak German. Most of the Prussians were out of sight or only partially visible in doorways and behind windows.

One young NCO was out in the open, checking his men; Ramsay shot him without compassion and ducked behind the chimney as the Prussians responded with a hail of shots.

"Good shooting, sir," Cruickshank said. He sounded more calm than usual and the wild anger was absent from his eyes.

"Keep working that rifle, Cruickshank," Ramsay said.

"Yes, sir." Cruickshank pulled back the bolt, sighted and fired.

The Prussian officer gave an order and a score of men burst out of the houses, bayonets fixed, while supporting fire ripped around Ramsay's positions.

"Here they come again," Cruickshank said. He was very calm as he sighted and fired. His bullet kicked splinters from a window frame a few inches from an advancing German. The man flinched and Cruickshank fired again. He grunted as the German staggered back and slowly slid down the wall.

"One less for Kaiser Bill." Cruickshank worked the bolt of his rifle.

The others were also firing in a wild cacophony of shots that splattered over the street, hitting the walls and the ground, but seldom coming near the Prussians.

Oh, I wish I had my Royals with me now. Niven and Aitken and Flockhart would make mince out of this lot. There are too many good men dead.

"Sir!" That was McKim's voice. "We are ready whenever you like."

The street behind Ramsay was clear. McKim had his men in position at the very edge of the village, facing every direction. "Into the street, boys, and run! Corporal McKim will cover us."

Timms led the rush down the road but Cruickshank remained in place. "Come on, Cruickshank. Don't play the hero!"

Cruickshank looked up and gave a small smile. "I better stay, sir. I'll cover you." He coughed and a spurt of blood erupted from his mouth and spattered the ground in front of him. "The bastards got me, sir."

Oh, God. That's another one gone.

"Is it bad, Cruickshank? Maybe it's only minor."

"I'm shot through the lungs, sir. I haven't long to go, but I'll take as many as I can with me." He spat blood and stifled a groan. "I'll be with the missus soon enough. Run, sir."

"Good luck, Cruickshank." Ramsay touched his shoulder. There was nothing he could do for him and he had other men who depended on his leadership.

He felt very exposed turning his back to the Prussians and literally running away, but he heard McKim's shouts of encouragement and the usual slogan:

"Death and hell to you!"

The street seemed to stretch for miles as Ramsay ran up it. Individual shots merged into a continuous roar of sound containing rifle fire, yells and the whine of ricocheting bullets.

Ramsay saw a man fall before him; he hesitated, but the man had been shot through the head. Ramsay jumped over the body and continued, hearing the breath rasp in his throat and feeling his legs weak with fear. He glanced behind him and saw Cruickshank half-rising and trying to thrust with his bayonet. He saw a Prussian shoot him, and another smash the butt of his rifle onto Cruickshank's head. Ramsay stumbled and fell, landed with a heavy thump on the cobbles and something hard grabbed hold of his shoulder and hauled him around a corner.

"Careful, sir," McKim growled. "The Fritzes are everywhere." He pointed to his right where a group of soldiers were probing cautiously around the corner of a building. "They're over that way as well." Another party of Germans were filing slowly from the left, keeping to the shelter of the houses as they approached Ramsay's position.

Ramsay swore. He had hoped for a clear run to the British lines, but the Prussian officer had outflanked him on both sides. He had two choices: make a stand and hope for help or run up the ridge with the Prussians in close pursuit.

He knew the Prussians would not be distracted by the prospect of loot. They would ignore their dead and march on until they were victorious. If he organised a fighting retreat his rearguard of crocks would not be strong enough to hold them back for more than a few moments. There was no choice, he would have to make a final stand.

"Get up to that farmhouse, McKim." The house was about three hundred yards away, set at the far side of a field. A narrow lane led straight to the door, with a tall boundary hedge for shelter.

"Sir." McKim nodded. "Same system, sir?"

"Yes." Ramsay loosed three shots at the Germans to his right. His men were in a confused clump, some firing one way and some the other. "Move, McKim!"

McKim clicked his magazine into place, rolled the pipe around his mouth and nodded. "Good luck, sir."

"Good luck, McKim."

Ramsay fired his last three shots at the Germans advancing up the street behind him and fumbled for cartridges. "Fire away, boys. Keep them back." He ducked as a bullet struck fragments from the wall above his head and watched as McKim led his men in a weaving run across the open field. One of the Germans on his left pointed to McKim and the others began to fire at the hideously exposed British force. Ramsay saw one man fall, and then another. McKim staggered, spun and fell, landing on his face in the muddy field. He looked ridiculously small there, an old man who should be sitting quietly by his own fireside, not a fighting soldier struggling through a foreign field.

Ramsay rammed home the last cartridge and fired at the Germans, hating them. Until that moment he had been detached from the war. He had survived in misery and fear, but had felt no personal animosity towards the Germans. They had been the enemies of king and country – fighting was an unpleasant duty and nothing else. Now, as he looked at McKim, elderly, intelligent and wise but shot like a dog, he experienced such a surge of hatred as he had never felt before.

"You Prussian bastards!" He rose from cover, firing. He saw one of the Germans fall and laughed. "Death and hell to you!" He borrowed McKim's phrase in an unconscious tribute to the corporal.

The Prussians were closing in on both sides. Their numbers had increased, there were at least thirty on the right, perhaps half that on the left and more pounding steadily past Cruickshank's prone body.

Without McKim to lead them, the first group of Ramsay's men had floundered to a confused halt outside the farmhouse. With the Germans advancing on three sides he had no time to waste.

"Come on, lads, follow me and don't stop for anything!"

He tried to sound confident as he led his group at a run up into the field and towards the farmhouse that already seemed so far away. He heard his men following him, the sound of their boots changing from the sharp crack of studs on stone to a softer thud as they sank into the mud and grass of the field.

"Keep going!" Ramsay urged as an overweight storeman struggled up the slope. He glanced over his shoulder. The

Germans were following, scores of them now forming a compact column that would surely batter through any defensive line he could create. They marched on the path, so confident that they began to sing.

"Into the farmhouse!" Ramsay put his hand on the storeman's shoulder and shoved. "Come on, man, don't give up now!"

There was another khaki-clad body on the ground, and another. Bullets were buzzing like bluebottles around a piece of rotted meat, but Ramsay knew he had to keep going or nobody would survive.

"Not far now, boys," he said as the walls of the farmhouse thrust up before them. He spotted McKim lying on the ground, but the small man was not still. He was twitching and trying to rise.

Ramsay halted. "McKim!" He flinched as two bullets thudded into the ground at his feet and another hissed past his face.

The corporal looked up, suddenly he looked very old and frail. "Go on, sir! Give them hell!"

I won't leave McKim behind.

"Up you get, McKim." Ramsay stooped and put an arm under the corporal's shoulder. He felt the surge of renewed fear as all his hatred and anger evaporated.

I have half the German army trying to kill me and here I am trying to save the life of a foul-mouthed soldier I had not even met a few days ago. What a bloody fool I am.

"Come on McKim!" Ramsay limped upwards, with McKim a light weight on his arm. "Not long to go now, man!"

McKim grunted. "My rifle, sir. I can't leave my bundook behind, I've had it since Mons."

"Forget your bloody rifle," Ramsay snarled, but he stooped and allowed McKim to scoop the weapon from the ground.

The Prussians had stopped firing now. Their officers had formed them into two smart columns marching slowly uphill. One column remained on the path, the other was making easy work of the slope.

Ramsay's men were scattered across half the field, some with rifles, some without. Turnbull was propped against the outside wall of the farmhouse holding a rock in his left hand as though he intended throwing it at the Prussians. Timms was nursing a wounded leg.

One column of Prussians was closer now; barely twenty yards away and singing. His Hauptmann was with them, tall and as immaculate as if he were on a parade ground somewhere in Berlin. He signalled for his men to halt and shouted, "Surrender, Lieutenant. You can do no more. Surrender and save the lives of your men."

Ramsay shook his head and struggled on. He had lost but he would not surrender. He had fought too long and too hard to give up now.

I am condemning them all to death. I am saving their honour. What the hell am I doing?

The terrible chatter of the machine gun deafened him. He ducked as the bullets sprayed down the slope of the hill, scything down the Prussians in their close formation. The Guards fell in scores, NCOs and officers were hit before they could give orders to their men.

Ramsay had just presence of mind enough to dive to the ground and take McKim with him. "Down, men!" he shouted. "Get down!"

The machine gun was manned by an expert; it produced a cone of fire that virtually wiped out both columns of Prussian Guards, hosing them as a fireman sprayed water on a reluctant fire, back and forth and back again. Then it turned its attention on the straggling looters who were watching from the broken shops of the nearest streets of Albert.

Having been on the wrong side of machine gun fire, Ramsay could only watch with admiration and some sympathy as the Germans fell. He heard the screams and cries of brave men who had no chance, but he stilled his sympathy. The Kaiser had started this war and these men had followed him to war with willingness and relish.

At last the hellish chatter died. Only the dead and writhing wounded remained in the sloping field. Those and a khaki-clad handful who staggered to their feet and continued their walk to the farmhouse.

"Up you come, lads." The voice was North Country English, boisterous and friendly. "We've been watching you for an hour."

As Ramsay supported McKim up the remainder of the slope to the farmhouse and the remnants of his men picked themselves up, a moustached captain led a file of men down to take prisoners from the shocked German soldiers. Ramsay saw the German Hauptmann being led away by a pair of grinning Northumberland Fusiliers. He tried to catch the man's eye, but the German had his head down in his shame at being captured.

"Where the hell did you spring from, lieutenant?" The captain bore the scar of an old wound across his face. "And who are you anyway?" He looked over the collection of men from different units who were staggering past him and into the farmhouse.

"Lieutenant Douglas Ramsay, sir. 20th Royal Scots." Ramsay would have saluted, but to do so would have meant letting McKim fall so instead he just smiled foolishly.

"Captain Regan, Northumberland Fusiliers." The captain introduced himself. "I heard that the 20th Royals were all gone to glory. How did you get here?"

"We followed the German advance," Ramsay said.

The Fusiliers were shepherding their prisoners past the farmhouse and up to the ridge. The Vickers machine gun fired an occasional burst into Albert whenever the crew saw any sign of movement.

"Are we making a stand, sir?" Ramsay felt as if he had not slept for a month. Now that he had reached comparative safety all the strain and fatigue of the last six days was catching up on him.

"Not here," Regan said. He jerked his head backward. "We are on the ridge up there. This is just an ambush to remind Fritz that we still exist." He watched as a couple of shells exploded on the far side of Albert. "We've done some damage and now we will withdraw. The line is still fluid to the north." He put out a hand as Ramsay swayed. "Best get you somewhere safer than this, Ramsay, and you can give us all the information you have gathered."

CHAPTER ELEVEN

29th March 1918

Ramsay jerked awake and looked around him in a half-panic, unable to decide where he was. He could hear the rumble of guns in the background, but that had been part of life for so long he barely took heed. There was chicken wire in front of him, holding back an earthen wall, so he was in an established dugout rather than a scrape in the ground or an old shell crater, and somebody was talking quietly nearby. He strained to hear the words, fearful in case they were in German and he had been captured.

He breathed out in slow relief when he realised the man was speaking English and he was safe, at least for the time being. He rolled over in bed, feeling the bounce and give of an actual mattress, and saw there were half a dozen men in the dugout, playing cards around a circular table by the light of an oil lamp.

"Ah, you're awake, Ramsay." A burly major stepped towards him. "How are you feeling?" He held out a hand. "No, don't try to get up or salute or any of that nonsense. We're all in the same boat here."

"I am fine, sir." Ramsay struggled into a sitting position and immediately wished he had not as his head began to pound. He put a hand to ease the pain and encountered a large bandage.

"Nasty knock you had there," the major said pleasantly. "You had quite a collection of cuts and bruises, but nothing too serious. That strange little corporal of yours tells me you were in the front when the Germans began their push and you brought your men home through enemy lines. Is that correct?"

Ramsay tried to nod but the movement brought fresh pain. "Something like that, sir. How is McKim?"

"Garrulous and wanting to get back to his regiment." The major grinned and perched himself at the foot of Ramsay's bed. "He's quite a character and tough as old boots."

"McKim is one of the originals," Ramsay told him. "He lives for the regiment." He smiled. "I'm glad he made it. We lost far too many good men in the last few days."

The major nodded. "We did indeed, but there are still stragglers coming in now and then. We have a couple of your men in the ranker's hospital and one or two have filtered back to our lines."

"I should go and see them." Ramsay swung his legs out of the bed. He was wearing a striped night shirt that certainly was not his own and he had been washed, and bandages applied to various parts of him. His uniform, washed, repaired and ironed, hung on a peg thrust into the wall. "How long have I been out?"

"You collapsed from loss of blood the moment you came through the lines," the major said. "That would be two or three days ago."

When Ramsay reached for his uniform the major shook his head. "If you insist on getting up, I'll have your servant fetch something for you to eat."

"I don't have a servant." Ramsay became aware of the

terrible weakness of his legs, while the pounding of his head was increasing with every passing minute.

"We found you one," the major replied.

"Have we stopped the Germans yet?" Ramsay asked.

"Not yet, but we've blunted their thrust," the major said. "They failed to break through our defence lines, but they certainly pushed us back miles. They dented Gough's Fifth army and now they have stopped. They will never take Amiens and when we have regrouped we will push them as they have pushed us."

"We've lost thousands of good men." Ramsay thought of his own dead.

"The Germans have lost more," the major said. There was great satisfaction in his voice.

It was two hours before Ramsay left the dugout, fully fed and feeling smart in his crisp uniform. He was about a mile behind the new British lines, in an encampment that was part tented and part dug in, although there seemed no intention of a permanent stay, to judge by the lack of fixed positions.

His servant was a fussy, cheery Geordie with bright eyes. He escorted Ramsay to the hospital tent and saluted punctiliously. He smelled of soap and was so immaculately shaved that his skin glowed. "Will that be all, sir?"

"Yes, carry on . . ." Ramsay hesitated.

"Gilmore, sir," the servant reminded.

"Carry on, Gilmore." Ramsay acknowledged his salute with a flick of his hand and entered the tent.

Men lay in parallel rows of cots, some quiet, others moaning or chatting to their neighbours. The sharp smell of disinfectant battled with gas gangrene and male sweat.

Ramsay ran his eyes along the shaved or bandaged faces and wondered if he would recognise his men in this state of cleanliness.

"Royal Scots!" he announced as he entered, and four faces turned toward him. Two he did not know, but McKim and Blackley stiffened to attention.

"At ease, men," Ramsay said. He had thought that Blackley was dead. "It's good to see you both again."

"There are a few more Royals turning up, sir." McKim looked naked without the broken pipe hanging out of the corner of his mouth. "I don't know if they are ours or not."

"Let's hope so."

Blackley was wounded in the arm and leg, but greeted Ramsay with a broad grin. "Blighty one sir. I'm going home!"

"Congratulations, Blackley." Ramsay held out his hand and accepted Blackley's somewhat tentative handshake. "I hope this war is over before you are fit enough to return."

Blackley shook his head. "Soldiering is my job, sir. I signed on for twenty-two years." He smiled again, "If I wasn't in this war I'd be in another one, sir."

"Good man." Ramsay was smiling as he left the hospital tent. A flight of aircraft left vapour trails overhead as they headed for the German lines.

Get them, boys. Send the Kaiser a message that he will never win this war.

Five men from an English regiment escorted a file of German prisoners through the camp towards a waiting lorry. "Get along there," the smallest of the guards snarled. He prodded the tallest of the Germans with his bayonet. "Pick your feet up, you lazy bastard!"

Ramsay watched the scene without interest until he realised that the tall German was his old adversary. "Enough of that!" He stepped forward and pushed the bayonet back from the German. "You treat this man with respect, you hear?"

The private looked at him in surprise. "But he's a German, sir. A murdering Hun!"

"This man is a gentleman and an officer," Ramsay made sure he spoke loudly enough for all the guards to hear him. "I want him treated with all possible courtesy."

He waited until the guards had acknowledged his order before he checked his pockets for a cheroot, but had none, so stood to attention instead and saluted the Prussian officer.

The officer slammed to attention, clicked his heels and returned the salute. "Thank you," he said. He did not smile.

Ramsay watched the prisoners boarding the lorry and took a deep breath.

What now? I suppose I had better report somewhere and get sent back to my unit, or what remains of them.

Ramsay realised that he was in that strange military position of not belonging anywhere. With the 20th Royal Scots no longer a viable unit, he had no local battalion to which to return, while the parent cadre was still in Scotland. It was unlikely that he would be posted there, but until the higher command remembered he existed, he could enjoy the relative security of this camp, wherever it was.

Cadging a cigar and a match from a passing Fusiliers captain, Ramsay lit up, shook the flame out and threw the match away. He looked around at the ordered array of tents and the disciplined khaki-clad soldiers and contrasted the scene with the chaos through which he had retreated for so many days.

Well, I survived. I survived the greatest retreat and the greatest German attack since 1914.

He drew deeply on his cigar and smiled.

"Lieutenant Ramsay?" The voice had the familiar cadences of Midlothian.

Another of my men turned up alive I hope!

Ramsay turned around, still smiling.

Sergeant Flockhart stood foursquare behind him with the thumb of his right hand hooked into the sling of his rifle. "Or should I call you David Napier?"

Ramsay felt the shock like a kick in the stomach but over three years in the army had taught him some self control. He removed the cigar from his mouth with as much appearance of calmness as he could muster. "I rather think you should call me sir, Sergeant. I do not know what you mean by that other name." He forced a smile. "It is good to see you again, Flockhart. I had thought you killed when the engine was hit."

"The last train to Waverley." Flockhart swung the rifle around and held it at the trail. The muzzle was pointing directly at Ramsay's stomach and Flockhart's hand was dangerously near the trigger. "I knew I had seen you before, but I could not remember where. It was at the station at Newtongrange, wasn't it, *sir*?"

"Pointing a rifle at a superior officer is a capital offence." Ramsay turned aside slightly and felt for his pistol, but he had not strapped it on. He was completely unarmed although in the middle of a camp of British soldiers he should be safe.

"Raping sixteen year old girls and leaving them pregnant is worse." Flockhart worked the bolt of his rifle. The sound was unheard amidst the general bustle of the camp, but Ramsay knew there was now a bullet in the breach.

"Don't be a fool, man!" Ramsay said.

"We're going for a wee walk," Flockhart told him. His eyes were steady and utterly merciless, "and you are going to tell me exactly what happened."

Ramsay grunted, "I do not know what you are talking about, Flockhart. Now for God's sake put that rifle aside. I think you are shell shocked, man. Come now, and I will take you to a doctor."

Flockhart slowly shook his head. "I could shoot you here and now," he lowered the muzzle slightly so it pointed at Ramsay's belly, "And take my chance with a court martial. I might be shot or they might believe that my rifle went off by accident." He shrugged. "Do you really think I care?" He prodded Ramsay with the muzzle of his rifle. "Walk in that direction, Lieutenant."

Nobody spared Ramsay and Flockhart a second look as they moved through the camp.

How can I get out of this? If I shout for help he might just shoot.

Ramsay looked over his shoulder and into the dispassionate eyes of Flockhart. They were the same colour as Grace's had been, but while hers had been bright and dancing with life, Flockhart's were utterly poisonous.

There was no dispute. Flockhart would shoot. He was a trained and experienced soldier with a longstanding grudge.

"Where are we going?"

"You'll see. Move." Flockhart nodded to the camp exit. "Out there and keep moving."

The camp was set in the midst of open countryside, the fields already bearing a sheen of green as the spring growth began. The guards on the gate merely glanced up as they passed.

"Be careful out there, sir. One of the Hun prisoners has escaped."

Ramsay barely heard the words. Flockhart led them off the pave road to a farm track, rutted and sunk between high hedgerows. A lark was singing, its song plaintive in the shaded gloom.

Will I see the summer blossom this year? Will I hear the liquidity of the blackbird over the gardens of Edinburgh?

There was a scattering of small villages in view,

undamaged and peaceful beneath the afternoon sun. A civilian led a horse through a field and a gaggle of children shouted as they watched a military lorry snarl past. It all seemed so normal that Ramsay wanted to reach out and embrace it.

"Over there." Flockhart shoved him in the back. "That old barn will be the place."

In the dark of a French barn in Picardy. Shot by one of my own men for a sin I committed as a youth. This is not the death of a soldier.

Flockhart sidled past him, keeping the muzzle of the rifle pointing at his stomach, and kicked the door open. The interior was dark and there was a sweet smell of damp hay. "In you go."

As Ramsay stepped in, Flockhart cracked him over the head with the barrel of his rifle, reopening his wound. Ramsay yelled and staggered until Flockhart pushed him to the ground. He sprawled face down and Flockhart kicked him in the ribs.

"Lie still, Ramsay, or Napier, whatever your bloody name is."

Ramsay groaned at the agony in his head, tried to roll away and swore when Flockhart kicked him again.

"I said lie still!"

When the barn door shut Ramsay could hardly see. He struggled to a sitting position just as there was the flare of a match and Flockhart lit a small lamp.

"It was pure blind luck that I came across you," Flockhart said. He kicked Ramsay again and hung the lantern on a hook situated on one of the wooden pillars supporting the roof. Yellow light pooled around them, emphasising the gloom beyond. Ramsay heard the rustle of rats in the straw.

Flockhart dragged across a three legged stool and sat

on it. The rifle rested across his knees with the muzzle still pointing at Ramsay's stomach.

Should I try and jump him?

He estimated the distance. It was about eight feet and Flockhart's finger was curled around the trigger of his rifle. He would not be able to muster the strength to leap and grapple with the man before Flockhart fired. It was better to sit tight, hear what he had to say and then try and talk him out of it.

"I really think you have the wrong man," Ramsay started, but Flockhart lifted the rifle to his shoulder and aimed it in the direction of his navel.

"Rab Moffat saw you with her in the field outside Aitkendean," Flockhart spoke in a conversational tone. "He did not know your name. You told wee Gracie that you were called David Napier."

Ramsay tried to shuffle into a more comfortable position but the rifle was steady on him and Flockhart's finger tightened on the trigger. He slumped down again. He was leaning against a pillar with his legs stretched out before him and his hands at his side. Light from the lantern highlighted the high cheekbones and determined jaw of Flockhart but revealed nothing of the barn outside. Ramsay felt as if they were trapped within their own world, separate from the greater slaughter outside only more personal and just as deadly.

"I am not David Napier," he said.

"You told Grace that you were, and she told Rab Moffat." There was no doubt in Flockhart's voice and Ramsay knew that denial was pointless. He decided on another tack.

"I would have married her, you know."

"She was too good for you," Flockhart said.

What? I am a gentleman, she was only a miner's daughter.

A nothing! She should have been grateful even to be noticed by me!

Ramsay's initial thoughts transported him back to the man he had been then. The wild, arrogant, irresponsible youth who had hunted women for sport, used them for his own pleasure and discarded them with a laugh or a curse.

He thought of Grace lying in the grass and despite his situation, he smiled. She was a lovely, lively and passionate woman. He had never loved her, but there was certainly a spark of affection that he had never felt for any of the other girls he had pursued. Except for Gillian, of course. She was on a completely different level.

"You are right," he surprised himself by admitting. "She was too good for me."

He thought of Gillian. Tall, elegant, sophisticated and fun, if shallow in many ways. He was promised to marry Gillian once this war was finished. He loved her. His feelings for Gillian were far different to his feelings for Grace or any of the others. He could see himself living with Gillian; he was comfortable with her as a friend as well as man and woman. He never had that depth of security with anybody else. Yet, he was a gentleman and he had wronged a woman. Grace was of a different class, but so were McKim and Blackley and Niven. They were good men, as honourable and honest as any of the officers he had ever met.

The decision struck him with all the force of a six inch shell landing a few feet away. He could not marry Gillian, he must break his promise to her. He had to do the right thing, although it meant condemning himself and Grace to a lifetime of misery as they tried to reconcile the irreconcilable and equalise the inequality of their class differences.

"Put the rifle away, Flockhart. We can still resolve this. I will do the decent thing and marry Grace, if she will have me now. I did offer already, you know."

"She's dead." Flockhart's words were brutal.

Oh, dear God. Poor wee Grace.

"Oh, God, I didn't know! How?" Ramsay stared at the sergeant. "How did she die?"

"In childbirth. My sister Grace died giving birth to your bastard."

"I did not know." Ramsay thought of her wide blue eyes and that childlike expression of innocence she had had. His feelings of compassion were much stronger than he would have believed possible.

"And the child, what happened to the child? Did it live?" Suddenly Ramsay was desperate to find out about his child.

Was it a boy or a girl? What was it like? Where was it now?

The prospect of something good coming of that dismal encounter was strong. Witnessing death in all its hideous forms day after day had created a desire to see life.

Flockhart's voice softened slightly. "Grace had a wee boy. He's being taken care of."

"A boy! Where is he?"

I have a son. Somewhere in the world there is a small part of me, somebody who will grow up, perhaps with my likeness and with some of my personality traits.

"I would have married her, you know," Ramsay said.

Of all the deaths he had been responsible for, this one would haunt him most. Death and new life intertwined and a nightmare that would continue.

"You lying bastard!" Flockhart rose. He slipped the bayonet from its scabbard and clicked it in place. Light flickered along the length of the blade. "You didn't even tell her your real name!"

Ramsay had guessed that Flockhart would make a sudden lunge and he threw himself sideways to avoid the stab of the vicious blade. He felt the tearing pain as the bayonet ripped up the side of his ribs and then Flockhart was standing over him with the bayonet poised.

"That was my sister, you bastard! You killed my sister!" The bayonet jabbed down, slicing into Ramsay's arm. He yelled and rolled over, but Flockhart followed with his bayonet held point up, ready for a killing stroke. Ramsay's blood dripped from the edge.

Killed by a British sergeant inside a Picardy barn. What will Gillian say to that?

The man came from outside the circle of light, launching himself at Flockhart without any hesitation. He did not say a word. Ramsay only saw a blurred shape as the figure grabbed hold of the sergeant's rifle.

They rolled out of the lamplight but Ramsay heard them fighting in the gloom. He heard Flockhart swearing, and the other man responding in German.

It's a German. It's that bloody Guards Hauptmann. I thought he was a prisoner, he must be the escapee the guards were speaking about.

Ramsay tried to rise, swore at the tearing pain across his ribs and his arm, and slumped back down again. He heard the two men fighting and caught the occasional glimpse of the struggle in the periphery of the lamp light. He placed his back against the pillar and pushed himself up, groaning in pain and feeling the blood run hot and sticky down his side.

"You dirty Hun bastard!" That was Flockhart's voice. Ramsay heard a long moan and saw one man standing in the gloom. He could not make out who still remained on his feet.

Ramsay slid out of the pool of lamplight. He was unsure what to do. He saw somebody move and then both were on their feet. They closed, grappling in the gloom. The door of the barn opened and three soldiers were silhouetted against the bright light outside.

"It's that escaped Hun!" One of the men raised his rifle and fired. The others joined him and the sharp crackle of multiple shots in the confined space deafened Ramsay. He felt the shock of the bullet entering his body but there was no pain. The impact slammed him against the pillar. He gasped for air and slowly slid downwards until he was on the ground.

The firing stopped. Five British soldiers pushed into the barn.

"There's one of ours in here as well," another of the soldiers spoke and fired a final shot into the body of the Prussian officer. "Jesus, there's two of ours. The Hun has murdered a British officer."

"You call me sir," Ramsay said, and fainted.

CHAPTER TWELVE

EDINBURGH

June 1919

There were no larks.

Ramsay shook his head to clear it of the images and realised that Gillian was looking at him.

"Is it the war?" Her voice was sympathetic.

"And other things," Ramsay said. That tune was still bouncing around his head.

> *"Après la guerre finie*
> *Soldat Ecosse parti*
> *Mademoiselle in the family way*
> *Après la guerre finie"*

Well, the *guerre* was *finie* now and his mademoiselle had been in the family way when she left him. He looked down at Gillian and smiled. This was his future now. Mrs Gillian Ramsay.

And what of his son? Ramsay thought of a little boy growing up in the mining community of Newtongrange. He thought of men such as Flockhart and McKim, Blackley and Niven. They were honest, forthright men, generous with their passions and loyal to their friends. Ramsay smiled as a hundred memories crowded and jostled through his head. He had gone to war feeling like he belonged to a different species from the men he would command. He had marched to peace with the humbling knowledge that they were better men than he. With men like that, and women like Grace, his son was in good hands.

I still want to see the little tyke though. I will keep looking for him. It may take me a lifetime but I will never give up.

Gillian hooked her arm through his.

"Come away, Douglas. The war is finished and done with. It is time to think about other things."

They walked away from the Botanical Garden and into the bustle of Inverleith Row. But the words were still circulating around Ramsay's head. He knew they always would.

> *"Après la guerre finie*
> *Soldat Ecosse parti*
> *Mademoiselle in the family way*
> *Après la guerre finie"*

HISTORICAL NOTE

There was no 20th Royal Scots and no Lieutenant Douglas Ramsay. However the German advance of March 1918 occurred and pushed the British Army back as far as forty miles. This was a major success in the First World War where advances were frequently measured in hundreds of yards rather than miles. The March Offensive, Operation Michael was also the beginning of the end of the trench warfare that had typified the war in France and Flanders since the autumn of 1914.

The Germans commenced their attack with a targeted five hour bombardment that was one of the heaviest of the war. General Erich Ludendorff had 72 divisions against the 26 British infantry and three British cavalry, although the French supplied a further 23 divisions in the latter stages of the battle. The Germans used infiltration tactics with storm troopers and flame throwers, aided by a thick fog and a lack of British manpower. They penetrated the British forward positions and pushed them back miles in some of the fastest advances of the entire war.

The British retreat was over the old battle ground of the Somme, a place of terrible memories. The battle, or rather series of battles, lasted well into April, when the heat went out of the German attack. The Germans did capture the town of Albert, and their advance was delayed by indiscriminate looting and British machine gun ambushes. The final stage of this phase of the German attack on the British 5th Army was an attack on Amiens, which the British and Australians repulsed. The Germans then turned their attention to the Third Army to the north.

These German attacks were their last of the war. Once the allies had held the line, they consolidated and went on the offensive. The British victory of Amiens in August was called the Black Day of the German Army and after that the Allies were on the offensive until the Armistice of 11 November 1918.

Malcolm Archibald
Pluscarden
January 2014.

Books by Malcolm Archibald

www.malcolmarchibald.com

Bridges, Islands and Villages of the Forth 1990
Scottish Battles 1990
Scottish Myths and Legends 1992
Scottish Animal and Bird Folklore 1996
Across the Pond: Chapters from the Atlantic 2001
Soldier of the Queen 2003
Whalehunters, Dundee and the Arctic Whalers 2004
Whales for the Wizard 2005, Dundee Book Prize 2005
Horseman of the Veldt 2005
Selkirk of the Fethan: Fledgling Press, 2005
Aspects of the Boer War 2005
Mother Law: A Parchment for Dundee 2006
Pryde's Rock 2007
Powerstone 2008
The Darkest Walk 2011
A Sink of Atrocity: Crime of 19th Century Dundee 2012
Glasgow: The Real Mean City: True Crime and Punishment in the Second City of Empire 2013
A Burden Shared: The Dundee Murders 2013